LOSING BET

Books by Mikhail Chernyonok

DETERMINED BY INVESTIGATION
KUKHTERIN DIAMONDS
UNDER MYSTERIOUS CIRCUMSTANCES
LOSING BET

LOSING BET

An Anton Birukov
Mystery by

MIKHAIL CHERNYONOK

Translated by Antonina W. Bouis

The Dial Press

DOUBLEDAY & COMPANY, INC.

GARDEN CITY, NEW YORK

1984

Published by The Dial Press

First published in issues 2 and 3 of SIBIRSKIE OGNI © 1979.

Library of Congress Cataloging in Publication Data
Chernyonok, Mikhail.
Losing bet.
Translation of: Stavka na proigrysh.
I. Title.
PG3479.5.H3715S7213   1984   891.73'44   83–18965
ISBN 0-385-27853-3

Losing Bet is one in a series of detective novels by Mikhail Chernyonok set in contemporary Siberia. Anton Birukov, Chernyonok's detective, began his career in the Criminal Investigation Division (CID) of the militia, or police, on the district level, in the village where his father was chairman of the state farm. Because of his intelligence and perseverance, Birukov moves up quickly through the ranks; by the time he is in his midthirties, he is a senior investigator in the capital of Novosibirsk Oblast [region], Novosibirsk, a city with a population of over one million.

In the Soviet Union, there are three agencies that carry out preliminary investigations of crimes: the KGB handles crimes against the state, and the militia and the Procuracy of the U.S.S.R. deal with other criminal acts. The militia, or police department, is under the Ministry of Internal Affairs. The Procuracy, or prosecutor's office, is similar to the U.S. Attorney General's office, but has greater power. In most cases investigators from the police and the procuracy work together, even though there is a long-standing rivalry between the two organizations.

Another aspect that differs from police procedure in the United States is the requirement that two investigation witnesses be present during a police search. The witnesses, usually neighbors, are chosen on the spot and must be over eighteen years of age and impartial—that is, not connected with the case. They must remain throughout the search and sign statements about any evidence the investigators find and remove. But like detectives everywhere, Birukov fights against time—fading clues, cooling trails, as well as pressure from his superiors—to solve the case.

A.W.B.

LOSING BET

1

On a stuffy August evening, frightening passersby with the heart-rending wail of its siren and alarming flashes of violet light, a militia squad car raced down the Railroad Station Highway of Novosibirsk. When it was almost at the station, it turned sharply onto one of the quiet side streets, rolled up to a high-rise in front of which a crowd had gathered, and came to a brake-squealing halt. Opening the doors on both sides, members of the operative team jumped out of the car. There were four of them: Anton Birukov, the lanky senior inspector of criminal detectives; Prosecution Investigator Makovkina, blond and wearing a dark-blue uniform that made her look like a stewardess; Vitaly Karpenko, the youngish medical examiner with a professorial beard; and Arkady Ivanovich Dymokurov, the tall, gray-haired forensics expert. Immediately a junior lieutenant of the militia came up to them and reported.

"Patrolman Igonkin. The scene of the incident hasn't been touched."

"Call in witnesses," Birukov said curtly.

"Yessir!"

The crowd stepped aside warily. Near the house, in the flower bed, a young woman in a dark-cherry bathing suit lay facedown. She looked as if she had been sunbathing and had fallen asleep with her arms spread out.

The detective and the medical examiner crouched next to the body and quickly looked over the woman. With Birukov's help, Karpenko turned her faceup. Framed by thick chestnut hair, the victim's face seemed waxen. A streak of dried blood was on the right temple.

"There's a pulse," the examiner said, holding her wrist. "We have to get her to a hospital fast. . . ."

A cautious voice came from the crowd. "I called an ambulance right away."

Turning, Birukov saw a thin old woman in an old-fashioned flowered dress, holding a string shopping bag containing a bottle of milk. Noticing the militia officer's attention, the old woman shyly adjusted her beret, as ancient as the dress, and spoke quickly and angrily, as if they hadn't believed her.

"Yes, yes, comrade officer! Right here, in the phone booth around the corner, I first called zero-three and then called for the militia."

"What happened here?" Anton asked.

The old woman's gaze darted up in fright.

"From up there," she said, pointing to a third-floor balcony, "the poor thing was either pushed or she jumped . . ."

Birukov looked at the balcony—the door was shut. The old woman must have noticed, and she got upset again.

"Yes, yes! After the woman fell, a man with white hair flashed by in the apartment and the door was shut."

Anton frowned and asked: "What man is this?"

"I didn't get a look at his face, but I remember his head: he had hair like a cap of foam."

Sirens blaring, the ambulance drove up. The orderlies started unrolling the stretcher. Birukov, after a talk with the medics, returned to the old woman. She began talking without waiting for a question.

"I was coming from the milk store, dearie, just then. I see that Yuri Pavlovich's balcony door is wide open. Just as I thought, 'So at last our neighbor's home,' the accident happened in a flash— the poor thing just flew out of the apartment—"

"Excuse me," Anton interrupted the chatty old woman. "What's your name?"

"Mine? . . . Ksenya Makarovna."

"Tell me, Ksenya Makarovna, who is Yuri Pavlovich and why is he home at last?" Anton said, stressing the "at last."

"Demensky, our apartments are on the same landing. He's a very charming man, a bachelor. He's an engineer. He was in Sverdlovsk a long time, studying. Yesterday he flew home, but he couldn't get into his apartment."

"Why not?"

"He had left his key with a friend," the old woman said with downcast eyes, and shifted the string bag from one hand to the other. "So, he left his suitcase with me and went off for the key. Two days have gone by since then . . ."

The orderlies, carefully lifting the stretcher, headed for the ambulance.

"Do you know the victim?" Birukov asked the old woman.

"I think her name is Sanya."

"Who is she?"

"It's hard for me to say. The day before yesterday, that is, exactly a day before Yuri Pavlovich came home, I heard a knock in the morning. I open the door and this sweet thing is smiling at me. Wearing one of those, you know, modern pink dresses and a black purse. 'Hello, granny,' she says. 'Hello, sweetie,' I reply. 'Is Yuri Demensky back yet?' 'No. And who are you, a friend?' 'My name is Sanya. I'm Yuri's wife.' Of course, that seemed curious to me. I say, 'I didn't know that my neighbor was married.' 'When Yuri returns, you'll find out.' "

"Did you tell Yuri Pavlovich about this?"

"Word for word, just as I told you."

"And what did he say?"

"Not a word. He hurried off to his friend's for the key."

"Take us to his apartment."

Catching her breath on the third floor landing, Ksenya Makarovna nodded at the door. Birukov knocked loudly. There was no answer.

"There's a bell," the old woman said helpfully. "Push the button."

However, Anton touched neither the bell nor the doorknob

until the lab expert took prints. The door was locked. They had to break in.

Demensky's small one-room apartment was furnished with inexpensive but modern furniture and glistened as if just cleaned for a party. On the polished table in the center of the room stood a vase with gladioli. The floor was covered with a thick gray rug. On the walls hung small engravings, two chased brass ornaments, and an age-darkened icon depicting the Crucifixion. There were several chairs, a large television set, and on top of it an expensive transistor radio. One wall was fully covered by shelves crammed with books; another wall, opposite the balcony door, held a chiffonier polished to a mirror gleam; next to it, covered with a shaggy plaid blanket, was a daybed on which lay a woman's pink rayon dress, and a new pair of women's shoes lay on the floor.

Birukov stopped in front of the dark Crucifixion. Turning to Ksenya Makarovna, he said, "Does your neighbor believe in God?"

The old woman merely waved a hand. "Who has faith nowadays! It's just fashionable to have icons and crosses."

"How old is Yuri Pavlovich?"

"Around forty."

After Dymokurov checked the balcony door, Anton Birukov carefully opened it and with Makovkina examined the balcony. There was a stool out there and on it a pan of murky water and a wet rag, which, apparently, was used for washing the windows.

"Anton Ignatievich, please come here," the fingerprint expert unexpectedly called from the bathroom.

Birukov went quickly, and looked over his shoulder into the tub—three empty vodka bottles labeled Extra lay in it.

The operative group went into the kitchen. Here, despite the open window, a strong smell of tobacco smoke hung in the air. On the table stood an unfinished bottle of cognac, two crystal glasses, a saucer with pieces of thinly-sliced lemon, an ashtray full of cigarette butts with lipstick on the filters, and a half-open box of matches with a picture of a bright red match burning against a black background.

"The cognac is from a restaurant," Dymokurov said, examining the purple stamp on the label. "Good cognac—Armenian."

Birukov looked around the kitchen. Near the garbage can he picked up a ballpoint pen that was broken in half and a wadded piece of paper. Smoothing it, he read with a frown: "To the Prosecutor of the city of Novosibirsk, from Kholodova, A. F. Statement." The writing had been crossed out nervously.

"They wanted to make a statement to your boss about something," Anton said, handing the paper to the investigator from the prosecutor's office. Makovkina looked at the scrawled handwriting and without a word put the paper in her briefcase.

The examination of the apartment yielded only puzzles. In the pocket of the pink rayon dress they found a telegram sent to Demensky four days ago from the resort city of Adler—"OB-TAINED THE ORDER MEET ME REVAZ"—and a letter without an envelope, addressed, as they surmised from the contents, to Demensky too.

> Sweetie, darling, hello!
> I spoke with you on the telephone today and I'm writing immediately, right from work. How are things? Are you getting over it? I ask, even though I know the answer is yes. That day when you left so angrily, I didn't know what to do, my heart was breaking. I was in a terrible state and stayed that way until you called. It's all my fault and I don't know what to do now. I miss you and think of you constantly. Everything's okay at home. Seryozha is growing persistently, often mentions his papa Yura—he misses you, too. Revaz isn't bothering me, everything's quiet for now.
> Come, darling. I'm waiting for you. Love and kisses,
>
> Your Sanya.

On the other side of the letter a stanza was written in a steady masculine hand:

> *And I began to regret*
> *That I loved and was loved . . .*

You're a bird of a different flight.
Where can we fly to together?

Under the poem a postscript in the same handwriting as the letter was nervously scribbled: "DAMN THE PAST! ALL OF IT! ALL!!!"

In the kitchen, behind the refrigerator, Dymokurov found a woman's robe.

"The buttons were torn off with the fabric, as if the robe had been pulled off by force," he said.

"Where did you find them?"

"All three were on the floor."

At Dymokurov's feet stood a stuffed red suitcase made of vinyl and a shiny black traveling case with a gold zipper. Squinting at them, Birukov asked, "What's in there?"

"In the suitcase, sheets and blankets waiting to be washed; in the case, two women's suits, a cotton dress, and a nightgown."

"No papers?"

"No."

Birukov went over to the bookshelf and looked thoughtfully over the ranks of books. His eyes lit on a row of old editions. He was attracted by a thick volume with curlicue stamping on the spine. Anton pulled the book out and opened it. It was a well-preserved Bible published in 1910. The heavy, shiny pages didn't have a single pencil mark on them. Only the title page had an inscription in neat handwriting, in the brown ink popular at the turn of the century: "Property of Darya Sipeniatina."

Having leafed through the Bible, Anton put it back and looked down at the bottom shelf. On the far left of the shelf was a big box. In it was a half-empty bottle of turpentine, over a dozen almost unused tubes of oil paint, and a variety of brushes. Next to them lay a new sketchbook and a hefty pile of sketch boards. Bending over, Anton picked up the top board. It was an unfinished oil portrait of a beautiful, smiling woman with bare shoulders. Something seemed familiar about the portrait.

Birukov held the board at arm's length and turned to Makovkina, "Do you recognize her, Natalya Mikhailovna?"

"The victim?"

"Yes."

"Yuri Pavlovich's work," Ksenya Makarovna quickly interjected. "He used to draw a lot, but lately he dropped art, he was busy with science."

Birukov looked through the rest of the boards. There were sketches of Novosibirsk streets and several landscapes infused with feeling. It was evident that the artist was confident of his ability.

Birukov glanced over at Ksenya Makarovna. The old woman was sitting next to the witnesses, tensely rigid, and kept readjusting her bag with the milk bottle on her lap. Anton caught her shifting gaze and asked unexpectedly:

"Ksenya Makarovna, why aren't you telling the complete truth?"

The old woman shuddered. Almost dropping the bag, she adjusted her beret and stared fixedly at the floor. For some time she seemed to be memorizing the design on the rug. Then, lifting her anxious eyes to Anton's face, she spoke.

"Today I saw the woman who fell, in the same pink dress, talking to an elderly man at the railroad station. I was seeing my daughter off on her vacation. The train from Adler came in and I think that man got off it . . ."

"Did he look like the one who shut the balcony door?"

"It's hard to say. Maybe with his white hair . . . The man, you know . . . looked like he was from the Caucasus, you know, Georgian or Armenian. Swarthy face, large nose, and hair as white as snow. Dressed in a railroad uniform. In his hand a new black briefcase with a gold lock. And next to her was that one . . ." Ksenya Makarovna pointed to the red vinyl suitcase in which, according to Dymokurov, there was laundry.

"You're not mistaken?" Anton persisted.

"I may be wrong, but it sure looks like it."

"The man was young or old?"

"Over sixty, for sure."

"What were they talking about?"

"I saw them from a distance. The man seemed to be convincing her, and she frowned and her eyes ran back and forth, back and forth, as though she was afraid."

"What time was this?"

"I told you, the Adler train had just come in. It must have been five thirty this evening."

Birukov looked at his watch—the accident had occurred almost three hours later.

"What time did you leave the railroad station?"

"As soon as my daughter left; the station clock said six."

"And did you go straight home?"

"No. First I looked in at a friend's house, on Irkutsk Street. I had tea, we gossiped. Then I stopped by the store on my way home, bought a bottle of milk . . ."

"Could Sanya have come home with that man from the station? Maybe he was the one who shut the balcony door?"

"It's hard to say; I didn't get a good look. I just noticed the white hair." Ksenya Makarovna was lost in thought.

"Do you know the woman's last name?" Birukov asked.

"How should I know that, dearie? She said her name was Sanya . . ."

"Had you ever seen her at Demensky's before?"

"Never."

"And Yuri Pavlovich had not mentioned her?"

"Never!"

Further discussion proved fruitless. Leaving a message for Demensky with Ksenya Makarovna inviting him to the station house, and sealing his apartment, the operative group left the scene of the incident close to midnight. Despite the late hour, the operatives ran a check on Yuri Pavlovich Demensky and A. F. Kholodova.

Demensky had been born in the Novovarshavsky region of Omsk Oblast, in 1937. In 1959 he graduated from the Tomsk Polytechnical Institute in electrical engineering. He arrived in

Novosibirsk from Cheliabinsk three years ago and worked as a senior research engineer in new technology at the Siberian Electric Transport Machinery Company. His dossier said: "Not married. No children."

According to the address bureau, A. F. Kholodova was not registered in the city of Novosibirsk.

2

The morning sun insouciantly created frisky sunspots. Anton Birukov moved his pile of papers so that the reflections from the glass desk top did not blind him, turned the calendar page to August 21, and as soon as the clock hands showed the beginning of the workday, picked up the telephone.

The personnel department at Siberian Machinery gave Demensky the most positive recommendation. It turned out that even with his higher education, Yuri Pavlovich took correspondence courses from the Urals Polytechnical Institute, finishing the program for automation early, and a month ago went to Sverdlovsk to defend his diploma project. He was supposed to start work in a week's time if he didn't take the postdiploma vacation that he was allowed by law.

Birukov put in a call to the Sverdlovsk Criminal Department and asked them to make a quick visit to the Polytechnical Institute to discover whatever they could about the distinguished correspondence student from Novosibirsk.

As soon as he finished that long-distance call, his door was flung wide open. A scrawny, smiling senior lieutenant, smartly saluting, clicked his heels and said: "Permission to speak, comrade captain!"

"Slava? . . . Golubyov!" Birukov was amazed and jumped up from his desk to embrace his visitor.

"Let go, you'll break my ribs!" the senior lieutenant said with a laugh.

"I've missed you, you village detective! I haven't seen you in over a year!"

"Almost two."

"That long?"

"Of course. You were transferred in September, and now, as you know, it's the end of August."

Anton sat down and pushed back the hair from his forehead. Seating Golubyov, he asked with interest, "How's life in the region?"

"As you see, we go on living."

"How's the work?"

"Normal; almost no crime."

"How's Gladyshev?"

"The lieutenant colonel is getting ready to retire. Wouldn't you like to come be our chief instead?"

"Are you here to recruit?"

Golubyov laughed: "To tell the truth, the lieutenant colonel did send me to talk you into coming back as our chief of the CID. But that's not my main reason for seeing you. I'm here for a month's work, to earn a promotion. Will you take me on as your assistant, like old times?"

"What a question!" Anton reached for the phone. "I'll arrange things with the department chief. There's a case right now—"

"Do you mean yesterday's incident?"

"How do you know?"

"I've just come from the chief. You don't have to call; we arranged things without your consent. What are the preliminary findings?"

"Nothing pleasant. It looks like a love drama. Actually, the operative group will be meeting in a few minutes—"

Birukov didn't finish the sentence. Investigator Makovkina came in after a knock. Like yesterday, she was wearing her uniform. Giving Golubyov a quick look, she said hello and turned to Anton. "Are you busy?"

"I'm waiting for the experts. Pick a comfortable seat, Natasha, they'll descend upon us any second," Anton replied and then nodded at Golubyov. "This is my former colleague in the regional department. He's come here for fieldwork."

Makovkina sat closer to the desk. Placing her file folder on her lap, she automatically smoothed her hair and, fixing her blue eyes on Anton, said worriedly, "I spoke with Dr. Shirokov. The victim is alive, but her condition is very serious."

Karpenko and Dymokurov entered the office together. While the ever-polite Arkady Ivanovich gallantly greeted Makovkina and was introduced to Golubyov, the energetic medical examiner handed his conclusions to Birukov with a broad gesture, straddled a chair, put his elbows on its back, and impatiently scratched his beard.

The medical examination had determined that the victim was in a state of light alcoholic intoxication. The fall had injured her knee joints and pelvis and given her a slight concussion. When Birukov finished reading, Karpenko added, "The flower bed saved her. If she had fallen on the concrete, it would have killed her instantly."

"Do you think she'll live?" Anton asked.

"It all depends on neurosurgeon Aleksei Alekseevich Shirokov."

"Is he a good man?"

"Wonderful, but brain injury, you know, is no joke."

"Tell me, Vitaly," Makovkina said, "were there any signs of rape?"

"No," Karpenko said quickly.

"Or beating?"

"Nope. It looks like the woman jumped from the balcony. Here's an interesting piece of information: she first landed on her feet, as if in a jump, and then fell face forward . . ."

Birukov looked at Dymokurov:

"And what do you have to say about that, Arkady Ivanovich?"

"The trajectory of her fall and the indentations in the flower bed confirm the doctor's supposition."

"Who shut the balcony door behind the woman? And pulled off her robe?" Anton paused. "And then, the statement to the prosecutor. What did Kholodova, A. F., want to reveal and why didn't she complete her statement? Did she change her mind or did someone disturb her?"

Dymokurov merely opened his hands.

After a pause Birukov asked again, "Arkady Ivanovich, what do the dactyloscopic tests reveal?"

The lab man opened a file and put several enlargements on the desk. "Here are the prints from the cognac bottle and one of the shot glasses. The same fingerprints were found on the deadbolt and the glass of the balcony door."

Examining the prints closely, Anton said glumly, "The fingers seem awfully scarred . . ."

"Probably the man had been imprisoned before and in an attempt to prevent identification through his fingerprints, he tried to change the pattern of his papillary lines," Dymokurov proposed. "And these, good for identification, were found on the bell and on the outside doorknob."

"Are these Demensky's little fingers?" Anton asked.

"We don't have his prints, nothing to compare them with."

"What are the handwriting expert's conclusions?"

"He's determined that the letter found in the dress pocket and the incomplete statement to the prosecutor were written by the same female hand. And the same woman added the postscript to the poem. The verse belongs to the poet Nikolai Rubtsov. Judging by the handwriting, it was copied by a man."

"Arkady Ivanovich, I was very interested in the matchbox from the Balabanov Experimental Factory, which was found on the kitchen table. In our oblast,* as far as I know, only Barnaul and Tomsk matches are distributed. Where did the ones from Balabanovsk come from?"

Dymokurov nodded in understanding. "The same question occurred to me, too. I found out that a small shipment of Balabanov Factory matches arrived in Novosibirsk two weeks ago. They were sold in the store near the Sukhaya Loga stop."

*An oblast is a political subdivision of a republic in the U.S.S.R.; Novosibirsk Oblast is 68,800 square miles in area and has a population of 2.5 million. (Trans. note.)

"Then we may surmise that Demensky was visited by someone from the other side of town?"

"We may surmise that."

The interoffice phone buzzed hoarsely. The desk sergeant reported that a citizeness calling herself Ksenya Makarovna was
looking for "the young officer from CID who was investigating
the hurt woman yesterday."

"Send her to me," Birukov said and, hanging up the phone,
looked at the people in his room. "Demensky's neighbor is coming."

A few minutes later Ksenya Makarovna timidly entered the
office. Just like yesterday, she wore the long, old-fashioned dress,
the same beret on her gray head, and carried the same string bag
in her hand. But this time, instead of the milk bottle, the bag
held a pack of Privet cookies. Anton asked the old woman to sit
down. She bowed gratefully, and, perching on the edge of the
seat, began speaking immediately.

"Yuri Pavlovich never did show up. I didn't sleep the whole
night, worrying . . ."

Birukov, listening to the woman, didn't utter a word. Ksenya
Makarovna sighed deeply.

"I came to confess—I hid the most important thing yesterday.
Yuri Pavlovich left the key to his apartment with me, but I gave
it to Anatoly Nikolaevich Ovchinnikov, an engineer from our
building management. He was fixing the plumbing in Yuri Pavlovich's apartment and, you know, he . . . brought women up
there . . ."

"So Ovchinnikov brought Sanya there?"

"No, no, Sanya is different. I'll explain . . ."

"Why did you hide this?" Anton asked reproachfully.

The old woman lowered her eyes.

"Ovchinnikov scared me. I reproached him once and he
showed a long screwdriver and said: 'You gab and I'll jab you
and let out all the air.'" Having said that, Ksenya Makarovna
seemed to bounce back. "Of course, Anatoly Nikolaevich may
have been joking; he likes to joke."

"Did Demensky know him?"

"All the residents of our building know him. He never refuses to do an emergency repair. Just show him a bottle of Extra and he'll be there in a flash." Ksenya Makarovna seemed to realize what she was saying again. "No, no! Anatoly Nikolaevich never takes bribes from the residents, but he'll do anything for Extra vodka."

"You say he works as an engineer in the building?"

"I can't say for sure. That's what our residents call him, but basically Anatoly Nikolaevich repairs the plumbing. And Yuri Pavlovich, leaving for Sverdlovsk, left a fiver with me along with the key and said to get Ovchinnikov to repair the plumbing. That's how it happened."

"Slava, find out about Ovchinnikov," Anton said to Golubyov, and when he left the room, Anton asked the woman once more, "Well, what happened with Sanya?"

"Sanya asked me for the key to Yuri Pavlovich's apartment," Ksenya Makarovna said in a doomed voice.

"And you gave it to her."

"No. I told her Ovchinnikov's address; he had the key."

"Did she go to see him?"

"I don't know, sweetie."

"You're not making anything up?"

"I swear!"

In parting, Ksenya Makarovna bowed low and left the office; then Golubyov came back in. Birukov took the note he brought and read with interest.

"Anatoly Nikolaevich Ovchinnikov was born in Novosibirsk in 1935. He has a middle-level technical education and graduated from the Novosibirsk River school as pilot and vessel mechanic. Registered on Cheluskintsev Street. Listed as fitter and plumber in the building. Conscientious worker. On vacation since August 19."

"Now we know about the pilot plumber," Anton joked and looked at Makovkina.

"Well, Natalya Mikhailovna, shall we get cracking? Let's start with Ovchinnikov, what do you say?"

"Yes, of course," she agreed after a minute of thought.

Birukov turned to Golubyov. "You, Vyacheslav Dimitrievich, have to get into it, too. Familiarize yourself with the evidence that Natalya Mikhailovna has. There's a telegram from Demensky from some Revaz in Adler, and Ksenya Makarovna's statement mentions some white-haired railroad worker 'of a Caucasian type,' age sixty. Talk to the station people at Novosibirsk Central and find out if anyone there fits that description." Birukov got up. "And now I'm off to Ovchinnikov's apartment."

Getting into his car, Anton had no idea that in a few minutes he would face a new mystery: Anatoly Nikolaevich Ovchinnikov had not been home for the last three days. Having received his vacation pay at work, he had disappeared. Neither his wife nor his mother knew anything about him.

3

Working blind, Birukov didn't even notice the first day of intense work slip by. Every new piece of information, instead of bringing expected clarity, only confused the issue even more. For instance, that was what came of the reply from the CID of Sverdlovsk. Demensky really had completed the curriculum early and had gotten an "excellent" for his defense. The dean of the correspondence division had given Yuri Pavlovich an excellent character reference; though this satisfied Anton, he was still made wary by two facts. First, although he had lived in Sverdlovsk for an entire month, Yuri Pavlovich was not registered either in the institute's dormitory or in the city's hotels. Second, Demensky had arrived in Novosibirsk yesterday, and, according to Ksenya Makarovna, he had flown in. But in the Sverdlovsk airport there was no record of a passenger by that name.

Slava Golubyov had worked all day with no results. Among the workers of the Novosibirsk Central Railroad station there were no men at all "of the Caucasus type" around the age of sixty. However, at the personnel department Golubyov did find several photographs of brunets gone gray and gave them to Ksenya Makarovna for identification. The old woman didn't recognize any of them as the man she had seen with Sanya at the railroad station.

The first swallow of spring was brought to Anton by forensics expert Dymokurov. Birukov and Golubyov were planning to call it a day when Arkady Ivanovich came into the office holding a small school file in one hand and several dactyloscopic photos in the other.

"I hit pay dirt," he said wearily, handing Birukov the photos. "The fingerprints on the doorbell and on the doorknob of Demensky's apartment belong to Sipeniatin, who's got a record."

"The first I've heard of him," Anton said with a frown, examining the enlarged contours of the papillary lines.

"For the last three years Sipeniatin was doing time for fraud. He forged icons and swindled lovers of antiquity."

"Is he out now?"

"He must be, if his fingerprints have appeared."

"What is he known for besides fraud?"

"Many other sorry deals. His underground name is Vasya Sivy. He's been arrested for hooliganism, holdups, break-ins, car and motorcycle theft. In a word, there's a lot on Vasya's conscience." Dymokurov put the file in front of Anton. "As a hobby, I collect unique criminal phenomena. There's some of Vasya in the collection. Take a look; maybe you'll find something helpful."

Opening the file, Birukov first saw the usual mug shots: right profile, full face, full length. Each photograph was labeled Vasily Stepanovich Sipeniatin and gave his birth date—1940. The flabby-lipped, pug-nosed face stared into the camera with a childlike curiosity and wariness, as though the subject were waiting impatiently for the birdie to pop out.

Besides the portraits, the file held photos of Sipeniatin's tattoos. Anton had seen various specimens in his time, but this was a first. Sipeniatin had a unique design. On his chest there was a grave with a large cross and the inscription: "SLEEP DEAR FATHER YOU GOT SQUASHED BY A TANK." In a semicircle above the cross there was another, equally ungrammatical phrase: "EVERY DAY THE SUNRISE AND EVERY DAY IT SET." On his right forearm there was a black sailor's cap with fluttering ribbons and the vow beneath: "I WON'T FORGET THE BOATSWAIN!"

"By the way, I have a photo of the boatswain, too," Dymokurov said and, digging through the file, handed Birukov a yellowed photograph.

Against the background of an approaching trolley a legless, big-headed man sat on a low dolly and extended a bandaged hand, as if begging for alms. The top of his head was covered by a flat, rimless navy hat with the ribbon of the Black Sea Fleet, and beneath the pea jacket sprinkled with buttons and medals peeked a muddy triangle of striped shirt.

"A fraudulent beggar?"

"Vasya Sipeniatin's teacher, if I may put it that way. Stepan Stepanovich Stukov, who worked in our directorate for twenty years before retiring, can tell you a lot about this man."

"Stepan Stepanovich!" Anton exclaimed happily.

"Yes. Do you know him?"

"I did my pregraduation practical work under him. And later when I worked at the regional department, we had occasion to meet." Birukov turned to Golubyov. "Slava, you must remember Stukov, too."

"Of course I do."

"We'll go see him right now; he lives nearby," Anton said and picked up the phone. "But I'll request more information on Sipeniatin first . . ."

A few minutes later they learned that Sipeniatin, V. S., born in 1940, was released from prison six weeks ago without permission to live in Novosibirsk. He was sent to the Toguchin region of Novosibirsk Oblast, where he arrived at the appointed time, received a passport, and got a job as a driver on the interstate farm route.

"Our region?" Golubyov was surprised. "Call Toguchin. I'll have a talk with the chairman of the road construction crew."

Long distance worked fast. Golubyov spoke briefly and, after hanging up, said, "Sipeniatin hasn't shown up for work for the last two weeks. They can't find him in Toguchin."

Birukov quickly went through the photos of Sipeniatin. Handing Dymokurov the full-face picture, he said, "Arkady Ivanovich, please have copies made. We have to find this citizen quickly."

Stepan Stepanovich Stukov lived in a five-story gray prewar building. The door was opened by an old man of medium height with a gray pompadour. Seeing Birukov, he clapped his hands in joy.

"Antosha! What winds bring you?"

"Work, Stepan Stepanovich," Anton replied. "How are you?"

"Hello, Antosha, hello," Stukov said and squinted nearsightedly. "Is that Slava Golubyov with you?"

"The same. You have a good memory."

"I can't complain. Why are we standing around in the doorway? Come in, come in. My family is at the dacha. I'll give you a bachelor repast; I'll put on the tea."

Having seated his guests near the coffee table, Stukov puttered in the kitchen. Soon he reappeared, sat opposite Anton, and asked, narrowing his eyes, "What work brings you to me?"

Birukov began telling him. Stepan Stepanovich listened attentively, asking a few questions. When the conversation reached Sipeniatin, the old detective was lost in thought, as though recalling something very old and serious.

As soon as Birukov stopped talking, Stukov asked with a smile; "Then Arkady showed you his collection?"

"He did."

"I got him started on that. I'll try to add something to it . . ." Stepan Stepanovich went over to the bookshelves, found a fat file with newspaper clippings, and handed it to Anton. "To learn about Vasya Sipeniatin, one should begin with his genealogy. This is from *Evening Novosibirsk*. Read it, Antosha; then I'll add to it."

A short article published in the section "From Our City's Past" was called "The End of Nakhalovka." Anton started reading.

"At the end of the last century, in the days when the Ob station was being built, which we now call Novosibirsk-Central, this unique part of our city also grew. Along the banks of the Ob River opposite the station, huddling up to one another, sprang up dugouts, mud huts, and even a few log cabins. Depot workers, railroad men, and indigents moved in.

"No sooner had the first independent builders arrived on the

bank of the Ob than the town officials showered them with
paperwork and demands for rent. The builders refused. The city
authorities tried everything to force the residents of the self-
styled settlement to pay taxes. But they couldn't do anything
with the local desperadoes. Angrily the city fathers named the
settlement Nakhalovka, or 'Obnoxious One.' They even showed
it that way on maps. Even on city maps printed in 1935 you can
still find the name Little Nakhalovka. For old times' sake, so to
speak.

"Among the residents of Nakhalovka were a few front-line
revolutionary workers, but, why hide the truth, there were plenty
of criminals, from petty thieves to real bandits and murderers.
The latter spent most of their time in the then-famous Darya's
Tavern, which belonged to a certain Darya Sipeniatina. The
owner did not care in the least who spent money there or where
he had gotten it.

"But for all that, Darya was a religious woman. Perhaps she
hoped to expiate her sins through prayer. But it was her religios-
ity that doomed her. They built a church on the station square,
which is now called N. G. Garin-Mikhailovsky Square. The
church pleased Darya! Every Sunday and some weekdays, too,
Darya was praying in the new church. The church was on the
other side of the tracks, and the overpass hadn't been built yet.
People made their way across the tracks and under the cars at
their own risk and fear. And once Darya was making her way.
She didn't look and gave up her soul to God without repenting,
under the wheels of a train . . ."

The article went on to discuss the changes in the neighbor-
hood that was once Nakhalovka. Anton finished the article and
asked Stepan Stepanovich with interest, "How is Darya related
to Vasya Sipeniatin?"

"His grandmother."

"And his parents?"

"The father died in World War Two. His mother, Maria Anisimovna—incidentally, a very fine woman—lives in Bugrinskaya
Roshcha, on Kozhevknikov Street."

"What's the relationship between Sipeniatin's criminal activity and his genealogy?"

Stepan Stepanovich tugged at his pompadour. "His last sentence had something to do with it. Here's what happened. A fat cat interested in antiquities bought an old icon with a gold frame and precious stones at the bazaar for two thousand rubles. He showed it to specialists—and they said it was a forgery. Naturally the icon lover went to the militia. When our experts examined the icon, they discovered a painted-over inscription: 'Property of Darya Sipeniatina.' "

Anton suddenly recalled the bookshelves at Demensky's apartment and the row of old books, among them the dark spine of the Bible published in 1910 and the brown ink on the title page.

"Stepan Stepanovich, has the CID come across any of Darya Sipeniatina's books?" Anton asked quickly.

"No, Antosha, they haven't." Stukov was silent a bit and then continued. "Having found the inscription on the icon, we naturally reproached our old friend. Vasya, as usual, put us off in the most obnoxious manner: How am I supposed to know who got hold of my grandmother's old icons; my grandmother died before the revolution. We had a lineup. The victim recognized Vasya without a doubt. And then something extraordinary happened: Vasya, betraying his traditional habits, took the whole blame on himself, even though, according to the experts, the forgery was the work of a qualified artist."

"What are Sipeniatin's traditional habits?"

"Confuse the investigation to the end and blame anyone else he can."

"Maybe his accomplice put a scare in him?"

Stukov shook his head.

"Vasya can scare anyone *he* wants. It was something else."

"What, Stepan Stepanovich?"

"Probably Sipeniatin had further plans. He knows the subparagraphs of the Criminal Code perfectly. He figured that he wouldn't get a long sentence for one icon, and he would need his companion in the future. That's why he didn't turn him in."

Birukov gave Stukov the yellowed photograph. "They say this boatswain taught Sipeniatin. I'd like to know more about his 'school.' "

Stepan Stepanovich, putting on thick hornrimmed glasses, looked at the picture with interest and, returning it to Anton, said thoughtfully, "The boatswain's school closed down a long time ago. Perhaps the old Novosibirians may remember the cripple. In the early years after the war he used to sit at the trolley stop near the TsK Sewing factory and shout hoarsely: 'Dear brothers and sisters! You won't even miss ten or fifteen kopecks, but to an invalid who suffered for his homeland, it's a fortune. Don't forget the Black Sea boatswain, citizens!' And he'd sing:

'I went ahead with machine gun in hand
When our unit went into battle . . .' "

"They say he didn't serve in the war."

"That's right. In thirty-nine he fell under a trolley, drunk, but not many people knew about it. By evening the 'boatswain' would get so stinking drunk he couldn't sit on his dolly."

"Why did the militia allow him to beg like that?"

"The militia had enough real work, Antosha. In those days lots of bums pretending to be war veterans crawled out onto the streets," Stukov said and took off his glasses. "They eventually cleaned things up, of course, and the 'boatswain' disappeared from the horizon. He lived beyond the Kamenka river, next to Sipeniatin. And as a young kid, Vasya fell under his influence. The 'boatswain' found the key to the lad's heart: he'd tell him about his war exploits, making up stories that he had seen Vasya's father throw himself under a Fascist tank with a grenade—"

"You mean the tattoo on Sipeniatin's chest is based on fact?"

"The tattoo is only part of the problem. What's terrible is that the boatswain, in order to get enough for his drinking, taught the local boys to steal. We stopped a lot of them, but Vasya Sipeniatin didn't straighten out. He was sentenced for the first time when he was fifteen, ended up in a colony for minors, and it was all downhill . . ." Stepan Stepanovich tapped his glasses on the file of news clippings. "I'm gathering facts bit by bit. I've become a lecturer in our youth groups, and I use Vasya's story often. There are no more 'boatswains,' of course, but there are still wheeler-dealers and drunkards out to destroy teenagers' souls, unfortunately." Stukov was lost in thought, twisting his glasses. He gave Anton a close look. "You say Vasya's fingerprints are at the scene of the crime?"

"Yes, Stepan Stepanovich," Anton said, smoothing back his hair from his forehead. "I'm wondering if Sipeniatin didn't attempt rape."

Stukov examined his glasses for a long time. Then he put them down on the coffee table and spoke.

"That's not a characteristic crime for Sipeniatin. Vasya can steal, finagle, try any deal, but as for women . . . He never had that weakness . . ."

The teakettle whistled loudly in the kitchen.

4

Early the next morning, hot on the heels of Anton and Golub-yov, a tall man came into the office wearing a fashionable striped shirt tucked into his trousers and a brass buckle on his wide belt. His curly hair was disheveled and his youthful face seemed tired, like that of an athlete who had just completed a heavy workout.

"Here—my neighbor gave it to me," he said in a deep voice, handed Birukov the message and without waiting for an invitation sank weakly into a chair.

"You're Yuri Pavlovich Demensky?" Anton clarified.

"Yes."

"Where were you for two days?"

"Looking for the key to my apartment."

"Where did you lose it?"

"My neighbor gave it to the handyman. I went to his place; he wasn't home. A friend suggested that Anatoly was planning to go to the Ob Sea for some fishing. So I went there. I checked all the fishing spots around Berdsk—"

"Yuri Pavlovich," Anton interrupted, "use the surnames of your acquaintances."

"Certainly. The plumber's surname is Ovchinnikov; his first name is Anatoly, as I just mentioned. Alik Zarvantsev is the fellow who told me about the fishing trip."

"Who is he?"

"An artist. He lives near the opera house." Demensky gave the address.

"Do you know why we asked you to come here?"

"My neighbor vaguely mentioned something, but I didn't understand, really."

Birukov got the pictures of the victim, taken at the scene, from his desk and handed them to Demensky. A thin film of sweat instantly appeared on Yuri Pavlovich's brow.

"Do you recognize her?"

"My ex-wife."

"Surname, name, patronymic?"

"Kholodova, Aleksandra Fedorovna."

"Where does she live and work?"

"I don't know a thing!" Demensky almost shouted, but got himself under control. "I can only tell you about the past. Shall I?"

Anton nodded. "Go on."

Yuri Pavlovich wiped his brow.

"I married Kholodova in Omsk. I was working in a factory there; Sanya was in charge of the bookstore. She had a year-old son, Seryozha, even though she hadn't been legally married before me. I was transferred to Cheliabinsk from Omsk. Sanya moved there with me, getting another job as head of a bookstore . . . May I smoke?"

"Smoke," Anton said, moving the ashtray closer to Demensky.

"At the end of seventy-two I was sent to Novosibirsk for two months. Just before New Year's I decided to pay a surprise visit home, give her a surprise present . . . It's only two hours by plane from Novosibirsk to Cheliabinsk. So, on December thirty-first at eight P.M. I was home. No one in the apartment. Two empty champagne bottles and glasses on the table, with a half-eaten box of expensive chocolates. The bed wasn't made, it was rumpled . . ."

Demensky took a deep drag and wiped his brow once again. "In short, I spent New Year's Eve pacing my apartment like a caged tiger. My wife appeared the next day. She arrived with a young pilot, drunk. Seeing me, she was stunned. She began lying naïvely, trying to tell me that she spent New Year's at a friend's house and that the pilot was the husband of her girlfriend, and he was just bringing her home because it was so late . . ." Yuri Pavlovich looked up at Anton. "I won't hide from you that I slapped her face and left the house. Then I got a permanent transfer to Novosibirsk. Kholodova remained in Cheliabinsk."

"And that was the end of your relationship?"

"Fully. I went to court and we were divorced six months later."

"You haven't seen Kholodova since?"

"No."

"Then how did she end up in your apartment?"

"I don't know."

"Yuri Pavlovich, a serious incident has taken place: we don't know if Kholodova will live. We have to find out if there was a crime involved in this or not . . . Do you understand? You know Kholodova and her circle of friends much better than anyone else. Help us . . ."

Demensky's jaws twitched. Squashing the butt of the cigarette he had smoked so quickly, he immediately lit another one. Inhaling deeply, staring at the floor, and speaking with reluctance, he said, "A day before the accident Ovchinnikov and Zarvantsev were at the Orbit Restaurant with Kholodova. They drank a lot there."

"Are they friends?" Anton asked.

Yuri Pavlovich snorted. "In their crowd friendship is a relative concept. If you need a person, you see him; if you don't, the contract is broken."

"What connects you to them?"

"Absolutely nothing. Ovchinnikov is simply—the handyman of our building. Of course, Anatoly keeps trying to become a friend. He even asked me once if he could bring a girlfriend to my apartment. To which I replied that I didn't run a house of assignations."

"And Zarvantsev?"

"About three years ago Alik worked as a designer at our factory and led the painting group at the factory House of Culture. That's where we met. At the time I was interested in art."

"When did you do the portrait of Kholodova?" Anton suddenly asked.

Demensky was embarrassed and replied, "Before leaving for Sverdlovsk. I was in a low mood, and I decided to check my visual memory."

"It seems to me you have a good mastery of the brush."

"No I don't . . . Compared to, say, even Zarvantsev, I'm just a dilettante."

"Zarvantsev is a good artist?"

"He's a marvelous designer, in a word, a pro."

"And as a person, what is he like?"

"Very modest, but knows what he wants . . . He likes to hang out with celebrities and powerful people. Of ordinary mortals, Ovchinnikov seems to be his only friend. Anatoly is basically a sweet guy. He says whatever is on his mind. And then he has irrepressible energy and astonishing optimism. That's just what Alik needs. Opposites attract."

"I see," Anton said. "Did you introduce them?"

"Just the opposite. I first met Ovchinnikov at Zarvantsev's. They were at school together."

"How did Kholodova get into the picture?"

"Zarvantsev says that Ovchinnikov brought Sanya to the Orbit. He doesn't know anything else."

"They talked about something in the restaurant . . ."

"I wasn't interested in their restaurant conversation."

"Where did Ovchinnikov disappear to?"

"I don't know." Demensky looked distractedly at his cigarette tip. "Maybe he headed for Razdumie—there's this little fishing spot on the Ob Sea. Anatoly has his own cutter with an outboard motor."

Birukov looked at the silently listening Golubyov and wrote him a note. "Call OSVOD.* Let them look for A. N. Ovchinni-

*The Soviet Coast Guard. (Trans. note)

kov in Razdumie. If they find him, have him sent immediately to Novosibirsk. We'll meet him here."

Golubyov read the note and left the office.

Watching Demensky nervously light another cigarette with the old one, Anton recalled the full ashtray on the kitchen table in Yuri Pavlovich's apartment.

"Does Kholodova smoke?" he asked Demensky.

"No," Yuri Pavlovich said curtly and then corrected himself: "Actually, when she's very nervous, she reaches for a cigarette . . . A strange question . . ."

"Nothing strange about it," Anton said calmly. "Forensics has determined that before the incident Kholodova had smoked almost an entire pack of cigarettes."

Demensky looked in bewilderment at the pack he held in his hand along with the lighter. "That's not like her."

"Did you buy matches from the Balabanov Experimental Factory?" Anton asked quickly.

"Which?"

"With green heads in a cardboard box."

Yuri Pavlovich showed him his elegant butane lighter. "I've been using this for many years."

Anton opened the file with the investigation materials, found the crumpled piece of paper with the unfinished statement to the prosecutor and, handing it to Demensky, asked, "Do you know the handwriting?"

Demensky furrowed his brow: "I think Kholodova wrote this . . ."

"What did she want to report?"

"Honest, I don't know."

Birukov showed him the letter with the verse. "And is this epistle familiar to you?"

Demensky seemed feverish. "Sanya sent that to me after the New Year's business. I added the poem from Rubtsov's collection. I wanted to mail it back to Sanya, but changed my mind."

"But the letter was found in Kholodova's dress pocket."

"Sanya must have been going through my books and found it

. . ." Yuri Pavlovich concentrated on the sheet of paper. "She's written something hysterical under the poem, that wasn't there before."

Birukov's eyes ran down the letter. "Listen to these two sentences, Yuri Pavlovich . . . First: 'I was in a terrible state and stayed that way until your call.' The second sentence is: 'Revaz isn't bothering me, everything's quiet for now.' " Birukov and Demensky met gazes. "What call is she talking about, if you severed all relations with Kholodova, and who is Revaz?"

Demensky was flustered, like a child caught lying, and muttered, "You see . . . it's like this . . . well . . . Actually, I did call her after the argument. To apologize for slapping her. You understand, hitting a woman . . . As for Revaz, he's—he's an acquaintance of Sanya's from back in the Omsk days."

"Who is he?"

"Revaz Davidovich Stepnadze. A pensioner. From Georgia. He lives in Novosibirsk in the Zatulinsky houses, on Zorge Street. In the summer he makes a little money as a conductor on passenger trains. He's a true book lover, and pesters Sanya with his orders for hard-to-get books."

"And what did you order through Revaz from Adler?" Anton asked, stressing the "you."

Demensky was obviously confused.

"Fruit . . . I asked him to bring fresh fruit."

"I think we've found the man from the Caucasus," Birukov thought with relief, going through the file for the telegram from Adler. Finding it, he handed it to Demensky and asked, "Please read it aloud."

"Obtained the order meet me Revaz," Yuri Pavlovich read without inflection.

"Did you meet him?"

"I was in Sverdlovsk. I've never seen this telegram."

Anton was silent. Then he spoke. "Yuri Pavlovich, is fresh fruit so scarce in Adler now that it has to be specially ordered and obtained?"

Demensky stared stupefied at the telegram. "I don't know

why Revaz Davidovich put it that way. Of course, it would have been more correct to put: 'I bought the order . . .' " And suddenly, as if finally guessing, he said: "Stepnadze probably doesn't have a good ear for the subtleties of Russian. Apparently 'buy' and 'obtain' are the same to him."

Observing Demensky, Birukov noted a characteristic detail: as soon as the conversation touched on Stepnadze, Yuri Pavlovich became a different man. He resembled someone unaccustomed to lying who was forced to do so by circumstances. In order to test his supposition, Anton changed the subject.

"Where did you live in Sverdlovsk, Yuri Pavlovich?"

"At my cousin's, on Minometchikov Street, number thirty-eight," Demensky replied quickly and, giving the apartment number, said with obvious relief, "You can check."

"We will," Anton said, putting away the telegram. "What is your cousin's name?"

"Her married name is Donayeva, Anna Sergeevna."

After he wrote down the address, Birukov looked into Demensky's eyes. "When did you appear in Novosibirsk?"

"August twenty-first. I flew in in the morning."

"You're not mistaken?"

For the first time in their conversation Yuri Pavlovich seemed to smile. "I'm of sound mind and body."

Birukov was silent and then said, "According to our information, you didn't fly out of Sverdlovsk on August twenty-first."

Unfeigned bewilderment appeared on Demensky's face. However, he dealt with it quickly and exclaimed with put-on chagrin, "That's right! I didn't fly out of Sverdlovsk on the twenty-first, I flew to Novosibirsk from Cheliabinsk."

"From Cheliabinsk?"

"Yes, I decided to visit some old friends there and spent two nights with them."

"Did you see Kholodova there?"

"No, I didn't. Why should I see her?" Demensky replied faster than was necessary and quickly looked over at the water pitcher. "May I?"

"Go ahead."

Yuri Pavlovich, almost spilling the water, filled a glass, brought it to his mouth, and emptied it with a few large gulps, as though he had been suffering from thirst for days. When Demensky had had his fill and sat back down in his chair, Birukov put a dozen police photos on the desk, among them one of Sipeniatin, and asked Yuri Pavlovich to look them over and tell him if he recognized anyone.

Demensky looked as if he had been asked to perform an incredibly difficult task. Finally Yuri Pavlovich just shook his head. Taking away the pictures, Anton looked into Demensky's eyes.

"Just one more question . . . Where did you buy the Bible that once belonged to Darya Sipeniatina?"

Demensky's eyebrows shot up in amazement; however, he answered without hesitation and, it seemed to Anton, rather sincerely, "Alik Zarvantsev got it somewhere for me about three years ago."

"Where specifically?"

"I didn't ask."

After a few more questions Birukov let Demensky read the transcript, and when he signed the statement, the inspector wished him well. Yuri Pavlovich headed silently for the door. Holding the doorknob, he suddenly turned.

"Tell me, comrade captain, will the doctors save Kholodova?"

"Don't worry," Anton said, evading the question.

Demensky bowed his head and left the office.

Soon after, an animated Golubyov appeared. OSVOD confirmed that Anatoly Nikolaevich Ovchinnikov owned a boat called *Progress* with a Whirlwind-30 outboard motor, but recently had his license suspended for boating under the influence of alcohol. Upon learning that Ovchinnikov had taken his *Progress* out onto the Ob Sea, the chief of the OSVOD navigation–technical inspection team promised to find the lawbreaker immediately and return him to Novosibirsk.

Having reported all that quickly, Golubyov asked Anton, "How was Demensky?"

Birukov pulled the statement over and frowned. "He's not telling everything, that Yuri Pavlovich. He's afraid of something."

"Did he say anything of value?"

"Of course."

"For instance?"

"For instance, we've cleared up the man 'of Caucasian appearance.' We were looking for him in the wrong place. Revaz Davidovich Stepnadze works as a reserve conductor and not at the railroad station."

"What do we do now?"

"There's plenty to do. First we have to get the prints from that glass." Anton looked at the glass Demensky had used and then at the ashtray. "Send the butts to the lab, too."

"Right."

"Then, Slava, get in touch with the CID in Sverdlovsk and ask them to find out when Demensky flew out and to what city and did he really live at his cousin's house on Minometchikov Street." He tore an old page from his calendar and wrote down the address. "After that call the Cheliabinsk CID. Let them find out what they can about Kholodova and check when Demensky left for Novosibirsk. When you've done that, take on Revaz Stepnadze. Find out about him from the conductor reserve force and try to meet him. I'll be interested to find out what Revaz Davidovich says about Kholodova. I think that he was the man Ksenya Makarovna saw talking with Sanya at the station."

"And what if Stepnadze is out of town now?"

"Then, to save time, try to get his picture at the reserves and have Ksenya Makarovna identify him. By the way, show her a picture of Sipeniatin along with the rest. Maybe the old woman happened to see Vasya near Demensky's apartment . . ." Anton thought for a bit. "But you know what, Slava . . . Before you do any of that, call Captain Yuri Vasilievich Ilynykh, Sixth Precinct militia chief. Have his men find out if Vasya Sipeniatin has appeared at his mother's house on Kozhevnikov Street. Got it?"

"Yes sir."

"Go on, then. I'm off to look for Alik Zarvantsev."

But the phone rang before Birukov could get up. It was Dr. Shirokov, Kholodova's physician.

"Criminal investigation?" Aleksei Alekseevich asked anxiously. "Please send one of your men over to the clinic immediately. Something very strange just happened here."

5

With his shaved head and thin frame, Dr. Shirokov gave the impression of being a wise but very meek man. Only his eyes, gazing with concentration beneath his thick brows, and his square chin, marred by an old scar, hinted that the doctor had not only brains but a willful personality. Meeting Birukov at the entrance, Aleksei Alekseevich hurriedly led him into an empty interns' room, sat him near a table that held a bouquet of gladioli in a liter-size glass jar, and gave him a small piece of yellowish paper, folded in half. It was a brief note, just one line, typed in capitals on a dilapidated machine.

"GET BETTER AND KEEP QUIET. GREETINGS FROM YOUR FRIENDS," Anton read.

"Yesterday morning an unknown man tried to pass this to the patient who entered our clinic under your auspices," Shirokov said and put a twenty-five-ruble note on the table. "That was a 'tip' for the nurses' aide, and the flowers, too." He pointed to the bouquet.

"Why were you silent about this for so long, Aleksei Alekseevich?" Birukov asked unhappily.

"The aide was silent," Shirokov said. Looking down the corridor, he called loudly, "Renata Petrovna! . . . Please come to the interns' lounge."

A minute later Birukov saw a very tall young woman with pitch-black hair plaited into a thick, long braid.

"Tell about how you took a bribe, Renata Petrovna," the surgeon said severely.

"I've explained, Aleksei Alekseevich, that I didn't take any bribes," the woman said huffily.

"Don't tell me, tell the detective."

Staring out the window, the aide shrugged crankily and began speaking. Putting questions to her, Birukov found out that the man who brought the note was middle aged—not old but no longer young, either. Tanned face. Dressed in a blue shirt with rolled-up sleeves and light trousers, and wearing patterned, fashionable shoes and a broad-brimmed hat, like a sombrero. The aide didn't see the color of his hair because of the hat. He had asked her to pass the note to the woman as soon as she regained consciousness. He didn't mention her by name at all; he merely said, "The one that fell from the third floor and was brought to the clinic in an ambulance yesterday."

"How did he offer you the money?"

"He said if the patient got well to drink to her health with my friends. I asked: 'Can't you do that yourself?' He smiled and said, 'You see, I'm off on a long business trip and I won't know when she gets better.'"

"Why didn't you tell Aleksei Alekseevich about it right away?"

"I thought the patient would get better soon."

Anton showed her several photographs.

"Did any of these men show up at the clinic?"

"No," the aide replied, going through the pictures thoroughly.

"May I?" Shirokov asked, reaching for the photos. At the sight of Sipeniatin's face, his thick eyebrows came together in concentration.

Anton released the aide from the lounge and said warily, "Is that a familiar face, Aleksei Alekseevich?"

"No. It's just that the fellow has a curious gaze," the surgeon replied, returning the pictures. "Sort of naïve."

"But the fellow's actions aren't naïve at all," Anton said, putting the pictures in his pocket. "If someone comes in about the patient, please let us know."

"Definitely."

The high-rise where Alik Zarvantsev lived was a stone's throw from the clinic. Finding the right apartment, Birukov pushed the bell several times. A lap dog seemed to bark in the apartment, but no one rushed to open the door. He had to ring again. Finally he heard footsteps in the entry, and the lock clicked twice. A man stood in the open doorway wearing a suit that looked brand new. The thick mane of hair, almost shoulder length, and the big-nosed face with the five-o'clock shadow did not match the youthful, trim body, and it was hard to determine the man's age at first glance.

"I need Albert Evgenievich Zarvantsev," Anton said.

The man looked flustered, nodded energetically, but drawled a greeting: "Come in."

Judging by the quiet, there was apparently no one in the apartment besides the man and the floppy-eared dachshund amiably wagging its rear end.

"Excuse me, with whom do I have the honor?" the man said with a blindingly white smile.

"Birukov. From the CID."

"May I see your ID?"

"A careful citizen," thought Anton as he got his papers.

The man studied the little red book thoughtfully, glancing several times at Anton, comparing his face to the photo, returned his identification, and made a sweeping gesture past the shut kitchen door to the open door of the living room.

"Come in," he sang once more, letting Birukov pass. "Albert Evgenievich Zarvantsev at your service. You may call me Alik."

The room into which Zarvantsev led Anton was remarkable for its murals. From ceiling to floor the walls were covered with provocative, big-breasted mermaids; nude beauties smiled and wept in various poses, and muscular gladiators with fig leaves stabbed sea monsters with daggers. The white spaces between drawings were filled with broad colored signatures.

In contrast to the loud wall "art," the furnishings were more than modest. A wide old-fashioned couch, a worn armchair, a table with crooked legs, a cracked wardrobe, and a pair of creaky chairs had either been inherited by Zarvantsev or bought for a song in a secondhand store. Between the wardrobe and the window stood a small TV, and on the floor there was an enlarger; several photos with curled edges were tossed one on top of the other on its base. Half the window was blocked by a paint-smeared, empty easel.

Offering Birukov the armchair, Zarvantsev sat on the couch. Loosening his tie, as though it had been choking him, and twitching the toes of his suede shoes, he froze tensely. The dog, which had dozed off next to him, suddenly looked up and yapped. Anton thought he heard the front door shut and at the same time heard quick steps going down the stairs.

"Just a minute." Zarvantsev ran out of the room. He turned the lock in the hall and returned quickly. As he sat down he seemed to perk up.

"We left the door open. The kids around here play tricks." He loosened his tie some more. "I'm listening, Comrade Birukov."

Anton met his guarded eyes. "I would like to listen to you, Albert Evgenievich."

"Excuse me, but about what?" Zarvantsev asked helpfully.

"About how you and Ovchinnikov and Kholodova spent time at the Orbit Restaurant."

Zarvantsev grew pale.

"We spent it normally, nothing excessive. Why, has something happened?"

"Yes."

"What precisely?"

Birukov told him. Albert Evgenievich, dumbfounded, never took his anxious and guarded eyes off Anton. Hearing him out, he asked in a shaking voice, "Why did you think I knew what was happening? I didn't see Sanya after the restaurant."

"Tell me how you met her," Anton said.

Zarvantsev bit a hangnail on his index finger and slowly, thinking over every word, began to talk. According to him, they met this way:

At noon on August twentieth Ovchinnikov called him and suggested they "wash down" his vacation. When Zarvantsev came to the Orbit, Anatoly Nikolaevich was already sitting there with a beautiful young woman who said her name was Sanya. Ovchinnikov added, "She's Yurik Demensky's wife; she flew in from Cheliabinsk to see him." Zarvantsev didn't ask for details. In the course of the whole evening Sanya drank only one shot of vodka. Ovchinnikov, however, drank heavily. Drunk, he tried to kiss Sanya and persisted in talking to her about going to the Ob Sea with him in the morning. He bragged constantly about his cutter. Finally Sanya got tired of it all, and she suggested they go home. Zarvantsev, feeling heavy all over, went home, and Ovchinnikov had "one for the road"—almost a full glass of vodka—and took Sanya home. The next day early in the morning Demensky appeared unexpectedly at Zarvantsev's house and asked questions about Ovchinnikov. Learning about the evening at the Orbit, he went out of his mind . . .

Albert Evgenievich raised his sorrowful eyes at Anton. "Imagine, Comrade Birukov, I was even afraid. I asked him: 'What's the matter with you, Yura!' Demensky answered: 'Alik! Sanya Kholodova is actually my ex-wife. I wanted to go back to her, but she's up to her old tricks. Mixed up with Ovchinnikov. Well, I'll show her. She'll remember for the rest of her life.' And he raced off." Zarvantsev assiduously bit off another hangnail. "Now I blame myself for telling him the truth. I knew that Yura was jealous . . . I admit that Ovchinnikov threw me for a loop. I thought he was making it up about her being Demensky's wife."

"Demensky hadn't mentioned her to you before?"

"Never. Yura is a clam. Now that I'm talking about him, I can tell you he's a very decent man. A talented engineer. He makes so much money! Anyone else would live the high life, but Yura lives modestly."

"Is he miserly?"

"Not at all. He just doesn't spend a lot. For instance, a taxi is a luxury for him; jewelry—a vestige of the past; furniture, rugs, and cars—bourgeois; resorts and drinking—a waste of time. In a word, almost anything you could spend money on doesn't interest Yura. What he likes is books. Speculators, knowing his weakness, charge him triple . . ."

"Do you know, by the way, how much Demensky paid for an old Bible with the 'autograph' of Darya Sipeniatina?" Birukov asked casually.

Zarvantsev, lunging forward, didn't seem to understand. "Whose autograph? . . . Ah-hah! . . . I got that Bible for Yura at the book market for a hundred and fifty rubles."

"Isn't that a bit high?" Anton asked.

"What can you do? The prices are crazy for unique editions. Not even unique ones! Books by contemporary popular writers go for ten to fifteen times the list price."

"Do you remember the man from whom you bought the Bible?"

"It was a long time ago, Comrade Birukov . . ." Zarvantsev appeared to be thinking. "Can you imagine, I don't even remember if I bought it from a man or a woman."

"Well, now what could have happened in Demensky's apartment, Albert Evgenievich?" Anton asked, returning the conversation to the incident.

"I have no idea . . ."

"You said that Demensky threatened Sanya."

Zarvantsev, as though protecting himself, threw up his hands in fear. "No, no, Comrade Birukov, not at all! Yura just said that in anger. When he's calm, I swear, he wouldn't touch a woman. Demensky is a sentimentalist, he likes to dig around in spiritual suffering, berate himself for trifling mistakes. It's as if he lacks a public scaffold and to punish himself, invents his own scaffold. No, Comrade Birukov, suspecting Yura of something bad is simply crazy!"

"What do you think of Ovchinnikov?"

Albert Evgenievich smiled slightly. "I can think whatever I want, but I can't say it all."

"I'm counting on your frankness."

"Anatoly and I went to the same school; he was three grades

ahead of me. What can I say about him?" Zarvantsev shrugged
and thought. "He used to be a soccer star. He wanted to become
a coach, but the vodka interfered. He went into river navigation,
almost made it to captain, but the drinking again . . . Now he
works for building management: he's either a locksmith or works
in supplies. He's pushy. And he adores women—"

The doorbell rang impatiently. The quietly dozing dog
jumped from the couch and yapped loudly as it rushed to the
door. Zarvantsev shuddered, but didn't hurry to open the door.
The bell rang even more persistently. Finally Albert Evgenievich, apologizing to Anton, reluctantly went to the entry and
clicked the lock twice. Immediately a woman's voice shouted
angrily: "Why did it take you so long?" Zarvantsev whispered
something, but the woman, laughing noisily, cut him off. "Don't
bullshit me! You must have a woman in here! I'll give her a
permanent!" There was a scuffle in the entry, the door flew
open, and a young woman resembling a lanky youth backed into
the room, wearing a white shirt and jeans lettered across the seat
in extravagant yellow gouache: TOLYA. Flopping down on the
couch, she stared at Anton with tipsy eyes.

"Hello," Anton said, unable to suppress a smile.

"Hi . . . Who are you?"

"Lusya, stop fooling around," Zarvantsev said in embarrassment, following her in. "This is a comrade from the militia."

"Oh-oh-oh," the woman said, pursing her lips and bugging
her large eyes. "I'm so-o-o scared."

Zarvantsev, sitting down next to her, smiled ingratiatingly.
"Are we a little drunk?"

"What? . . . Did you give me liquor?"

"Stop it. The comrade will think badly of us."

"I don't give a damn!" Lusya squinted and burped. "I don't
give a damn, Alik, what people think of me . . . Give me the
phone . . . I'll call Tolya. His wife will answer, and I just sigh
. . . It scares her, and how! Isn't that a great joke, hah?"

" 'Jokes' like that will land you in jail. It's called hooliganism."

"Jail?" Furrowing her forehead, Lusya turned to Anton. "Can

you put me in jail, really? . . . It's scary there, oh-oh-oh . . .
Alik! Bring something to drink . . . We'll wash down my re-
lease ahead of time." And extending her thin neck, straining, she
sang:

> *"Two winters! Two springs!*
> *I'll do my time and come back . . ."*

"Why are you here?" Zarvantsev said, losing his cool and
turning pale. "To brag that you're as drunk as a skunk?"

Lusya stared at him. "Not like a skunk . . . Yura Demensky
only bought one bottle of cognac . . . Understand? Tomorrow
I'm quitting the barbershop, Yura will set me up as a desi—
designer at his factory. I'll make over two hundred a month! I
don't give a damn for your crummy three rubles! Understand?"

Zarvantsev's face contorted painfully. However, Lusya, leaving
sweaty hand prints on his white trousers, continued.

"Well, tell me how you and Yuri's wife caroused at the Orbit?
. . . What are you staring at, like the bourgeoisie at the working
class? . . . You and Tolya killed Yuri's wife. You killed her,
right? You bastards! Crawling vipers! . . . Mama!" Lusya, face
buried in the couch, started crying hysterically. Completely un-
nerved, Albert Evgenievich sat like a statue.

"Give her some water," Anton prompted.

"She'll get over it, this isn't the first time," Zarvantsev said,
his face coming back to life. "She'll be snoring like a horse in a
few minutes."

Lusya really did calm down very quickly. Bringing her knees to
her chest, she tucked her folded hands under her cheek and
snored deeply. Zarvantsev moved away fastidiously.

"Who is she?" Anton asked.

"Lusya Priazhkina. She cuts hair and gives shaves at the railroad station barbershop. She sometimes poses for me. I give her
three rubles out of my own pocket for two sessions . . . I can't
understand why Demensky went to her with a bottle of cognac
. . . Could he have suspected me? . . . Now that's jealousy

that knows no bounds." Zarvantsev looked askance at the snoring Priazhkina. "And this weirdo comes in here drunk . . ."

"Does she often drink?"

"Rather. The girl has a complex. She's in love with Ovchinnikov. You see the name Tolya on her jeans—it's a cry from the heart . . ."

"Do they know each other?"

"They say they lived next door."

"Where?"

"In Bugrinskaya Roshcha somewhere. Anatoly moved to Cheluskintsev Street recently. He recommended Lusya as a model to me."

"We didn't finish talking about Ovchinnikov, Albert Evgenievich. Lusya interrupted us," Anton said.

Zarvantsev, gathering his thoughts, was silent. Then he spoke. "What is there to say about him? Anatoly is a drinker, likes to play around, but—this is true—he's totally harmless. A lot of it is put on, for show, and inside he's a gentle and in his own way unhappy man. I, for one, pity him."

"What did he and Kholodova talk about?"

"Once he had something to drink, Ovchinnikov, as usual, began some frivolities, but Sanya quickly turned him off. Then Anatoly switched to jokes. He's a virtuoso in that genre. Basically, it was a banal restaurant chat—no more than that. Sanya was mostly silent."

"There was nothing unusual in her behavior?"

"Absolutely. It seemed to me that Kholodova had come to the restaurant out of boredom. Of course, she did try to talk about Demensky several times, as if she wanted to learn something about Yuri. But Ovchinnikov did not go along with her attempts and took the conversational lead."

"Did she mention Revaz Davidovich Stepnadze?"

"Why should she?" Zarvantsev blurted, and he looked as though he had committed an unforgivable error. "No, Comrade Birukov, there was no conversation about Revaz."

"Do you know Stepnadze?" Anton asked.

"He's my uncle."

"So that's how it is!" thought Anton and, controlling his amazement, asked calmly, "Do you know anything about his relationship with Kholodova?"

"Absolutely nothing!" Zarvantsev almost shouted. And then to fend off any more questions, he added quickly, "I haven't had anything to do with my uncle in over five years."

"Why?"

"Nothing in common."

Lusya Priazhkina moaned and turned over. Apologizing to Zarvantsev for taking up his time, Birukov said good-bye. Opening the door for him, Albert Evgenievich had a lot of trouble getting the key in the lock.

6

Slava Golubyov followed Birukov's plan. Turning over to forensics the butts and the glass used by Demensky, he called Captain Ilynykh about checking on Sipeniatin. Then he called CID in Sverdlovsk and then in Cheliabinsk and, having spoken with his colleagues, headed for the conductors' reserves office.

From his conversation with the head of personnel—an elderly, coughing railroad man—he found out that Revaz Davidovich Stepnadze, despite his pensioner's age, had been working for many years in the summer, when there is an increase in passenger travel, as a conductor on the long-distance lines to the south and to central Asia. In years past he worked on trains headed for Tashkent, Alma-Ata, Simferopol, and Odessa. This year since June he had been on the Novosibirsk–Adler train. He returned the last time on August 21 ("The day of Kholodova's incident," Slava noted), and the next day took off on another trip, even though it wasn't his shift. No one in the management could say precisely why that happened, although they did suggest that Stepnadze might have traded shifts with someone else. Stepnadze's work record was excellent.

"We could use more pensioner conductors like him," the personnel director said.

Getting a photograph of Stepnadze, Golubyov went to see Demensky's neighbor without further ado. Ksenya Makarovna wasn't home. Slava went down into her courtyard and sat on an empty bench and waited impatiently. Time passed, and the old woman still didn't show. Golubyov began thinking that he should find a more discreet place to wait, so as not to parade in front of the entrance in his militia uniform, when he saw Demensky, walking slowly.

Reeling, Yuri Pavlovich came abreast of the bench where Slava sat, stopped, and asked in an unsteady voice, "May I . . . join you?"

"Please do," Golubyov answered, moving over.

Demensky swayed and sat down. Taking out a cigarette, he sighed deeply, as though trying to get rid of the alcohol smell. Lighting up, he turned to Golubyov and said, "I recognized you. You were in the office at headquarters where the captain questioned me. Right?"

"Right," Golubyov confirmed.

"Why is the militia keeping from me the name of the clinic where Kholodova is?"

"Instead of looking for Kholodova, Yuri Pavlovich, you'd be better off telling the truth about her."

"Do you think that I lied at headquarters?" Demensky asked challengingly, leaning back against the bench.

"You didn't lie, but you didn't tell all, either."

Yuri Pavlovich laughed drunkenly. "Is that all you want! The complete truth . . . on a platter with a ribbon. I don't know the complete truth myself."

"Do you at least know one or two of Kholodova's acquaintances in Novosibirsk?"

"Sanya didn't have any acquaintances here except for me and Revaz Stepnadze. I only fudged one thing at the questioning: when the captain showed me photographs of some criminals, I was afraid to name a fellow."

"Which one?"

"I bought the Crucifixion from him at the book market before leaving for Sverdlovsk. I paid him ten and didn't have another five on me. I gave him my address, but he didn't come by for what I owed him before I left."

"Do you know the fellow's name?"

"How should I? I only bargained with him for ten minutes or so."

Golubyov, after some hesitation, took out a pack of photos. "Look, is he in here?"

"There he is." Demensky pointed to Sipeniatin.

"Why did you keep quiet about this at headquarters?"

"Because I was as frightened as a schoolboy. I was afraid to admit it."

"And you're not afraid now?"

"Now I'm brave, I'm not afraid." Yuri Pavlovich brought the smoldering cigarette to his lips, took a drag, and then pulled out Stepnadze's picture. "And this is Revaz Davidovich, who sent me the telegram from Adler."

"Could Kholodova have met him at the station?" Golubyov asked, taking the picture back.

"If the telegram fell into her hands . . ."

The butt burned Demensky's fingers. Grimacing, Yuri Pavlovich ground out the yellow filter with his heel and then, recalling something urgent, lurched and got up. Without another word he strode to the driveway.

Golubyov had to wait another half hour for Ksenya Makarovna. The old woman unhurriedly approached the house, carrying her eternal string bag and looking up at the balconies as if she expected another woman to fall. Slava quickly found two witnesses to be present at the identification and went into the old woman's apartment with them. He explained and put the pictures on the table.

After a brief look, Ksenya Makarovna pointed at Stepnadze's picture. "That's the man!"

"Which one?" Slava wanted clarification.

"The one Sanya met at the station. You see, his head is as white as foam . . ."

"You can dye foam, granny."

"But you can't hide a Caucasian face. He's the one; I don't have a single doubt."

Golubyov asked the old woman to look closely at the other photographs.

Squinting nearsightedly, Ksenya Makarovna stopped at the

curiously wary face of Vasya Sipeniatin and said uncertainly; "I think this citizen came to see Yuri Pavlovich twice while he was away. He asked me when my neighbor would be back. But he doesn't have a crew cut, like on the photo, but white hair . . ."

Golubyov grabbed at the thread.

"Was this a long time ago?"

"Last week."

"How about the day the incident took place—did you see this citizen?"

"No, dearie, that day I didn't."

Golubyov returned to headquarters late in the evening. Birukov was sitting at his desk and reading telegrams, peering at one and then the other alternately. In his usual rapid speech, Slava reported on his results.

Having heard him out, Anton doodled on his calendar and said nothing for a long time. Then, crossing out his scribbles, he said, "Listen to what the reply is to our inquiry from Cheliabinsk . . . Aleksandra Fedorovna Kholodova, born 1942, has been living in Cheliabinsk since 1972. Her character references in general and at the bookstore are excellent. On August eighteen she took her vacation. She was planning to go to the city of Aleksin in Tula Oblast to see her parents, where her seven-year-old son lives. But a check at the airport reveals that on the night of the eighteenth on flight 3324, Kholodova flew to Novosibirsk without telling her neighbors about it. On the morning of the twentieth, Yuri Pavlovich Demensky came to the neighbors, who know him as Kholodova's ex-husband. He was interested in her behavior, and insisted on knowing where Kholodova was at present. The neighbors, who gave a good account of Kholodova, said they thought she had gone to Aleksin. At the airport it was established that passenger Demensky left Cheliabinsk for Novosibirsk on flight 3324 on August 21."

"What does Sverdlovsk have to say?" Slava asked.

Birukov picked up the other telegram. "Demensky's stay at the apartment at Donayeva at the address you gave us is confirmed by neighbors. We checked: passenger Demensky, Y. P., left Koltsovo Airport in Sverdlovsk on the morning of August 20 for Cheliabinsk. No other passengers with that surname were registered at the airport in the three-day period."

"Yes, a charade," Golubyov said dispiritedly. "Yuri Pavlovich flew on Kholodova's heels. Did he catch her? Well, and what about the fingerprints and butts?"

"According to forensics, there are no butts of Demensky's among those found in the ashtray in the kitchen." Anton set aside the telegram. "I'm very concerned by Revaz Davidovich. Remember, in Kholodova's letter there's the phrase: 'Revaz isn't bothering me, everything's quiet for now.' That was written in 1973. A lot of water under the bridge since then. I wonder if the 'quiet' hasn't ended?"

Golubyov paced decisively around the office. "We have to show Demensky the telegram from Cheliabinsk. He told you that he was visiting friends . . ."

"Should we reveal our cards to Yuri Pavlovich ahead of time? Demensky is either shocked by the incident or hiding a secret . . . Let's give him a day or two to calm down and then we'll see how he behaves."

"What hypothesis are we going to go on?"

"Let's call it Foam. According to Demensky, Stepnadze is an avid bibliophile . . ."

"Right!" Golubyov picked up quickly, pointing at the photograph of Revaz Davidovich. "Look, there's a cap of foam on his head. Could he be the one who shut the balcony door behind Kholodova?"

Birukov picked up Sipeniatin's photo from the desk and laughed. "Vasya has a lot of 'foam' on his head now, too."

Golubyov thought. "So what?" he asked suddenly. "Vasya could have done the job himself. Let's say he comes to Demensky for the money owed him, finds Kholodova alone in the apartment . . . You can expect that from a hardened criminal—the robe with the torn-off buttons . . ."

Birukov said nothing. On a clean page of his calendar he concentrated on printing in block letters the word: "FOAM."

"Why aren't you saying anything?" Slava asked impatiently.

"Revaz Davidovich Stepnadze is worrying me," Anton said, underlining the word and looked up at Golubyov. "Slava, how about a trip for you to the Black Sea? The train that Stepnadze is on will arrive in Adler tomorrow. If you leave Novosibirsk in the morning, you'll get there in time to meet Revaz Davidovich. Meet him and don't let him out of your sight."

7

The head of the inspection team of OSVOD kept his word. More than that, he offered the use of his speedboat, on which Birukov raced from Oktiabrskaya harbor to the Bugrinsky beach, as they say, on a breeze.

The morning sun played and shimmered on the Ob waters. A light haze hovered barely noticeably over the sandy beach. Awaiting Ovchinnikov, Anton had time for a swim, and after combing his wet hair, he settled in the shade of a mushroom umbrella. The beach wasn't at all crowded. Not far from his umbrella some tanned men were playing with a volleyball. When one of them lost the ball, a skinny teenager hanging around the players immediately ran after it.

Ovchinnikov's *Progress* turned out to be a standard metal motorboat. He appeared from the side of the Ob sluice of the Ob Hydroelectric Station accompanied by a hydrofoil with an OSVOD flag. Sharply reducing speed, both vessels hit the sandy shore at the same time. Ovchinnikov, tanned to a bronze, wearing nothing but bright orange swim trunks, straightened to his full six feet four inches. Spreading his arms wide, he stretched, then stepped heavily overboard and with a single tug pulled the boat, without any strain, almost halfway up onto the sand.

Birukov, coming over to the hydrofoil, at the wheel of which sat a severe-looking man in a captain's cap, introduced himself.

Squinting over at Ovchinnikov, the captain whispered, "I'll just make out the ticket and I'm done."

While the OSVOD captain wrote the ticket, Anton looked over the powerful physique of the former soccer player. His balding head and noticeable paunch suggested that Ovchinnikov's soccer career had ended at least ten years ago.

After the hydrofoil left the shore, noisily roiling the water around it, Anton came over to Ovchinnikov and said, "I'm from the CID, Senior Inspector Birukov. Hello."

"Hello, chief," Ovchinnikov said. Confusion glimmered in his big gray eyes, but he laughed immediately. "Boy, the controls are squeezing down on a lone boat owner. I can understand OSVOD, they're worried that I'll sink. But what does the CID care? That I might fly up into the clouds?"

"We need to know about your health," Birukov said in a joking tone.

"Hangovers give me a terrible headache every time."

"You should drink less."

"I pay for my own. Whose business is it?"

"This is our business and it's serious." Birukov, sitting on the *Progress*'s side, looked into Ovchinnikov's eyes. "Anatoly Nikolaevich, where did you spend the night after your evening at the Orbit and also the following day, August twenty-first?"

"The twenty-first, early in the morning, I was pushing away in my corvette from the shores of Novosibirsk and heading for Razdumie. Right? Right. Where did I spend the night? At home, probably, where else . . ."

"You haven't spent the night at home in a long time," Anton said, looking at the matchbox in Ovchinnikov's hand.

"Chief, shoot me—I can't remember. I put away so much at the Orbit that . . . I walked the plank and there wasn't any."

"Where did you buy those matches?"

Ovchinnikov stared at the box as if seeing it for the first time. Anatoly Nikolaevich's face expressed surprise, but he replied calmly, as if nothing had happened, "In Novosibirsk."

"Where exactly?"

"Exactly, chief, I memorize only where I can buy Extra vodka. Actually, what's going on?"

"Somebody left matches just like that on Demensky's kitchen table."

"At Yurik's? . . . I could have," he said. Then his large eyes darted anxiously, as if he belatedly realized that he had said too much.

Trying to calm him down, Anton changed the subject. "You used to be an athlete?"

"I confess. I chased a soccer ball around until I was thirty-five and worn out. I had to apply for a job in building management."

"But you do have a diploma as a pilot and ship's mechanic."

"Who needs a specialty like that? All summer—water, water, everywhere . . ." Ovchinnikov took a deep drag on his cigarette. "I blew it with sports, though. I could have been a coach on a kid's team . . ."

Just then the escaped volleyball rolled toward the water. The skinny teenager came running after it. Watching him, Ovchinnikov said sadly, "I could have trained kids like that to be first-class." Suddenly he jumped to his feet and shouted, "Hey, twerp! Bring the balloon here!"

"What?" The boy picked up the ball and didn't understand.

"The ball, bring the ball, I say! I'll show you a trick."

The boy came over to the boat. Ovchinnikov put on his shoes, got an empty bottle out from under the seat, and, stepping heavily from the boat onto shore, walked along the beach, flexing his muscles. Finding a level spot and putting the bottle on the sand, he measured eleven paces from it. He set the ball at his feet and turned to Anton. "Watch this, chief!"

He took a short run and kicked with his right foot. The ball, in a smooth trajectory, knocked over the bottle. Ovchinnikov gave Anton a triumphant look.

"Would you like to see me do it with the left?"

Recalling his fascination with soccer in his student days, Anton said with interest, "Do it!"

The ball didn't hit "with the left" but shot past so close to the bottle that it fell again. Once upon a time, while he was in training, Birukov himself had liked doing tricks with the ball. Of course now he wasn't in shape anymore and had other concerns, but he wasn't going to miss a chance to show off to the old soccer star and gain his confidence. Anton decided to try the experiment. As though giving in to a moment's fancy, he easily swung over the boat and shouted to the kid chasing after the ball, "Bring it back again!"

The boy caught the ball and kicked it back. Then he set up the bottle and ran off to the side, stopping short. The volleyball players were also interested in the experiment. Noticing their curious gazes, Birukov slowly walked away from the ball, took a running start, and kicked with his left foot. The ball seemed to lick up the bottle buried in the sand.

"Are you a lefty?" Ovchinnikov asked in surprise. "Can you do that with your right, chief?"

Right kicks had come harder to Anton in his college days. He decided not to take the risk and smiled. "Better stop while I'm ahead."

"Do you have a letter?"

"Yes. But not in soccer. In wrestling."

"Let's wrestle."

"Some other time . . ."

"Well, you're okay, chief!" Ovchinnikov pointed to his boat. "I have a bottle of lemonade on board left over from fishing. It's called Extra. How about a glass each to tone us up?"

Anton squinted at the sun. "It's kind of hot for Extra."

As they talked they walked over to the boat. They resumed their seats, opposite each other. Ovchinnikov pulled out his Belomor cigarettes. He looked sideways at Birukov as he smoked.

"You're wrong in suspecting me of some vile deed, chief. The night of August twentieth I wasn't at American intelligence headquarters but in a Soviet drunk tank. After the Orbit I came across a volunteer patrol." He smoked in silence. "How did CID find out that I was partying at the Orbit? Were you watching me, or what?"

"Zarvantsev told us."

"Alik? . . . What did I do to him?"

"Somebody did something to Sanya Kholodova," Anton said.

Ovchinnikov was stunned. "What happened, chief?"

"She got hurt, falling from Demensky's balcony."

Ovchinnikov's big eyes became almost spherical. "Are you kidding? Was she drunk?"

"Why drunk?"

"A sober person would never fall off a balcony."

"How did you meet Kholodova?"

"No tricks, chief." Ovchinnikov looked away and took several drags on his cigarette. "Yurik Demensky asked me to fix his shower and faucets in the tub before he left. Well, I got the key from his neighbor, did what was necessary, and then I forgot to return the key. I got my vacation money on August twentieth—I had to wash down an occasion like that. Alik Zarvantsev and I were going to meet at six at the Orbit. As soon as I hung up the phone, who do you think appeared: a cute lady in pink asking for Ovchinnikov. I was stunned. 'I'm Comrade Ovchinnikov,' I say. 'What's up, sunshine?' She smiles, offers her hand, saying, 'Nothing's happened. I'm Sanya Kholodova, Yuri Demensky's wife. Do you have the key to his place?' We got to talking. I walked her to Yuri's apartment. She showed me her passport with registration in Cheliabinsk—everything was in order. She said that Yuri had called her from Sverdlovsk, asked her to come and told her that if he wasn't back in Novosibirsk, the key would be with Ksenya Makarovna, his neighbor. Really, chief, it all fits together, the way it really was. I could see she was a friendly dame, and I invited her along to celebrate my vacation pay. No way! It took me half the day to convince her to have dinner at the restaurant. She barely agreed. Alik and I put it away, naturally, but she wasn't having any . . ."

"Was she in a bad mood?" Anton asked.

"I wouldn't say that . . . She was careful, I think; we were mere acquaintances."

"And Kholodova spent the whole evening there with you?"

"You think it was boring? Women are never bored with me, chief. You want to hear the latest jokes? You'll fall down laughing."

"Why don't you tell me what happened after the restaurant."

"After the restaurant the fakir was drunk and the trick didn't work. I bid Sanya a gentlemanly farewell at the front entrance to Yuri's building. As soon as I got on the Railroad Highway, the volunteers, may they always be hung over, showed up . . ."

"Where did you spend the two nights before that?"

Flicking his cigarette into the river, Ovchinnikov looked into Anton's eyes. "I have a girlfriend—she'd make you lick your fingers! Yurik Demensky even called her that—who was the Roman goddess of beauty?"

"Venus."

"No. What other celestial beauty was there?"

"Aphrodite."

"That's the one!"

"That's Greek mythology, not Roman."

"It's all the same! In fact, it's all Greek to me." Ovchinnikov laughed, but quickly grew serious. "I can tell you don't like my humor, chief. Let's be more concrete. I paid my fine at the drunk tank, and then I went to Razdumie to relax. I didn't do anything bad there and I wasn't planning to set fire to the Ob Sea with the matches left behind at Demensky's. What does the CID want with me?"

"There is a supposition that Kholodova didn't fall on her own from the balcony," Anton said. "She was pushed."

Ovchinnikov's left cheek twitched nervously. "Well, what do I have to do with it?"

"Circumstances indicate that you were one of the last people to see Kholodova before the incident."

"Chief, I wasn't in Novosibirsk on the twenty-first! I tell you, I moored at Razdumie that morning."

"Who can corroborate that?"

Ovchinnikov hesitated for a second. "The girlfriend who looks like Aphrodite."

"Who is she and where does she work?"

"Frosya Zvonkova. She works in a grocery store by the Sukhaya Loga stop."

"So that's where the Balabanov matches came from!" Anton

thought and, looking into Ovchinnikov's eyes, asked, "Did you do some drinking in Demensky's apartment?"

"That was a sin before Kholodova came. I admit it—I had Extra with girls I know. But I didn't do any tricks. I'm not one of those who speak to the weaker sex from a position of power. I have a principle: if it doesn't work, drop it."

"And who drank cognac with Kholodova in the kitchen?"

"What cognac?" Ovchinnikov asked in amazement.

"Armenian, five stars."

"You think I'm stupid, that I should throw money away? You can buy three bottles of Extra with that! No, chief, that's not my system."

Further conversation revealed that at the restaurant Kholodova had had a black patent leather purse that held her passport and "a pile" of money. Sanya even wanted to pay for the whole group, but Ovchinnikov paid out of "gentlemanly considerations."

"The search of Demensky's apartment did not reveal that purse," Birukov noted to himself, and asked Ovchinnikov where the purse might have gone. He didn't have any idea. When asked about Stepnadze, he replied that he'd known Revaz Davidovich a long time, since he was in school with Zarvantsev, but he didn't maintain a special relationship with the old man.

In conversation Ovchinnikov kept furrowing his brow, trying to recall something important. Suddenly, slapping his bare knee, he exclaimed; "Chief! I left the matches at Yuri's."

"When?" Anton asked, listening for false notes.

"Before going to the Orbit with Sanya. I remember I didn't have any matches at the restaurant; I had to keep bumming."

"One–zero, not in my favor," Anton thought and asked once again, "Did Kholodova mention Stepnadze?"

"No, I don't think so . . ." Ovchinnikov scratched his bald spot. "Now a telegram came for Demensky from Revaz. Two days before Kholodova appeared. I was working on the plumbing when it was delivered. I remember I put it on the table in the room."

"The one with the gladioli?"

"What gladioli? Yuri didn't have any gladioli in his apartment." Ovchinnikov pouted and frowned. "Listen, chief . . . Revaz loves gladioli. Maybe he was with Kholodova on the twenty-first, hah? Stepnadze is a hot old man when it comes to women."

"Why did Kholodova come to Novosibirsk, do you know?"

"It's obvious why wives come to see their husbands."

"Demensky and Kholodova were divorced."

"Sanya said they were thinking of getting back together."

"Anatoly Nikolaevich," Anton said, "why does Lusya Priazhkina advertise your name on her jeans?"

"That Lusya is nuts . . . If you want to know more about her, drop by the juveniles' room of the Sixth Precinct. She has a record there."

"I see. I have a request: please stay in Novosibirsk for the next few days. We may need you as a witness."

"Come on, chief . . . What kind of witness am I?"

"A very needed one."

Birukov said good-bye. Ovchinnikov watched his receding back a long time, as though rethinking their conversation. He lit up nervously, regarded the empty matchbox from the Balabanov Experimental Factory with surprise, and then angrily tossed it far into the river.

8

Every time the unraveling of a crime brought him in close contact with intimate human relations, Anton Birukov felt an unpleasant sensation. It was either fastidiousness at the uncleanliness of out-and-out lowlifes, or discomfort arising from the fact that his work made him an unwilling witness to deep secrets of basically decent people. In these cases Anton almost always recalled Stepan Stepanovich Stukov, who had worked almost a half century as a detective. Once, lecturing young inspectors, the old operative said, "You must have a clean conscience and clean hands, but in order to find out, say, the contents of a criminal's suitcase, you may have to dig around in dirty laundry, dear comrades. Every crime is a tragedy, and tragedies are not done in watercolors. Be clean yourselves, but don't turn up your noses fastidiously at someone else's dirt, because in most cases it's the dirt that leads people to crime." After the talk with Ovchinnikov, Anton Birukov realized that there would be more than the usual amount of dirty laundry in this case.

Ovchinnikov made an ambiguous impression. On the one hand, he was a hail-fellow-well-met, from whom it was not difficult to learn the truth. On the other hand, the amorous adventures and constant drinking of Anatoly Nikolaevich were such a part of him that probably he himself couldn't tell anymore when he was telling the truth and when he was lying. In order to cut down the list of suspects, Anton decided to determine right away when Ovchinnikov had set off for Razdumie. If he had really pushed away in his corvette from the shores of Novosibirsk on the morning of August 21, then he had an alibi and his involvement in the incident with Kholodova could only be tangential. According to Anatoly Nikolaevich, his departure time could be confirmed by the as-yet-unseen Aphrodite, who worked in the grocery store at the Sukhaya Loga stop. Therefore as soon as he got to his office Birukov looked up the grocery store in the phone directory and dialed the number. A weary female voice answered.

"Tell me, is Frosya Zvonkova working there?" Anton asked.

"Oh my God," the woman said with a sigh. "I just told you in plain Russian: Frosya is off today, call her at home."

Birukov was alert. "You didn't tell me anything. This is my first call here."

After a pause the woman said, "Excuse me, I confused your voice with someone else's. A minute ago some man was asking for Frosya."

"Does she have a phone at her apartment?"

"Yes," the woman said and gave him the number.

"Thanks," Anton said and, hanging up, started leafing through the directory.

The Zvonkova, E. V., with that telephone number lived on Petukhov Street. Birukov called for a car immediately.

The building in which Zvonkova lived was at the beginning of the street. Finding the right entrance, Anton went up the stairs, watching the numbered doors. Between the third and fourth floors a woman of twenty-five or so, dressed up and with extraordinarily fine features, came down the stairs toward him.

"Are you Zvonkova?" Anton asked almost intuitively.

The woman stopped. Looking Anton up and down in surprise and adjusting her purse strap on her shoulder, she said in bewilderment, "Yes. What's the matter?"

"I must talk to you."

"Excuse me, I'm in a hurry."

Anton showed her his ID. After looking at it, Zvonkova shrugged. "I'm listening."

"This isn't the best place for a serious talk."

Zvonkova hesitated and then said, "Let's go to my place."

On the fourth floor she dug her key out of her bag. Opening the door, she spoke curtly. "Come in."

Anton, letting the woman in first, came into a bright, tastefully furnished apartment.

Seeing his hostess's inhospitable mood, Anton said, "I must talk to you about Anatoly Nikolaevich Ovchinnikov. Do you know him?"

Zvonkova cast a sidelong glance at the phone, looked embarrassed, but replied calmly, "I do."

"When did you last see him?"

"Three days ago."

"Be more precise."

"More precisely . . . August twenty-first, in the morning, when Anatoly went to Razdumie in his boat."

"Had he slept here the night before?"

Zvonkova blushed, but she replied as calmly as before, "Two nights."

"How about the night of the twentieth?"

Zvonkova shrugged. "I don't know." And then, turning beet red, added, "Oh, I remember. Anatoly was here too."

Pretending not to have noticed her forgetfulness, Anton asked, "May I use your telephone?"

"Please."

Birukov called the medical sobering unit and asked the man on duty to check the files and see whether on the night of August twentieth they had held Anatoly Nikolaevich Ovchinnikov, locksmith, picked up in a drunken state on Railroad Station Highway. When he got a positive reply, he looked at Zvonkova, who turned away in embarrassment.

"So . . . You didn't tell me the truth," Anton said slowly. "And it was Ovchinnikov who told you to lie to me, calling you before I got here. But you didn't understand him correctly, did you?"

Zvonkova, with her back to him, was silent. Her face was flushed and splotchy. Finally she mustered her courage, tossed her purse on the bed, and sighed softly. "Right."

"What exactly did Ovchinnikov ask you to do?"

"If CID asked, I was to confirm that Anatoly spent two nights here and that on the morning of August twenty-first I saw him off to Razdumie."

"Then he didn't sleep here and you didn't go to Razdumie with him?"

"Of course not." Zvonkova started bustling. "Why are we standing! We should sit down!" Moving a chair up for Anton, she smiled ingratiatingly. "Sit down, please."

"How did Ovchinnikov explain his request?" Anton asked, sitting opposite Zvonkova.

"He said that something had happened to a woman and the CID thought—oh, what do you call it—suspected him, that is, Ovchinnikov."

"Do you have a close relationship?"

"With Anatoly? I really need bald men!"

"Then why did he turn to you with this request?"

Zvonkova jerked her shoulder. "We've known each other a long time. Anatoly once dated my older sister, before Nina got married, but nothing came of it."

"Do you know Demensky, Yuri Pavlovich?" Anton asked.

"I do. Yuri is the complete opposite of Anatoly. He's smart, so well read that you feel a total fool around him."

"Have you ever met his wife?"

"Is he married?" Zvonkova was surprised.

"Probably," Anton said, avoiding a direct answer.

Zvonkova shook her head. "No, Yuri's a bachelor. He's like Alik Zarvantsev—you'll never get them married."

"You know Zarvantsev, too?"

"Of course. Alik is the nephew of the husband of my older sister, the one Ovchinnikov dated in her youth."

"Your sister is married to Revaz Davidovich Stepnadze?" Anton asked, controlling his amazement.

"Yes. She found a husband thirty years older than herself, as if there weren't younger suitors." Zvonkova laughed. "Of course,

Nina wasn't looking for love but for furniture, a car, a dacha.
Revaz has all that in the highest degree."

"They live well?"

"Snug as bugs in a rug. Revaz worked in the Far North a long
time; he buried his old woman there. Then he moved to Siberia,
got good money there, too. He retired at fifty-five and gets a
hundred and fifty rubles a month . . ."

"And earns more as a conductor," Anton added.

"He's bored with riches. 'You see, dear, I can't live without
work,'" Zvonkova imitated him. "And Nina supports him:
'Well, really, what will you do all day long in the house? Go
south for the summer, lie in the sun.'"

Anton smiled and said: "You don't like your sister."

"What is there to like about her—her greed? Last year she
lent me an eighty-ruble ring to wear and I lost it. Nina practically broke my neck. I had to pay her back out of my vacation
pay."

"Is Revaz Davidovich like that, too?"

"No, Revaz is simpler. It's Nina that's putting the squeeze on
the old man. If not for her, the old man would probably shower
everyone with his money. He's really old, but he makes eyes at
women no less than Ovchinnikov."

"Is the nephew like his uncle?"

"Alik is dishwater. He blushes like a schoolboy around
women."

"They say he's pals with Ovchinnikov."

"Alik makes good money, and Anatoly hangs around him. He
can borrow fivers without paying them back. Anatoly himself, if
he ever has a ruble, drinks it away with friends."

Birukov took out photographs. Handing them to Zvonkova,
he asked, "Have you met any of these men among Ovchinnikov's friends?"

Zvonkova, thin brows arched in surprise, began examining the
pictures. When she got to Sipeniatin, she cried out, "Oh! But
that's Vasya Sipeniatin! . . . His mother, Maria Anisimovna,
lived right in the next apartment. And Vasya lived with her.

Then he was put in jail for speculating with an icon. Maria Anisimovna is old, it was hard for her to climb up to the fourth floor, and she traded apartments. Now she lives in Bugrinskaya Roshcha. Sometimes I drop in on her . . ."

"Where did Vasya get the icon?"

"You know," Zvonkova said animatedly, "the Sipeniatins moved here from Kamenka. And when they were razing their old house, Vasya found a trunk full of his grandmother's icons in the attic. There were all kinds of them! Little ones, like toys, and medium ones, and big ones. There was an enormous one, in a darkened brass frame. Vasya touched it up and they say got several thousand for it."

"What happened to the other icons?"

"He sold them all off quietly, and he got caught on the last one. He speculated on church books, too. That Vasya is such a crook, let me tell you! For instance, listen to this: A month ago, when he got out, he comes to me in the store. 'Hi, sweetheart!' Vasya calls me that. 'Hello, bunny,' I say. 'Are you out?' 'Good behavior. Listen, lend me ten rubles till tomorrow.' 'Is that all?' I say. 'I know your tomorrows.' Vasya looks around—there's no one in the store. He gives me a jar. 'If you don't want to lend it to me, then buy this for a tenner. It's priced by the state.' I look, it's a regular jar with a factory label: 'Black Sturgeon Caviar.' He said they were selling it at Gastronom Number One." Zvonkova laughed. "I knew that Vasya was a crook, but he was giving me such an innocent look . . . So I gave him the ten, and instead of black caviar the jar held Hiker's Breakfast, which costs pennies. Do you think I was the only one he tricked? My friends at the Gold Key store told me that they bought up twenty jars of the 'caviar.' That makes two hundred rubles Vasya picked up! Just think what a rip-off! Where he got the factory labels . . ."

"We're getting off the subject a bit," Anton said. "Do Ovchinnikov and Sipeniatin know each other?"

"I don't know."

Suddenly the phone burbled softly. Zvonkova moved to get the phone, but then, flustered, sat down again.

"Are you afraid of something?" Anton asked.

"That's probably Ovchinnikov," Zvonkova replied, lowering her eyes. "We were supposed to meet, but I was held up with you. Anatoly promised to tell me about that woman who had the unpleasant incident."

Anton immediately had a risky but very promising idea.

"Frosya," he said, using her name for the first time, "go meet him, help out the CID."

"Oh!" Zvonkova said in fear. "I don't know how to lie; I blush. Anatoly will be able to tell right away."

"Don't say anything; just listen."

"Oh, I won't be able to . . ."

"Try," Anton cajoled. "But most important, not a word to Ovchinnikov about our conversation."

"Anatoly isn't a criminal. I assure you."

"Well, then, let's prove it."

9

A second chat with Demensky, held right after Birukov returned to headquarters from Zvonkova's, yielded absolutely nothing. Yuri Pavlovich denied everything with melancholy. He seemed depressed and asked the same question several times: "Tell me, will Sanya make it? Will she live?"

Anton asked the medical examiner to join them so that he could observe Yuri Pavlovich during the conversation. After Demensky left, the examiner said, "It looks like reactive depression. Apparently he's concerned about Kholodova's fate."

"How long can this last?" Anton asked.

"As long as the traumatizing circumstances. As soon as Demensky hears that Kholodova is better, the depression will disappear."

"And what if Demensky is worried that Kholodova will survive?"

"Then he'll calm down when he learns of her death."

Frosya Zvonkova called. Putting together her confused story, Anton saw that Frosya hadn't dared ask Ovchinnikov a single question, and he had told her much less than Birukov already knew. Anatoly Nikolaevich, as Anton realized, probably had spent most of his time convincing Frosya that he wasn't guilty of anything and had asked her help in "getting out of this stupid business."

Then Anton concentrated on rereading the work references for Ovchinnikov, typed in dancing heavy letters on the old building management machine. The text was covered with purple-ink commas. Apparently the machine's comma didn't work and the typist had inserted them by hand. Suddenly something clicked for Anton. He recalled that the note left by the stranger for Kholodova with the nurse's aide was typed on an old machine, too. Birukov found it quickly. The type was the same, but the darkness of the ink was different. It looked as if someone had changed the ribbon after dashing off the note and only then had typed Ovchinnikov's references. But the paper was the same: slightly yellowed, plain, the kind used in photocopiers.

Turning the reference and the note over to forensics, Birukov went to the management office a half hour later. The first thing he noticed was a large bouquet of gladioli on the windowsill.

In the empty reception room a middle-aged woman with flame-red hair, lips tight in concentration, typed a bank statement with two fingers on an old portable Moskva typewriter. Indifferently glancing at Birukov's ID, she explained that she was a bookkeeper, but since they didn't have a typist on staff, she had to do that job, too.

"Did you type Ovchinnikov's references?" Anton asked.

"I did," she replied calmly.

"Did you change the ribbon before typing?"

"Yes, I did; the old one was just no good anymore."

"After getting his vacation pay, did Ovchinnikov show up here again?"

After a pause the woman said, "Anatoly Nikolaevich got his vacation pay on the twentieth . . . Then, I think. Yes, he did. He spent half the day here on the twenty-first. He was waiting for the mail, got a letter, and I haven't seen him since then."

"What letter?" Anton frowned.

"In an ordinary envelope. He read it, looked happy, stuffed it in his pocket, and said good-bye."

Anton, pretending to be interested in the gladioli on the windowsill, asked, "Did he buy the flowers?"

"Yes, to celebrate his vacation."

"Do Ovchinnikov's friends drop by here?"

"Endlessly."

"Any men of Caucasian appearance among them?"

"I don't ask nationality, but in general there's loads of people here from early morning on."

"Who else besides you uses the typewriter?"

"Whoever isn't too lazy to do it."

"How about Ovchinnikov?"

"I never saw him. What does a locksmith have to type?"

"They say that he also handles supplies for you."

"That happens infrequently, when we have to get something really rare. But I always type all the paperwork."

The bookkeeper had replied in a monotonous voice with such indifference that not a trace of emotion crossed her face the entire time. "She's a robot, not a woman," thought Anton. Looking at the pile of plain yellowish paper near the Moskva, he asked, "May I type something?"

"Go ahead."

Birukov took a piece of paper, folded it in half, put it in the carriage, and with one finger typed all the lowercase and uppercase letters and then all the punctuation marks. The comma was blank.

Anton left the building management office in a foul humor. By the time he reached his office, the forensics team had established that the note and Ovchinnikov's references were typed on the same paper and on the same machine. Tests showed that the paper from the management office had the same chemical analysis as the one used for the note and that the typeface was identical. Unfortunately, the lab men could not determine the most important question: who had typed the note.

In his own office, Anton stared for the umpteenth time at the line "GET BETTER AND KEEP QUIET. GREETINGS FROM YOUR FRIENDS." The telephone interrupted his concentration. As soon as Anton answered, Dr. Shirokov's worried voice came on the line.

"Comrade Birukov, I have to see you urgently."

"What happened now, Aleksei Alekseevich?"

"Either blackmail or provocation—I can't tell."

Anton looked at his watch. The workday was almost over.

"I'll be right there."

A few minutes later, when Birukov appeared at the clinic, Shirokov was nervously pacing the reception area with his hands in the pockets of his snowy coat. He said hello and then silently led Anton to the empty interns' lounge, shut the door carefully, as if afraid they'd be overheard, and asked, "Let me see the photograph of that fellow with the naïve look, the one you had last time, when you showed it to the aide."

Birukov took out Sipeniatin's picture. Shirokov, as though unable to believe his eyes, stared at the photo, and Anton noticed that the ridge of the scar on his chin went from pink to burgundy.

An unexpected thought came to Anton. "Did he give you the scar?" he asked.

"No," Shirokov replied quickly. "The scar is from the war, but this criminal type met me near my house today and broadly suggested that I shouldn't treat Kholodova. That is, she had nothing to live for . . ."

"He mentioned her name?"

"Yes."

"What did you reply?"

"I sent him to hell!" Shirokov returned the picture to Anton and, stuffing his hands in his pockets, paced the lounge. "The fellow started threatening me: if Kholodova lives, we'll finish you off. Then I saw a militiaman and shouted: 'Comrade! Help me detain this criminal!' While the patrolman ran over, the man whisked around the corner and disappeared."

"What does he look like now, this man?" Anton asked.

"Like on the picture, only his hair is long. The color is unusually light."

"White?"

"Unusually so, as though he used peroxide." Shirokov paused. "This wasn't the end of my tribulations. An hour ago an unknown citizen called and said with an accent: 'The ticket is in your mailbox. Don't be late.' It sounded as if he was calling from a public phone at the railroad station—I could hear a public announcement about the arrival or departure of some train."

"What did you say?"

"Not a word. The man, saying only those two sentences, immediately hung up. I called my wife and she brought this . . ." The surgeon took out a blue rectangle of paper and handed it to Anton. "A ticket to the Aurora Movie Theater for tomorrow night's eight o'clock show."

"You have to go to the Aurora."

"Why? It seems to me the easiest thing is to block all roads out of Novosibirsk and detain the white-haired man."

"The easiest isn't always the wisest, Aleksei Alekseevich. First of all, it's not easy to block all the roads. Second, the man may only be an unwitting go-between, and we need the one who's taking such a big risk to keep Kholodova from testifying. Will she get better, Aleksei Alekseevich? Can we count on her help?"

"She's approaching the crisis. Count on the worst," the surgeon said curtly. "That's why I'm afraid of getting into a messy business at the theater."

"Our people will be there. We'll try to take control of the situation."

"Can you at least tell me what all this means?"

"Unfortunately, I don't know any more than you do right now," Anton admitted frankly and, in order to encourage Shirokov, added, "We still have twenty-four hours, Aleksei Alekseevich. I hope something will be cleared up in that time."

Birukov left the clinic with a heavy feeling, as if it were his own fault that a very dangerous criminal had escaped and was about to create a lot of trouble. The case was twisting into a tense spiral. If Sipeniatin's fingerprints on Demensky's door could have been explained away by accident, now Vasya Sivy seemed to be attracting police attention intentionally. This was puzzling. What was making an old criminal hand take this risk: profitable work as an intermediary or fear for his own skin?

Musing, Anton walked along Red Prospect. The day was coming to an end. The newsstands were doing good business with the evening paper, people were squeezing into buses at the stops, the store doors almost never closed. Not far from the ancient turreted building of the Orbit Restaurant an elderly artist in a thick, shaggy sweater worked over an open sketchbook.

"I have to talk to this master about icon painting. Maybe he knows Zarvantsev, too," thought Anton, coming closer to the artist.

The artist put his last strokes on the sketch. Evaluating his work, he threw his hairy head back and, as if addressing Anton, muttered, "Well, how is it?"

"I think it's terrific," Anton said, using the opportunity to strike up a conversation.

"And I think it's just a colored photograph," the artist grumbled.

"Is that bad? It's really lifelike, it resembles it."

"In art, young man, everything must be like it is in life and not like it is."

"Excuse me, what's your name?"

"Nikolai Ivanovich."

"Are you a professional, Nikolai Ivanovich?"

"I'm an artist, not a Canadian hockey player."

Anton laughed. "I have a friend who considers himself a professional artist. Do you know Albert Evgenievich Zarvantsev?"

"The artist Zarvantsev died five years ago."

"Died?" Anton asked, puzzled.

"As an artist, naturally."

"And as a man?"

"As a man, Albert Evgenievich is alive and well and making big money. He was tempted by easy money."

"If it's no secret, what money is this?"

"You should know; he's your friend."

"We recently met."

Nikolai Ivanovich, as though puffing an invisible pipe, wheezed. Putting aside his sketchbook, he looked at Birukov's shoulder boards.

"Are you from the speculation and embezzlement squad?"

"I'm a senior inspector in the CID."

"Zarvantsev never used to have friends in the CID."

"He's a witness in a case."

"Witness?" Nikolai Ivanovich, pulling the strap holding his sketch box over his shoulder, nodded at the path in the park that began at the foot of the Orbit.

Birukov walked next to him unhurriedly. Despite his external grumpiness, Nikolai Ivanovich turned out to be a garrulous man. He had known Zarvantsev a long time—from the day Alik finished art school and appeared in Novosibirsk and started working in the studios of the Art Fund. Alik was outstanding among the beginning artists, with his heightened perception of color and phenomenal visual memory. All he needed was to look closely at someone for a few seconds and he could draw the portrait from memory. For about ten years Zarvantsev worked happily in the studios. He did a lot of creative work in that period, appeared in several regional exhibits, but suddenly cooled toward art and took on design work. He started in that field at the factory, and now traveled from region to region doing commissions.

"Did Zarvantsev ever work with icons?" Anton asked.

"Who needs them?" Nikolai Ivanovich looked surprised. "There aren't any churches nowadays; you can't make money painting icons."

"I mean the icons that are chic among collectors now," Anton said, clarifying his question.

"Zarvantsev isn't a crook. And he doesn't need to take on the risk of forgery. Alik makes plenty by elementary hackwork."

"Is designing on commission hackwork?"

"Obviously. Everything's done by stencil."

"You can't make that kind of money in creative work?"

"Creativity is constant seeking and sleepless nights; it's the maximal expenditure of nerve cells and a mass of doubts, broad periods of failure. In creative work you don't capture fortresses at a single bound and you don't achieve success thinking only of money. Success comes with years of intense, painstaking work. Not everyone has the patience for it."

"Zarvantsev didn't have enough?"

"He cracked somehow . . . He started degenerating, hitting the bottle. And when a monied man starts drinking he instantly attracts a crowd of failures and sneaks."

"I, for one, found Zarvantsev modest and decent," Anton said.

"Yes, you can't deny Alik that for now," Nikolai Ivanovich said.

"Why 'for now'?"

"Because the paths along which an unsteady man may slide down are inscrutable."

10

The operatives appeared at the Aurora Movie Theater an hour
before the show was to start. The film *Esenia* had attracted a
large audience, and people looking for extra tickets darted
around the entrance. Particularly active was an elderly Gypsy
woman with large earrings. Getting tangled in her long skirt, she
rushed headlong to every passing man, each time calling out,
"Handsome one, sell me your extra ticket!"

The Gypsy ran up to Birukov, dressed in mufti, with the same
request. Receiving a negative reply, she burst out in one breath,
"Then give me a cigarette, darling, there is a big change in your
future."

"I don't smoke," Anton said, moving on.

"A change for the worse," the Gypsy woman called after him
and hurried to the next man.

"Handsome one, sell me a ticket!"

The Café Minutka next to the theater was the most conve-
nient observation point. Buying two glasses of hot coffee,
Birukov took a corner table. The long minutes of tense waiting
began.

Events started unfolding a half hour before the show. First to
appear, from somewhere behind the theater, was thin, leggy Priazhkina. Like the time she dropped in unexpectedly on Zarvantsev, Lusya was wearing a white shirt and jeans with TOLYA written in large yellow letters. After a few frantic minutes at the
cashier's box, she went around the corner of the glassed-in café
and from her hiding place began watching the people who came
up to the theater. The first bell pealed in the foyer. The crowd

started moving through the wide open doors, creating a bottle-neck. Just then Birukov saw a grim Frosya Zvonkova approach with an insouciant Ovchinnikov in an unbuttoned black suit. Ovchinnikov gave the Gypsy a cigarette and patted her on the back as he lit up himself.

The rest happened very fast. The Gypsy, like a hawk, swooped down on Dr. Shirokov when he appeared. Anton, grimacing in dismay, saw the confused Aleksei Alekseevich hurriedly hand her the ticket. She paid and, sweeping the asphalt with her long skirts, the Gypsy floated into the crowd being sucked into the theater. Ovchinnikov merrily offered his arm to the still-grim Zvonkova and, quickly finishing his cigarette, also headed inside. After observing the entire scene, Priazhkina speedily disappeared behind the theater. Practically running out of the café, Birukov raced after her.

Taking back alleys, never once looking back, Lusya came out on Blukher Street right at a parked light gray Volga. As soon as she got into the backseat, the Volga roared off.

Anton looked around. Seeing the green light of an approaching taxi, he raised his arm. The driver, who had pulled over, began explaining that he was on his way back to the garage to turn in the cab, but seeing Anton's ID, asked knowingly, "Where to?"

Birukov pointed to the Volga ahead. "Follow that car and don't lose it."

"Can I floor it?"

"Go ahead!"

The driver shifted. The Volga was quite a distance from them. Racing out onto Vatutin Street, it made a left turn, went around the Tower Square, and sped toward the Sibiriakov–Bvardeitsev Highway. The taxi, going over the speed limit, was noticeably gaining on the car. Anton could make out the Volga's license plate—31-42 NSU—but just then the light turned red. The brakes squealed; a crowd of pedestrians came into the intersection. The Volga, which had managed to cross before the light, swiftly passed a gray Moskvich and disappeared in the flow of cars filling the highway. The wait seemed interminable to Anton. No sooner had the taxi passed the light that had finally turned green than an enormous truck came out of Vertkovsky Street, roaring threateningly, and blocked the road as it started to turn around. The driver swerved left, but an oncoming trolley jangled its bell in alarm. Behind the trolley a loaded dump truck rumbled on an upgrade. Maneuvering between them like a slalom skier, the cab driver managed to pass the illegally maneuvering truck and, making up for lost time, raced off to the Motodrom stop.

The unexpected occurred instantly. Just as the cab began speeding away from the truck, Lusya Priazhkina appeared as if out of the ground, with her arms held high. Jolted against the back of the front seat, Anton Birukov heard the squealing brakes and right in front of the car's radiator saw Lusya's terror-contorted face as she fell backward.

The driver, thrown against the wheel, swore in a doomed voice.

The car was instantly surrounded by people who had run over from the stop. A fat-cheeked highway patrol officer with lieutenant's shoulder boards appeared out of nowhere on a yellow motorcycle and sternly demanded the cab driver's license. Anton showed his ID.

The lieutenant saluted. "Excuse me, comrade senior inspector, but—"

"Call the investigative unit and the ambulance. We're not going anywhere," Anton said, interrupting the lieutenant curtly and throwing open his door.

Priazhkina lay flat on her back, arms flung wide, eyes shut. Her face was completely white. Birukov, leaning over, felt Lusya's wrist for a pulse and saw the corner of a ten-ruble note in her clenched fist.

It was getting close to midnight when a conference began in the division chief's office on the incident at the Aurora Theater.

The first to speak was the investigator who had checked on the circumstances of the car accident.

"The ME has determined that the victim was intoxicated. The taxi did not touch her, and the loss of consciousness was caused by striking the back of her head against the asphalt—Priazhkina was trying to get out of the car's way but, being intoxicated, lost her balance and fell backward. Measurement of the braking vehicle's path and numerous witnesses at the Motodrom stop indicate that in the unexpected circumstances it would have been practically impossible to change the road situation." That was the dry official language of his report.

The chief of the division turned to Birukov. "How did Priazhkina get to the Motodrom stop and why did she run to your car?"

Birukov rose and spoke. "Witnesses testified that Lusya got out at the Motodrom stop from a light gray Volga—the one we were pursuing. The Volga raced off, and Priazhkina tried to hail passing cars. None stopped . . ." Anton paused. "I think that Priazhkina had to get home. She lives in Bugrinskaya Roshcha."

"Couldn't the driver of the Volga have brought her closer?"

"Apparently it wasn't in his interest."

"Who owns the Volga?"

"Revaz Davidovich Stepnadze."

"So that's how it is!" The chief was surprised. "Have you been to see him?"

"Of course. There isn't the slightest sign of forced entry in the garage, and there's no one in the apartment. At least the door wasn't opened after repeated ringing. We couldn't get anything accurate from the neighbors. They say Stepnadze's wife lives in a dacha in Shelkovichikha and he's on a trip. According to my calculations, Revaz Davidovich should be on his train somewhere around Rostov right now . . ."

The division chief picked up a telegram from his desk. "While you were busy with the theater, we got a message from Golubyov. Listen." He started to read:

"At Rostov-on-Dov Stepnadze got off train. Spent half the day

walking around technical schools, took interest in the work of
admissions committees, then disappeared. According to the train
foreman, Stepnadze's brother in Omsk is very sick. I caught up
with the train in Millerovo. Golubyov." The division chief was
silent for a minute. "This dispatch was sent at noon. In that
time Revaz Davidovich could get not only to Novosibirsk but to
Vladivostok."

"We urgently have to check on Stepnadze's brother in Omsk,
comrade lieutenant colonel," Anton said quickly.

"We already have. There are no residents with that surname.
It seems as if all this was prearranged."

"I gave orders to the district inspector to await the appearance
of either of the Stepnadze spouses and to inform us immediately."

The division chief put the telegram on the desk. "All right,"
he said, "let's hear what the others have to say."

A series of laconic reports ensued. Birukov tried not to miss
the tiniest significant fact. However, there were almost no facts
at all. The Gypsy who got Dr. Shirokov's ticket was from a camp
of Gypsies who were waiting for the morning hydrofoil at the
river station and had come to the movies out of boredom. The
seat intended for Shirokov was next to Zvonkova and Ovchinnikov, but the presence of the Gypsy did not elicit any surprise
from them. At one point in the show Zvonkova turned to her
neighbor and asked rather loudly, "Could you sit normally?"
There wasn't anything off about the question, since the Gypsy
was giving free rein to her emotions. After the movie Ovchinnikov seemed to have an argument with Zvonkova. Leaving her at
the bus stop, he took a taxi and went to midtown. Zvonkova,
highly nervous, took the number 15 bus to her house, and the
lights went out in her apartment soon after her arrival.

When the reports ended, Anton Birukov, addressing the inspectors, asked, "Neither Sipeniatin nor Demensky appeared at
the theater?"

"No," the two inspectors replied in unison.

The division chief looked at Birukov. "What do you think of this business with the theater?"

Anton gathered his thoughts before he spoke. "I think, comrade lieutenant colonel, this business is the product of an amateur criminal's mind. And it's almost impossible to guess what will come into an amateur's mind."

"Whom do you suspect?"

"According to the latest data, both Stepnadze and Ovchinnikov are mixed up in this, but both candidates elicit doubts in me. The first uses his car too blatantly, the second goes to the theater without any cover-up . . . The third suspect is Sipeniatin; however, Vasya Sivy is no amateur in crime. His thoughts could be divined, but in this case they're not divinable yet."

"What about Demensky?"

"Yuri Pavlovich gives the impression of being a decent man mixed up in his relationship with Kholodova. I think that he lied about something in his first interrogation, and now, trying to cover it up, he's doing one stupid thing after another."

The intercom light on the division chief's desk came on. The lieutenant colonel pushed a key, and the duty officer's loud voice came over the speaker.

"The district precinct on Zorge Street is calling. Stepnadze's wife drove up to the house in a taxi. There's a man with her. Tall, balding, in a black unbuttoned suit. They went right into the apartment; the lights are still on. The officer wants to know: should he drop in, ask a few questions?"

Birukov lunged forward. "No, comrade lieutenant colonel! That sounds like Ovchinnikov with Mrs. Stepnadze. The militia should keep an eye on him, as much as possible."

"What if Ovchinnikov is our amateur?" the division chief asked in a huff.

"We'll try to play with him."

"We won't lose?"

"I don't think so."

"Watch it . . ."

The lieutenant colonel gave the desk sergeant his orders.

Turning off the intercom, he asked Birukov, "What's Ovchinnikov like?"

"A hail-fellow-well-met—and a dirty fellow."

The chief picked up a red pencil from the folder. Twirling it thoughtfully in his fingers, he looked up at Anton. "Did you find out about Stepnadze's past?" he asked.

Anton nodded. "Revaz Davidovich worked for a long time in Far East Construction as legal counsel."

"Does he have a law degree?"

"In applications he writes: 'Incomplete higher education,' even though all there is for that is a forty-year-old reference confirming that Stepnadze, R. D., third-year law student at Moscow Law Institute, was off on summer vacation." Birukov paused. "In 1960 Revaz Davidovich got a job as a representative of a Tashkent furniture factory and settled in Novosibirsk. Here he dealt with lumber firms and 'obtained' wood for his factory. Stepnadze's personnel record for that period is excellent. But here is something that I think merits attention."

"What's that?"

"In the spring of '62 in Tomsk there was a major trial in which several workers in the lumber industry were accused of taking bribes. Stepnadze was in the dock right next to them. But he didn't accept bribes; he gave them. In the trial Revaz Davidovich proved convincingly that the bribes were extorted from him, that he acted purely in the interests of the furniture factory and didn't put a single cent of government money in his pockets. He got off lightly—two years suspended sentence."

"He wasn't tried for anything else?"

"No."

The phone on the chief's desk rang. The lieutenant colonel picked up the phone, and Anton noticed his face grow grim. The conversation was brief.

"Try to keep this a secret for now, Aleksei Alekseevich. Is that possible? . . . Fine. Thank you for calling me right away." The lieutenant colonel squinted at his watch, slowly hung up, and, meeting Birukov's questioning gaze, said dryly, "Kholodova just passed away."

11

According to the information from the Novosibirsk conductors'
reserves, Stepnadze was supposed to work in car 8, and Golubyov
saw him immediately, as soon as the train stopped at the Adler
station. The white-haired, distinguished conductor attracted attention without trying. With his partner—a young girl with dark
eyebrows—he gallantly helped the passengers get off. Observing
from a distance, Slava noticed that without exception every passenger saying good-bye to Stepnadze seemed to be parting with a
very good friend.

When the car was empty, Stepnadze, smiling, exchanged a
few words with his partner and lightly leaped back up into the
car. Having changed from his uniform into a light polo shirt and
light-colored trousers, he left the car about five minutes later
with the same ease and, waving a new black briefcase with a gilt
lock, unhurriedly strolled along the empty platform to the city
exit. Following at a distance, Slava thought that Revaz Stepnadze looked much younger than his age and did not behave at
all like a pensioner earning a little on the side as a conductor on
long-distance trains. Crowned with a noble mane of white hair,
Stepnadze looked more like a successful businessman.

Seeing that Revaz Davidovich had gotten in line at the taxi
stand, Golubyov grew anxious. All Stepnadze had to do was get
in a car, and Slava might as well look for the wind in a field.

"I'll have to commandeer a private vehicle," Slava decided,
quickly looking around the parking lot, which was empty now
that the train had come in.

From the platform, swinging car keys on a chain on his index finger, a tanned, pleasant-looking man was headed for his cherry-colored Zhiguli. Golubyov hurried over to him, but the man, guessing his intentions, didn't even let him open his mouth. "I'm not in competition with the government."

Golubyov took out his ID. "Criminal Investigation. I need you desperately."

After a peek at the red book, the man opened the car door. "Get in."

Settling in next to him, Slava pointed out Stepnadze. "Over there, the white-haired man—don't lose him."

"Who is he?" the man asked, putting the key in the ignition. "He's respectable-looking, like an assistant professor."

"That's what he is," Golubyov said, having decided not to be too frank.

"Taking bribes?"

"What makes you think that?"

"What else can a professor do to attract the attention of the CID?" The man was talkative. "The only thing he can do is arrange for some blockhead to get into an institute for a fee. You know that joke? It's old, but to the point. A man gets into a taxi and drags a turkey in with him. The driver says, 'Where do you think you're going with that turkey?' 'What turkey?' the man replies. 'My turkey has been accepted in the institute, and this is the bribe that got him in.' "

Golubyov laughed.

The man held out his hand. "Let's get acquainted. I'm Viktor Pashkov. I'm an engineer in a construction company." He winked slyly. "By the way, I'm connected with the militia, too." He opened the glove compartment and showed Slava his auxiliary militia ID. "There, see that . . . So you can count on my complete cooperation. Of course, I don't know any judo holds, but I can trip your professor if its necessary."

"Thanks," Slava said with a smile.

"You're welcome," Pashkov said, winking again.

Just then a free cab with a checkerboard on its sides pulled up at the taxi stand. Stepnadze quickly pushed through the crowd, whispered with the driver, and got into the cab, all alone.

Slava asked, "Do you know the city well?"

"Like the back of my hand."

The cars set off almost simultaneously. Turning onto the highway, both accelerated at once. The sides of the road were filled with bright, motley, tanned crowds.

"Your professor is here to blow money?" Pashkov asked.

"We'll see what he's planning to do," Golubyov replied musingly, trying not to lose sight of the taxi racing ahead of them.

"People who like an easy buck flock here. The ones who flash money are always easier to fleece . . . Now I keep wondering: where do these parasites come from? They're leeches, not people. They clamp on and suck your juices, growing fat until the militia put the squeeze on them. The point is, they can't stop on their own. Is it some disease with them, or what? Something like alcoholism, maybe?"

Golubyov didn't have time to reply. Without warning the endless, deep blue sea opened up on the right and a long row of high-rises stretched along the shoreline amid greenery. The taxi, its turn signal blinking, turned off onto a paved ramp on the right.

"The prof is headed for the holiday hotels," Pashkov said, turning the steering wheel to the right.

After that it was sheer mystery. Leaving the cab, Stepnadze rounded a luxurious flower bed and strode toward the hotel down a shady path. He walked calmly, his new black briefcase swinging in rhythm with his steps. Revaz Davidovich's taxi, as though killing time, slowly rolled along the asphalt that extended in a straight ribbon along the wrought-iron hotel fences.

"Will you wait?" Slava asked Pashkov.

"Let's go together," Pashkov said, winking.

In the empty vestibule of the hotel, which they saw through the wide, tall windows, Revaz Davidovich joyfully greeted the super on duty—an old man with a white handlebar mustache. They even embraced, slapped each other's backs, and then sat down in the rattan chairs near the desk. Stepnadze opened his briefcase and with an elaborate gesture handed "Mustache" a book with a light green cover. The man smiled broadly, patted the book, flipped through a few pages, and put his hand to his heart gratefully. After that, as though in exchange, he handed Revaz Davidovich a book with a black cover. Stepnadze, without looking, shoved the book into his briefcase. After a chat that took no more than ten minutes, he rose. The super graciously walked him to the door, returned to his desk, and buried himself in the new book. Revaz Davidovich headed for the beach with measured tread.

Pashkov took Golubyov by the sleeve. "I know that old man a bit. Should I ask him about the book trade?" he asked.

"Fine," Golubyov agreed. "Meanwhile I'll stroll behind the professor. If we get separated, we'll meet at the car."

"Got it."

Despite the fact that it was late August, the beach was full of vacationers, its pebbles covered with colorful mats. The becalmed sea seethed with swimmers by the shore and resounded with a multitude of voices. Revaz Davidovich, apparently looking for someone, slowly walked along the beach.

At the very end of the beach, apart from the main mass of vacationers, under a tent improvised from a sheet and stakes, lay a prone woman, gone to fat. Next to her, nose buried in a book, sat a girl wearing glasses and school bows tied in her thin braids. Coming abreast of them, Stepnadze stopped. Slowly getting a newspaper from his briefcase, he spread it on the rocks and began undressing. Then, turning to the girl, he asked her something. Pleased to have someone to talk to, the girl instantly shut her book. The woman immediately broke into the conversation. She turned on her side and began smiling sweetly at Revaz Davidovich. After some talk the woman and Stepnadze suddenly rose and, stepping carefully on the pebbles, went toward the sea together.

Without losing time, Golubyov sat next to the girl. A Russian grammar book lay at her feet. Glancing at it as though looking for a banal conversation opener, Slava said, "Studying?"

The girl looked at him with interest. "I'm taking my final exam in two days. I'm going to attend the Sukhumi Pedagogical Institute."

"You came to Adler from Sukhumi to study?"

"Mother's resting here at a hotel."

"And your father, too?"

"What father?"

Golubyov looked out at the sea. "The one who went swimming with your mother."

"He's as much my father as you are. Just a vacationer."

"A friend?"

"Never saw him before in my life."

"He was telling you something interesting . . ."

The girl shrugged and said, "We were just talking out of boredom. Turns out he has a relative who heads the department at the institute in Sukhumi. Naturally Mother was interested. She is terribly worried that I'll flunk the last of my exams."

"What if you really do?"

The girl's bespectacled eyes flashed angrily. "Bite your tongue!" she said. "I've gotten straight A's in Russian. Understand?"

"Then why is your mother worried?"

"Ask her. She's gotten it into her head that I won't get into the institute without protection, and that's that."

Pashkov appeared from the hotel. Golubyov looked at Revaz Davidovich. Standing near the water, he was chatting with the woman, and it looked as if they weren't going to go in at all. Slava, wishing the girl luck, gallantly bowed and headed to meet Pashkov.

"I'm reporting completion of my mission," Pashkov said laughingly. "The professor brought the superintendent a collection called *God's Little Acre:* Caldwell, Faulkner, Macdonald and another three American writers. And for a trade he took *Foreign Mysteries.*"

"That's it?"

"That's what he said, but who knows what really went on."

"Even your friendship with the super didn't help?"

"Here's the extent of the friendship . . . Last winter we did major repairs on the hotel, and the old man followed us around and 'supervised.' " Pashkov looked around. "Where is the prof?"

Golubyov nodded toward the sea. Stepnadze had gone in after all. After a short swim he came out on shore and returned to the tent with the woman. After he dried off, he dressed slowly. Before parting, Revaz Davidovich handed the woman what looked like his card and, bowing, headed farther along the beach.

Pashkov frowned. "The super says the prof is here frequently."

"Did you ask about their relationship?"

"They're both bibliophiles."

"Where's he going? The beach ends here."

"You can get to all the hotels along the shore here."

"You get the car. I'll follow him," Slava said quickly.

The rest of the day Stepnadze spent in bookstores. He seemed to know every door in Adler that bore a "BOOKS" sign. Golubyov and Pashkov, alternately tailing Revaz Davidovich, noticed that in every store Stepnadze had clerks who were his friends—as a rule, female clerks.

The Adler–Novosibirsk train was leaving in exactly fifty minutes. The platform was jammed. September was around the corner, and vacationers like birds caught in bad weather were flocking from the southern beaches to their familiar nesting grounds. Golubyov had gotten a return ticket ahead of time through the major of the transport militia. There was no rush, and Slava invited Pashkov to join him for a snack at the station buffet. Pashkov accepted and, swinging his keychain on his index finger, headed toward the station with Golubyov. Suddenly there came rushing toward them an elderly man, round as a ball, in enormously wide trousers, dragging a huge shopping bag.

"Taras Tarasovich!" Pashkov exclaimed, catching the keys in his fist.

"Hi, Vitek," the man said, letting the bag hit the ground with relief. "Listen . . . Do you know anybody at the station? I'm desperate for two tickets to Novosibirsk. My Dusya is in line, but I'll tell you, it's as crowded as herring in a barrel over there . . ."

"Why are you going to Siberia?" Pashkov asked in surprise.

"Our genius wasn't accepted into the Siberian Construction Institute—the exams. We got the telegram today . . . He's applied to some NETI, whatever that is, and he writes there's a shortage there and they're taking all sorts of fools."

"You've decided to check if that's so?"

"You know my Dusya, she starts wailing, 'Let's go save our son!'—and won't hear of anything else. I had to ask for emergency leave." The man wiped sweat from his brow. "Vitek, you know everyone in the city. Help me get on a train."

Pashkov gave Golubyov a questioning glance. "Could he buy tickets through your colleagues? This is Taras Tarasovich Yarko —the best work superintendent at our construction administration. He could be of use to you on the trip."

"I certainly will be!" Taras Tarasovich quickly added and nudged the overflowing shopping bag with his toe. "Dusya packed such goodies for the trip—you'll lick your fingers!"

"I'll go find out," Slava said with a smile.

12

The tickets turned out not to be so hopeless to obtain after all. There were plenty of empty seats on the train, and with the intervention of the transportation militia duty officer, Golubyov quickly got seats for the Yarkos at the military ticket office, where there wasn't a long line, in his compartment in the very same car number 8 in which Stepnadze was conductor. The ecstatically happy Taras Tarasovich introduced Slava to his Evdokia Nilovna—a thin woman with tear-swollen eyes. The fourth passenger in their compartment was a tall young man who gave his name as Kostya and who was also traveling all the way to Novosibirsk.

Settling on the lower seat, Taras Tarasovich, red with exertion, thought a bit, pulled out a cellophane-wrapped chicken from his overflowing bag and, oblivious of the boarding bustle, started breaking the chicken into pieces with a crunch.

"You could wait until people are seated," Evdokia Nilovna said.

"We're all seated," Taras Tarasovich said, as if in surprise.

"But boarding isn't over."

"So what? You could die of hunger before it's over."

Evdokia Nilovna, sighing in dismay, went into the corridor. Taras Tarasovich, watching her go, smiled compassionately.

"She's worried about our son," he said. Turning to Golubyov and Kostya, who were sitting together at the window, he asked, "You boys studying or working?"

"I'm studying," Kostya said, "at Novosibirsk Railroad Engineering Institute."

Taras Tarasovich shifted his gaze to Golubyov. "You're in school, too?"

"Yes, I'm studying, too," Slava said, deciding to be less than frank.

"Good for you, boys! You can't take a step without an education nowadays, and our genius flunked his entrance exams." He looked up at Kostya. "Listen, did you get in without any pull?"

"Of course," Kostya replied with a smile.

"Do they rake you over the coals in the entrance exams?"

"It's tough."

"And do sneaks manage to squeak through?"

"It happens sometimes. But they get thrown out of the institute after the first semester if they don't have the knowledge."

"That's what I keep telling my Dusya: what are we going to do at that—NETI? The Novosibirsk Electrotechnical Institute? What can we say? If that's the way it is, that our boy doesn't have suitable training, then he has no business at the institute. He should join the City Technical School. They feed you for free, the food's good now, they clothe you from head to toe. What more do you need? If he can't learn to be an engineer, let him learn stonemasonry. All trades are respected here. I began as a mason myself . . ."

Evdokia Nilovna appeared in the doorway of the compartment. Surprisingly, she looked happier. She addressed her husband tenderly. "Tarasik, come out for a minute."

Taras Tarasovich wheezed grumpily, made his way out from behind the table, and followed his wife. He returned quickly. Squeezing into his seat, he began wrapping the remains of the chicken angrily.

"Something wrong?" Golubyov inquired.

"She's something! Completely nuts . . ." Taras Tarasovich grumbled. After a silence he quickly added, "Now you ask at the Adler Construction Administration: 'Who is Yarko?' First thing they'll say: 'He likes to eat.' 'And how does he work?' you'll ask. 'There's no better work supervisor,' they'll say, 'to be found on the Black Sea coast.' That's who Taras Tarasovich Yarko is! Understand, boys? I change the face of the earth, with honest labor I earn money and Dusya just whispered to me in the corridor, 'Let's give the white-haired conductor five hundred rubles.' You see, the dean of NETI, where our boy has applied, is his best friend. They go fishing together. Well, there was a time when I caught almost a full hopper of gray mullet with the deputy minister himself! Why doesn't anyone give me any dirty money!"

Trying to hide his excitement, Golubyov asked, "Did the conductor hint at a bribe?"

Taras Tarasovich frowned and replied, "He doesn't hint at anything. Dusya wants to give him the money herself. She's ready to throw away half a thousand for her son as easily as take a breath."

Slava, climbing up onto the top berth, started thinking about Stepnadze. He was troubled by Revaz Davidovich's relative at the Sukhumi Pedagogical Institute and his dean pal at NETI. What was that? An ordinary coincidence or an extensive bribery scam?

Early in the morning the train pulled into Rostov-on-Don. Trying to avoid being seen by Revaz Davidovich, Golubyov came out onto the platform. The day, just begun, was so fresh and sunny that he didn't want to think about last night's concerns. After a short wait in the line at the newspaper kiosk, Slava bought a copy of the oblast paper *The Hammer,* still smelling of printers' ink, and without hurrying walked back to his car. The departure of the train was held up. From the conversation among conductors bored by the open red flags, he could tell that a belt had broken on one of the cars and it was being changed.

Running into Kostya on the platform, Golubyov stopped. Not far away Stepnadze was talking to the brigade leader of the train.

Holding onto the handles, sleepy Taras Tarasovich stuck his head out of car number 8. Seeing his compartment neighbors, he called loudly, "Hey, fellows! Come on, we'll have some chicken!"

"Be right there!" Kostya replied.

Taras Tarasovich disappeared into the car. Wearing a red cap, the station master approached Stepnadze and the brigade leader. Greeting both men and shaking hands, he handed Revaz Davidovich a piece of paper that looked like a telegram. Stepnadze frowned after he read it and immediately handed it to the brigade leader. Both began talking animatedly. The leader nodded, and Revaz Davidovich hurriedly went up to his car. In about five minutes he came out dressed the way he had been in Adler. He was carrying the same black briefcase. Shaking hands again with the brigade leader and the station master, Stepnadze walked quickly along the platform.

Golubyov did some fast thinking; there wasn't much time. Shoving the newspaper he had just bought into Kostya's hand, Slava said to the confused young man, "If I stay behind, tell the conductor to save my seat, and you keep an eye on my briefcase. I'll catch up with the train."

Kostya, who had understood absolutely nothing, watched him with bewildered eyes.

Apparently Stepnadze didn't even consider the possibility of being tailed. He never looked back or revealed any anxiety by gesture or look. Only a man with a clear conscience could behave this way, and Golubyov thought in dismay that he was wasting precious time.

Deep in his unhappy thoughts, Slava almost lost sight of Revaz Davidovich. He saw him near an ancient brick building with a gilt sign announcing Rostov University. Stepnadze was talking with a tall, youngish woman. Slava grew wary. The musing look left Revaz Davidovich's face. He was smiling charmingly and, once again, as in Adler, he no longer resembled a humble conductor but a successful businessman.

Suddenly Stepnadze pulled out an expensive note pad from his briefcase and wrote down what the woman was telling him. When he finished, the woman took out a notebook from her purse and asked a man standing next to her for a pen. But Revaz Davidovich offered her a tiny piece of paper that resembled a calling card. The woman slipped the paper into her notebook

with a grateful smile. Stepnadze, bowing, strolled away from the
university, back the way he had come. He took a trolley-bus at
Voroshilov Prospect. He got out a few stops later, waited for a
bus, and went to the Railroad Institute.

"He knows Rostov well, he's like a fish in water," thought
Golubyov, following Revaz Davidovich into a gray building filled
with recent high-school graduates. But at the institute he
flubbed it and lost Stepnadze.

Having checked all the dead-end hallways filled with huddled
packs of students, Golubyov left. Not far from the entrance,
lounging on a bench, sat a young man with a pompadour, smoking and looking over the crowd at the bus stop. Slava approached
him and asked, "Listen, comrade, did you just see a distinguished gray-haired man with a black briefcase?"

"Gray-haired? With a black briefcase? . . . Listen, I didn't
see him."

"What if it's serious?"

"If it's serious . . . He just took off in a taxi," the man said
and pointed right, up the street. "In that direction."

Golubyov sank wearily onto the bench.

He spent the rest of the day making trips around the populous
city. He visited all the institutes, branches, and even technical
schools, but didn't see Stepnadze anywhere. Tired of fruitless
seeking, Slava did some thinking. There were two options: fly to
Novosibirsk and be there in five hours or catch up with the Adler
train and be stuck on it for almost three days.

The Rostov airport, despite the regular flights, was filled with
passengers. Having learned from the duty officer of the transport
militia that he could pass the Adler train on the "corn run" that
took off in an hour for Millerovo, Golubyov chose this option.
Waiting for the officer to fill out his traveling papers, he left the
terminal and, with nothing to do, started looking at the planes
that were humming at a pitch approaching a whine. Barely audible over the noise, the PA system muttered ceaselessly: "Last
boarding call for flight 6129 Rostov-Cheliabinsk-Novosibirsk."

Soon, its lights blinking, the handsome TU-134 rolled out onto the runway. After a short wait the jet's turbines roared, and it accelerated and flew up into the darkening southern sky. Watching the dot disappear from view, Golubyov didn't suspect that right on board flight 6129, sucking on a mint, was the gray-haired man with the black briefcase.

13

In the morning, as was his usual habit, Birukov first dropped in on the duty room, where all the latest information was gathered. After reading the report, he cheered up a bit. Ovchinnikov had stayed with Revaz Davidovich's wife. He left her at three in the morning, looking very angry, stopped a car traveling late, and talked the driver into giving him a lift to Cheluskintsev Street. He hadn't been out of the house since. Apparently, catching up on sleep, Stepnadze's wife hadn't left her apartment either.

"How's Lusya Priazhkina?" Birukov asked.

"Under medical care. The trauma isn't serious, but they won't allow her to be questioned yet. They say she's in an alcoholic depression," the desk sergeant said and laughed. "She must have really tied one on yesterday."

"We have to keep an eye on her. They may try to contact her."

"The doctors have been alerted."

Birukov picked up the list of traffic incidents in the last twenty-four hours. After the laconic report on Priazhkina, Stepnadze's name and license number almost leaped off the page: 31-42 NSU. "Detained by public inspector of the Highway Patrol for speeding coming off Sibiriakov-Gvardeitsy Square at 20:25 local time." Anton read in amazement and noted almost automatically that Priazhkina's accident had occurred almost simultaneously with the Volga being stopped. That meant that after dropping Lusya at the Motodrom stop, the Volga had tried to get away from its recent passenger as fast as possible. Immediately calling Highway Patrol, Birukov learned a rather curious fact: the owner of the car himself had been at the wheel.

"That's not a mistake?" Anton asked, frowning.

"No way," the officer replied. "Little Kolya turned in his driver's license . . . It says in black and white: 'Stepnadze Revaz Davidovich.' What I can't understand is why this Stepnadze hasn't dropped in for his license. Kolya warned him—"

"Who's this Kolya?"

"Kolya Polozov—he's an engineer, one of our more active volunteers. We call him Little Kolya around here."

"Can you send Polozov over to me quickly?"

"We'll try."

"And have him bring Stepnadze's license," Birukov said. "And if the Volga 31-42 NSU appears on the city streets, inform me immediately. Is that clear?" After he hung up Birukov said to the desk sergeant, "Send a car for Demensky."

Little Kolya, as Polozov was called over at Highway Patrol, was tall enough to almost reach the ceiling, even though he couldn't have been over twenty-five years old. Introducing himself, Polozov handed Revaz Davidovich's driver's license to Anton and started recounting in a deep bass voice how he had detained the Volga with the number 31-42 NSU.

At first he was going to let him off with a warning, but then since Stepnadze's license had two punch holes in it for violations, he decided to take it away and turn it over to the local Highway Patrol, so that they could have a little chat with the driver. Stepnadze didn't argue, but he didn't show up, either.

Hearing out Polozov attentively, Anton then spread out several photographs on his desk and asked him to pick out Stepnadze. Polozov pointed to Revaz Davidovich uncertainly.

"I think he's the one."

"Why think?" Anton asked.

"It's the railroad uniform . . ."

"How about the face?"

"I think it's the same."

Birukov looked into Polozov's eyes. "This is a very serious

matter and I have to know for certain: was it Stepnadze himself driving the Volga or someone who looks like him?"

Polozov hesitated in embarrassment and said, "I didn't look at his face. The driver was wearing a railroad uniform and was an elderly, distinguished man . . . He wouldn't have brazenly handed me someone else's license, would he?"

"I see," Birukov said.

The telephone rang. Anton gave his name and heard the hurried voice of Dr. Shirokov.

"Comrade Birukov, I was just called by a man who said he was Demensky and wanted to know about Kholodova's health."

Anton stood up. "What did you tell him, Aleksei Alekseevich?"

"As the lieutenant colonel has requested, I had to tell him that Kholodova would live."

"You did the right thing. Did the man's voice resemble the one that invited you to the Aurora film theater?"

"Not in the least."

Birukov hadn't had time to mull over the surgeon's information when the intercom buzzed.

"Comrade captain, Sipeniatin is on the horizon!" the desk sergeant reported heartily. "Maria Anisimovna Sipeniatina's neighbor just informed us on zero-two that Vasya was hiding at his mother's. We just have to look for him . . ."

"What's the neighbor's name?"

"He refused to give it. 'Who needs you,' he said, 'dragging me through courts'—and hung up."

"Has the car with Demensky arrived yet?"

"Not yet."

"Get the driver on the radio. What's holding him up?"

"Just a minute." The sergeant tuned the radio. Anton heard hissing, crackle, a muffled conversation, and then the sergeant's clear voice in the telephone receiver again. "The car is at the city Aeroflot office. Demensky has been on the public phone there for over ten minutes."

Controlling his sudden irritation, Birukov said dryly, "Tell the driver to bring Demensky to me urgently."

Without letting go of the intercom, the sergeant spoke on the radio with the driver. "Yaremenko! Do you hear me, Yaremenko? . . . Demensky's finished making calls. Invite him into the car —go ahead! Hurry right over to Captain Birukov. Instantly!"

Hanging up the intercom receiver, Anton picked up the city phone and called the chief of the Sixth Precinct.

"Captain Ilynykh," he heard after the first ring.

"Hello, Yuri Vasilievich. Birukov here."

"Greetings, Anton Ignatych! Happy to hear from you."

"Listen: you have to get over to Kozhevninov Street quickly, to Maria Anisimovna Sipeniatina. Do you know her?"

"I do. What's happened there?"

"We've been told that Vasya Sivy is hiding there."

"I'm putting on my cap."

"Thanks for the cooperation," Birukov said and smiled.

About five minutes later there was a careful knock on the door. Demensky came in, sat down carefully on the chair Anton offered, and froze tensely, as though facing a camera.

"Who were you calling for so long?" Anton asked unexpectedly.

"I had to be at the factory at ten. It's already nine. I wanted to let them know I'd be late."

"Did you?"

"I didn't get through—the driver rushed me."

"How about Dr. Shirokov?"

"I reached him. He gave me hope that Sanya will live. Is that true?"

"Shirokov's the doctor—he should know."

Yuri Pavlovich's earlobes grew red. "Last time I was stunned by events. I was afraid that the responsibility for Sanya's death, if she died, would fall on me. That's why I lied, denied the obvious. In brief, I behaved like a coward. Actually my relationship with Sanya isn't at all the way I made it sound last time . . . Despite the divorce, there was no animosity between us."

"Then you flew to Cheliabinsk to be with Kholodova?"

"Yes, but I didn't find her there. I had called Sanya on the telephone before. I suggested that we forget the past and that she should come live with me. Sanya was pleased. She said she would see to Seryozha and fly straight to Novosibirsk. I told her that if she arrived before me, she could get the apartment key from Ksenya Makarovna, my neighbor."

"There's a discrepancy here, Yuri Pavlovich. You flew in from Cheliabinsk to Novosibirsk on the morning of August twenty-first. Kholodova was in your apartment at the time—she had slept there. All you had to do was ring the doorbell and—"

"I swear, when I found out from Zarvantsev that Sanya had gone to the Orbit with Ovchinnikov, I was blinded by jealousy and instead of coming home I rushed out to find Ovchinnikov."

"What did you order from Revaz Davidovich Stepnadze from Adler?"

"I lied last time. Of course I didn't order fruit. When I talked with Sanya on the phone, she asked me to get four skeins of blue-gray royal mohair. And that's what I ordered from Revaz Davidovich. I sent him a telegram from Sverdlovsk."

Anton asked Demensky to tell him more about Revaz Davidovich.

Demensky started talking in what seemed to be a frank way, but he didn't add a single thing to his previous statements. He also revealed very little about Lusya Priazhkina. "An excellent men's barber, sometimes poses for Zarvantsev, likes to drink. Did I give her cognac? Yes, I did. I wanted Lusya to find out from Zarvantsev the truth about Ovchinnikov and Sanya. What did she find out? Nothing. She got drunk and slept at Alik's. Does Priahzkina know Stepnadze? I don't think so."

Demensky looked at Anton guiltily. "Believe me, this time I'm not lying."

"I believe you and I want you to talk to me just as frankly about the relationship between Kholodova and Stepnadze. Are they connected only by books?"

Demensky's face twitched. "I know only about books, but

. . . Every time a letter came from Stepnadze, Sanya got feverish."

"What were those letters?"

"Very laconic and proper, usually with a request for some book or other. And I can't understand why Sanya was so afraid of them."

"She didn't hide these letters from you?"

"Never."

"Why didn't you ask what was frightening your wife?"

Demensky frowned. "I did ask. Sanya is very sociable and open, but every time the conversation turned to Stepnadze or Seryozha's father, she shut up morbidly. Once, losing control, I suggested that Revaz Davidovich was Seryozha's father. Sanya grew white and said that if I made up things like that we would be better apart. We never touched the topic again."

"Can you add anything about Ovchinnikov?" Anton asked after a certain pause.

Yuri Pavlovich laughed. "Ovchinnikov is Ovchinnikov. In a word, a womanizer and woman stealer."

"What is his relationship with Stepnadze's wife?"

"With Nina? None."

"Are you sure?"

"One hundred percent. Nina, you know, is the kind of beautiful woman who has an instinct for choosing a wealthy husband. She would never risk losing the trust of Revaz Davidovich over an impoverished womanizer like Ovchinnikov. That's number one." Demensky paused. "And two, if there were something between Nina and Anatoly, then Anatoly would have gabbed about it long ago. Female conquests are his only solace after his lost soccer fame."

"He seems to be interested in Nina's younger sister?" Anton asked carefully.

A mocking smile appeared on Yuri Pavlovich's face. "Using Ovchinnikov's own words, it's a waste of time. Frosya Zvonkova is a trusting silly. She's prepared to fall in love with the first man who promises to marry her. But that's not because she's promiscuous but because of her age. She's pushing thirty, after all, and as far as I know, she figured Anatoly out a long time ago."

"Nevertheless, she continues to go out with him . . ."

"Ovchinnikov is very pushy, and Frosya gets bored alone."

The intercom rang. The sergeant reported that Captain Ilynykh was asking him to hurry to Sipeniatina's.

"What's happening?"

"He says it's serious."

Signing Demensky's pass, Anton thought, "What calmed down Demensky? Dr. Shirokov's report that Kholodova will get well? Or did some other source reveal to him that Sanya was already dead?"

14

Introducing Anton to the owner of the apartment, Ilynykh made a request. "Maria Anisimovna, tell this senior inspector of the Criminal Investigation Department what you told me."

The woman, clasping her work-roughened hands, looked at Anton with a nearsighted squint and began speaking unhappily. It turned out that last night her son did actually drop by around nine. He offered her some money, but Maria Anisimovna refused the "handout." Her son was in a hurry and quickly left the house. After him, about two hours later, a former neighbor dropped by. Just when they started having a good chat, a strange man looked in. He asked for some Ptechkins or Chechkins. Maria Anisimovna replied that she didn't know anyone of that name. The man asked for a glass of water. He drank half, thanked her, and left. And her old neighbor stayed for the night.

"How Vasily managed to put that bag in the niche, I don't know. I only noticed it this morning," Sipeniatina finished up her story grimly.

"Which bag?" Anton asked.

Ilynykh stepped up fast. "Come on, I'll show you."

Out in the narrow corridor, he turned on the light and pulled back a flowered curtain from a deep niche in the wall. There, at the threshold, on the floor, stood a woman's black purse. Its patent leather sides, even in the artificial light, readily showed heavy fingerprints and several elongated smears, perhaps left by cotton dipped in cologne or alcohol. Opening the purse, Anton whistled. It was stuffed with skeins of gray-blue mohair with bright imported wrappings. Going back into the room, Anton carefully dumped the contents on the table. Besides the four skeins of royal mohair, there was also a new cosmetics bag filled with makeup, a key on a chain, an empty envelope addressed to Fedor Fedorovich Kholodov in the city of Aleksin in Tula Oblast, and a passport made out to Kholodova, Aleksandra Fedorovna.

"Apparently she was writing to her father," Ilynykh said, pointing to the envelope.

"Looks that way," Anton agreed and turned to Sipeniatina. "So, you didn't see your son put the purse in the niche?"

Maria Anisimovna spread her hands helplessly. "I opened the door for him myself. Vasily seemed to come in without the purse. Maybe I didn't notice it—my eyes are getting bad."

"None of your son's old pals came by recently?"

"I keep racking my brain. No one seems to have come by . . ."

"And who was this neighbor who slept over?"

"We lived next door to each other on Petukhov Street. Her name is Frosya, Zvonkova's the last name. She's a very sweet girl, considerate. We're very close, like mother and daughter."

Trying to control his excitement, Anton asked, "What time did Frosya arrive?"

Sipeniatina, squinting, looked at her ticking watch. "Around eleven."

"What brought her over so late?"

"She said she came home from the movies, was getting ready for bed, when there was a call. It was Vasily's voice saying that I was sick and asking her to come. Frosya is trusting and despite the hour, hurried over."

"Could she have forgotten her own purse?" Anton had to check.

"She didn't have one. When Frosya saw that I was all right, she threw her arms around me right at the door."

"What did the man who came right after Frosya look like?"

"Distinguished, with a briefcase . . . He was wearing sunglasses that reflected like mirrors. I even thought, 'How does he ever see at night?' Glasses like that are only for looking at the sun."

"How was he dressed?"

"A gray jacket, like a railroad worker's, but the cap was a pilot's with wings."

"Now the railroad personnel have wings on their caps, too," Anton hinted.

"I don't know much about uniforms."

"Did Frosya talk to him?"

"She didn't even see him," Maria Anisimovna said and gave Ilynykh an anxious look and then looked back at Anton. "Something's wrong with Frosya. When the man knocked, her face changed. 'Dearest, don't open! That's for me!' I was confused. The knock was repeated louder. My neighbors knock like that. I opened and it's a man in dark glasses! I confess, my heart jumped. But he talked politely, drank the water, and left. I came back to my room—Frosya is peeking out from behind the window drape, her face whiter than white. I barely managed to calm her down. In the morning we were drinking tea, and she started talking about some woman who was thrown from a third-story window. 'And that will happen to me, too,' she says, 'soon. Oh, such terrible things go on in this world, so terrible!' And then she ran off to work. I didn't understand a thing."

Anton took out the pictures of Ovchinnikov, Demensky, Stepnadze, and Alik Zarvantsev. Handing them to Sipeniatina, he asked, "Is that man among these?"

Maria Anisimovna brought each photograph up to her nose and shrugged her thin shoulders with a guilty air. "I don't think so. I didn't get a good look at him. He only spent a half minute in the foyer while I brought him water from the kitchen."

Anton put the pictures away and asked, "Do you know Frosya Zvonkova's older sister?"

"When I lived next door to Frosya, I used to see her. A handsome woman, severe."

"Do the sisters get along?"

"They're different. Frosya says whatever she thinks, but the elder is full of secrets. So they're not friends."

A half hour later, completing the necessary formalities related to confiscating the woman's purse, Birukov and Captain Ilynykh left Sipeniatina's apartment. Anton asked Ilynykh to come into his car and showed him the photograph of Priazhkina.

"Was this girl on your juvenile records?"

"Yes."

"What was her infraction?"

Ilynykh laughed, tilting his cap. "She was sixteen . . . She dropped out of school, didn't have a job. I called her in and offered her a place at the factory or the opportunity to go to a trade school. She looked me up and down with her indifferent, cloudy eyes and asked, 'What for?' 'To learn a trade and work,' I said. 'Why should I work?' 'To eat well and dress decently. Don't you want that?' She smiled. 'Men will bring me food and clothes.' We kept talking. I managed to get her into barber courses. Why are you suddenly interested in her?"

"She's mixed up in an ugly story, looks like."

"Lusya could mix up anyone she wanted to herself."

The radio in the car buzzed. Birukov picked up the receiver. Through the static he heard the desk sergeant's voice.

"Captain Birukov? . . . I have the chief of the Toguchin transport militia on the phone. They're holding Sipeniatin on our all-points bulletin. He arrived in Toguchin on the morning commuter train from Novosibirsk. When they checked his papers, he tried to run. He has three thousand on him . . ."

15

Ovchinnikov's apartment was on the second floor of a well-kept building. Birukov rang the doorbell and held it a long time. He heard an approaching baritone behind the door, singing a bawdy song.

The lock clicked and the door swung open and the monumental figure of Anatoly Nikolaevich appeared, dressed in sweat pants baggy at the knees and a sleeveless T-shirt hugging a rounded belly. The sight of Birukov flustered Anatoly.

"Chief?" But the round face immediately spread in a wide smile. "Come in! You'll be a guest, but if you bring a half liter of Extra, you'll be the master!"

Besides Ovchinnikov himself, there was no one in the standard, modestly furnished two-room apartment. In the middle of the room a half-empty pack of Belomor cigarettes lay on the floor and on top of it, a box of matches, and under the window by the radiator, half painted with a bright red oil paint, a stool held a pail of paint with a brush sticking out of it. Ovchinnikov, still smiling, asked, "You probably came to see if I had run off, right, chief? . . . Don't have to worry. I've spent the last cent of my vacation money, and you can't go far without money."

"Money can be made," Anton said.

"That's for sure!" Ovchinnikov seconded. "Lately I've been trying not to earn it. Judge for yourself: when you have a lot of money, you get all sorts of ideas that lead to a night in a drunk tank."

Smiling insouciantly, Anatoly Nikolaevich was nevertheless nervous and talked incessantly, as though trying to steer the conversation. Anton purposely said nothing, figuring that the temperamental and not very clever Ovchinnikov would be unable to stand a long silence and would talk about whatever was on his mind. And so it went. Practically choking on a deep drag, Anatoly Nikolaevich said, as though justifying himself, "Last time I told you the whole truth about Kholodova."

"The whole truth?"

"You don't believe me, chief?" Ovchinnikov was bewildered. "You think I'm covering up? Or has something new appeared?"

"Anatoly Nikolaevich, tell me about last night, starting with when you bought tickets to the Aurora and ending with how you got home."

Ovchinnikov, pulling the pack of cigarettes across the floor with his foot, took out a new cigarette. He lit it, turned the matchbox over in his hands like something he'd never seen before, and began talking reluctantly. Asking more specific questions, Anton learned that yesterday, in the middle of the day, Alik Zarvantsev dropped by in his Zaporozhets car to see Ovchinnikov and asked him over to pose for some urgent commission. Around five Lusya Priazhkina showed up at Zarvantsev's. She had tickets to the eight o'clock show of *Esenia* at the Aurora. Alik, busy with his rush job, refused to go to the movies, but at Ovchinnikov's behest, bought two tickets from Lusya. Priazhkina said that she still had one more ticket to sell, and left quickly. Ovchinnikov left Zarvantsev's around six. He dropped in at his place, changed, and went to Zvonkova's.

The rest, basically, Birukov knew, but he didn't interrupt or hurry Anatoly Nikolaevich. He related things rather accurately until the moment when, after arguing with Zvonkova at the movie's end, he took a taxi instead of taking her home. He stopped.

"Why didn't you see Zvonkova home?" Anton asked.

"What am I, a boy? Go all the way to the sticks?"

"So, you took a taxi . . . Then what?"

"Nothing, chief." Ovchinnikov began examining the matchbox with great concentration again. "I gave the driver three rubles and rolled off home in style."

That was a lie.

Anton pretended to believe his story and started from left field.

"Anatoly Nikolaevich, do you know Zvonkova's older sister?"

Ovchinnikov was surprised. "Nina? . . . I've known her for a long time. Since the days when I chased around a soccer ball and she hung around the stadium."

"Tell me more about her."

"A woman with female logic. There's a joke about female logic."

Anton looked at his watch. "I don't have time for jokes."

Ovchinnikov looked down. "I don't have anything particular to tell about Nina. When I met her I had better girls. True, we did date a bit. I could tell she was looking for her prince. And what kind of a prince am I? . . . I introduced her to Alik Zarvantsev. He fell in love with Nina up to his ears, but he wasn't a prince, either. Nina kicked Alik away and married his uncle, Revaz Davidovich. She got herself a prince thirty years her senior."

Birukov grew interested. "Why did she choose such an older man?"

"To each his own, said the Indian and married a monkey," Ovchinnikov replied with a laugh, but he grew serious quickly. "Nina is a practical broad. She worked as a waitress in a restaurant. She has no special education, her erudition is the size of a cat's sneeze. She thought about it: why would a real prince bother with her? And Revaz is a rich old man, he'll hang on for a decade and then give up his skates. Revaz has no close heirs, and Nina will instantly become the rightful owner of a four-room co-op apartment, and a luxurious two-story dacha, and a new Volga. And the old guy has lots of money in the bank! Now that's logic, chief."

"These are your suppositions?"

"Of course they are," Ovchinnikov said proudly.

"What does Zarvantsev have to say about this?"

"Alik is a wimp. When Nina pulled that trick, he began drinking out of grief. Forgot his work, started hanging out in villages, putting up hack work and making money. Now of course he's calmed down—he doesn't see Nina and doesn't ever mention her."

"They don't see each other?"

"No."

"And where did you meet Nina yesterday?"

Ovchinnikov, like a petty thief caught red-handed, looked terrified, his eyes darting.

"Honest, chief, I don't know why Nina lured me to her place yesterday. You see, it was like this . . . I came to Frosya Zvonkova's place an hour before the movie. I see Nina's there—came to visit her sister. When she heard that I had two tickets to *Esenia,* she bragged, 'Well, I'm going to the opera tonight.' And gave me a brazen look. I'd never seen her like that. I figured she was bored with the old man. You know the old saying—A young wife's better off with an arrow in her side than an old husband by her side . . . I didn't resist, of course. I figured, maybe I'll catch up on what I missed with Nina when we were young! Frosya went into the kitchen to change. I say to Nina, 'I can pick you up at the opera tonight.' She whispers, 'I was going to ask you that myself. I'm afraid of going back to Zatula alone at night.' We winked, and it was all set! I sat through the movie with Frosya as proper as pie, and then . . . Hopped a cab and to the opera. The taxi stopped, pulled up to the theater, and the princess floated out . . ."

"Alone?" Anton asked.

"Of course. We came to her house. She offers me a bottle of cognac, smiling like an actress on a poster. We had a drink, followed with lemon." Ovchinnikov scratched his bald spot and laughed at himself. "And here, chief, the comedy started. Just as I pursed my lips to kiss her on the cheek, she slaps me in the face —pow! I saw stars—she's a strong broad. I stare at her—she's wagging her finger at me and says, 'Tolya, I'm a married woman.'

What an actress, I thought! I spent my last fiver on the taxi for her, and she's playing Miss Untouchable . . . While I regained my senses, Nina told me the whole opera—it was like being at the theater department of a public university. I gulped down three glasses of cognac. I felt better, but Nina keeps on about Prince Igor, whom she saw in the theater. I thought, 'Does she take me for a punk, wet behind the ears?' "

"Speed it up, Anatoly Nikolaevich," Anton said.

"Okay, chief, I'll get to the end . . . So, after the fourth glass I made another pass at Nina, but she raises her eyebrows and puts her finger to her lips. 'Quiet! Someone's trying to open the door.' Now that's a fine situation, I thought. I did some fast thinking: I'm no Tarzan to jump from the fourth floor; I'll have to storm the door chest first. If Revaz comes swimming toward me, I'll flatten him like a destroyer hitting a sloop . . . Nina turns as white as the wall with fear, whispers, 'Wait, Tolya. The door is on a chain, it won't open. I'll let you out later.' I whisper back, 'Is that your lover scratching at the door?' 'What lover? I think Revaz is back from his trip earlier than planned. I'll really get it now—the old man is exhausting me with his suspicions.' And so that's how I spent my time there until almost three A.M."

"Did someone really try to open the door?"

"Who the hell knows? Maybe Nina imagined it."

"Did you hear it?"

"What can you hear after a bottle of cognac? Just a pleasant buzz . . ."

"Was the cognac from a restaurant?"

"How can you tell?"

"Was there an ink stamp on the label?"

"I didn't look close, just noticed the five stars." Ovchinnikov lit another cigarette with the butt of the old one. "You see, chief, Nina told me this last night . . . Revaz returned from the last trip quite drunk and upset. Maybe he pulled a wily Caucasian trick on Sanya, hah? . . . Revaz is a sprightly old man . . ."

"We'll see to Revaz Davidovich, but first we have to see to you," Anton said, looking Ovchinnikov in the eyes. "Why did you say last time that you left Novosibirsk for the Ob Sea on the morning of August twenty-first?"

"Because that's what I did."

"No, you didn't, Anatoly Nikolaevich. On the twenty-first you waited for the mail at the building management office almost until one P.M. and left there only after receiving a letter."

Ovchinnikov frowned, as though smoke had gotten into his eyes. Looking away, he said with a guilty air, "I swear, chief, I lied without thinking of the consequences. I wanted to get the letter from the drunk tank to keep it from reaching the bosses. They don't pat you on the head for stuff like that."

"Then when did you leave Novosibirsk?"

"On the twenty-first, after lunch."

"Where did you spend the two nights before that?"

Ovchinnikov looked as if he had to choose the lucky matchstick out of several. Then, totally unexpectedly, he laughed.

"I give up, chief! You've got me against the wall. I spent two nights with Lusya Priazhkina. Of course, I could have admitted that honestly in the first place, but I was ashamed."

"You weren't ashamed about Zvonkova?"

"Frosya is a decent and beautiful girl . . . And what's Lusya? A cuckoo alcoholic."

Anton chuckled. "Interesting logic."

"My eyes aren't frozen yet. I get ashamed sometimes, too. I'd like to look good in people's eyes."

The bell rang in the hallway. Ovchinnikov, pleased with the interruption, went to the door and let in the driver of Anton's car, who silently handed Anton a message.

"Radio report that Frosya Zvonkova is looking for you urgently. Wants to tell you something. Very nervous, calling from the pay phone in her store."

Anton read the message and scribbled with his ballpoint: "Bring her to headquarters. I'll be there soon."

He returned the note to his driver. Without a word the driver left.

Watching him go, Ovchinnikov asked anxiously, "What happened, chief?"

"Business," Anton replied evasively and continued the interrupted conversation as if nothing had happened. "So, you say you are sometimes ashamed of your actions?"

Ovchinnikov frowned. "Of course. When I'm sober I denounce myself, but when I drink, I want adventure so bad it hurts. I've consulted doctors. They tell me there's a disease like that . . . I forget its medical name . . . A passion for wandering, basically. Chief, if Frosya says I spent two nights at her place, don't believe her. I told her to say that. I swear I was embarrassed to admit it about Priazhkina."

"Kholodova received a message typed on the machine at your office . . ."

Ovchinnikov's large, protruding eyes grew even larger. For a few seconds he stared at Anton without blinking, as though dumbstruck. Then, coming to his senses, he spoke fast.

"Personally I have nothing to do with the typewriter at our office. The bookkeeper uses it, sometimes tenants drop in to . . ." And suddenly he exclaimed: "Chief! Revaz typed his calling cards on our machine."

"Calling cards?" Anton said warily.

"Right! Revaz makes lots of new acquaintances on the trains and so he makes up cards, like a nobleman, instead of writing his address over and over. This was a month ago. Alik Zarvantsev and I were drinking at the office after work and Revaz banged away at the typewriter the whole evening."

16

Zvonkova entered Anton's office about ten minutes after he had told the desk sergeant to let her through without any problems. Frosya really was out of sorts. Mouthing a barely audible hello, she took the proffered chair, smoothed her short summer skirt with a practiced air, and, without looking into Anton's eyes, sighed.

"I've let you down."

Birukov, filling out the official part of the transcript, said nothing. This urged Zvonkova on. Nervously squirming in the chair, as though trying to stave off events, she started to talk.

"I warned you, didn't I, that I'm a terrible coward! I warned you. And now we're all mixed up in this story. They descended on me so unexpectedly yesterday that I didn't have time to call you. Then it got so horrible that I didn't sleep the entire night—"

"Let's start from the beginning and do it calmly," Anton interrupted. "Who are 'they'?"

"What do you mean, who?" Zvonkova said in surprise. "Nina and Anatoly, naturally. First Nina showed up in her Volga. So sweet. 'Blahblahblah, how are things, Frosya dear?' While I listened to my sister, Ovchinnikov shows up! 'Come on, Frosya, let's go see *Esenia* at eight o'clock.' I was so scared before and now I just gave up, I was in a cloud. I just sat there through the movie, and on my right some terrible Gypsy woman kept jabbing my ribs with her elbow. I don't remember how I managed to wait to the end. For the first time in my life I asked Anatoly to see me home, but he seemed to know that I had promised to help you. He began giving me a story—his mother had a heart attack, he had to get over to a pharmacy urgently. It made me sick. He must have guessed that I told CID, I figured . . . And Anatoly's changed, he's not sincere anymore, he's hiding something . . ."

"What?"

"I don't know, but there's something abnormal in his behavior. He was whispering with Nina about something while I was changing in the kitchen, and after the movie he practically insulted me."

"Maybe he and Nina have a secret?"

"Try again! Nina never took Anatoly seriously. Now, she did like Alik Zarvantsev once."

"Why did she choose his uncle instead?"

"Because Alik is unserious and, frankly, rather poor. Nina likes a man with worldliness . . . And that night, just when I was about to go to sleep, the phone rings. My heart jumped. I picked up the receiver—it's Vasya Sipeniatin's voice. 'Hi, sweetheart! My mother's sick, she begs you to come and spend the night with her.'"

"Are you sure it was him?"

"No one but Vasya calls me sweetheart."

Birukov showed her Kholodova's purse. "Did you leave this at Maria Anisimovna's?"

"Oh, no! I've never seen it before. Is it stolen?"

"Why do you think so?"

"If Vasya dropped by his home, it was because he had to hide something there."

"You think it's Vasya's work?"

"Of course! He's never out of prison."

Throughout the conversation Zvonkova was so spontaneous that he wanted to believe in her sincerity, but still cats clawed at Anton's soul.

"How did you get up the courage to go to Maria Anisimovna at eleven at night?" Anton asked her.

"It was scarier being at home alone. That's why I spent the night at her place."

Everything was explained, everything was logical in Zvonkova's statement. Finding nothing false in either her voice or expression, Anton said, "I'll be questioning Sipeniatin now and perhaps I'll need you to confront him. Do you agree?"

"If—if it's necessary, of course."

Anton brought her into the next office and called Sipeniatin in for a preliminary interrogation.

Vasya Sivy came in accompanied by a guard, his hands behind his back out of habit, his head of white, flaxen hair bent low. Fresh scratches were healing on his flattened wide nose and round chin. His collar and sleeves were tightly buttoned to hide the tattoos, Birukov guessed. Sitting down without being asked, Vasya wearily shrugged his broad shoulders and turned his full-lipped face to the guard, as if determined to see him leave the office.

When the sergeant was gone, Anton, looking at the scratches, asked him, "What happened to your face?"

Vasya, turning to the window, laughed. "Learning to walk on my eyebrows."

"Why did you try to run when they checked your papers?"

"Ah, I was dumb, and the lieutenant tripped me. I have no complaint. That's how it is in sports: one wins, one loses." Sipeniatin stared at Anton from under his brow. "But in general, citizen inspector, I protest injustice. I was returning to my place of residence and work in a legal fashion. Why was I arrested? I did my time for my past sins."

Birukov met Sipeniatin's gaze. "Let's figure it out. What were you doing in Novosibirsk?"

Vasya's gaze shifted. "I came to see my mother. I ran into some old pals and partied."

"Give me their names and addresses."

Sipeniatin got huffy. "I'm not turning in my pals, citizen inspector."

"That's up to you," Birukov said indifferently and, trying to figure out Sipeniatin's connection to the Kholodova case, started asking his prepared questions.

Experienced in dialogues with investigators, Vasya responded laconically but with so much apathy you would have thought he didn't give a damn about anything in the world. Naturally, he fully denied any connection with Kholodova. When Anton switched to concrete details, the apathy left Vasya's face and sincere bewilderment flashed in those naïve, baby blue eyes. He looked through the photographs curiously and pointed a fat finger at the picture of Demensky.

"Now that guy I know."

"How did you meet him?" Anton asked.

Sipeniatin repeated Yuri Pavlovich's statement word for word about buying the Crucifixion, then, after a silence, added that on August 21 in the evening he went to Demensky's house to get the fiver he owed him, but, despite his repeated rings, the door wasn't opened even though there seemed to be someone inside. His statement was so on the mark that in one fell swoop it explained Vasya's fingerprints on the doorbell of Demensky's apartment and seemed to confirm that he had no connection with the incident.

"You say someone was in the apartment?" Anton asked.

Vasya shrugged. "I thought a woman screamed and her mouth was shut."

"You thought or you really heard?"

"I think I heard."

"Were you at the door long?"

"I don't have a watch."

"Approximately . . . a minute, two?"

"One and a half," Vasya cracked.

"Was the cry repeated?"

"It was like they were all dead in the apartment."

"Where did you get the Crucifixion?" Anton asked.

Sipeniatin replied with a ready answer, as if he had been waiting for just that question.

"My grandmother left me a trunk full of all sorts of icons and church books. Mother told me the old woman was religious."

"What did you do with the books?"

"Sold them secondhand." Vasya chuckled. "Eccentrics grabbed them up."

"Did you sell them expensively?"

"Ten each."

"How much did you sell the Bible for?"

"I sold everything at ten rubles."

"Do you remember who bought the Bible?"

Vasya guffawed condescendingly. "Is that a joke, inspector? You think my head is the Council of Soviets, that I can remember everything?"

"All the icons and books of your grandmother were inscribed 'Property of Darya Sipeniatina,' " Anton said, almost in passing.

"Granny knew writing like her Our Father."

"But the Crucifixion doesn't have that inscription."

Vasya frowned in puzzlement and then belatedly recalled. "The Crucifixion isn't Granny's icon. I'll explain that right away, citizen inspector . . . In Toguchin District, where I was sent to live, there's a village called Vysoka Griva. We were . . . uh . . . building a cattle yard there. You can call Toguchin, check, I'm a driver for the state farm administration." Sipeniatin, gathering his thoughts, was dragging things out, and Anton sharply interrupted.

"I know where you work and how long you've been away from work. Answer quickly."

Vasya made an injured face. "Quickly, citizen inspector, in that village I dropped off a load of wood for a religious old lady. In gratitude she gave me the icon."

Birukov looked into Vasya's innocent eyes with a rebuke. "You weren't in Toguchin district six weeks ago. You had just gotten out of prison then."

"Then I made a mistake." Sipeniatin, looking around, smacked his forehead with his hand. "Right, citizen inspector! A pal gave me the Crucifixion."

"Who?"

"I won't turn in a pal."

"Did he give you the money, too?"

"What money?"

"The three thousand found on you."

Sipeniatin looked downcast but immediately started making up a story. According to him some Georgian man gave him the money to hand over to some doctor so that he wouldn't treat some woman who had fallen from the third floor. The story was like a child's babble. It didn't mention a single name, but everything that had to do with Sipeniatin's meeting with the doctor agreed with Dr. Shirokov's story.

"What's this Georgian's name?"

"You think I asked to see his passport?" Vasya pretended to be surprised. "We met at a railroad restaurant, drank some cognac."

"And he handed you three thousand rubles?"

"Why not? . . . Obviously the fellow was pressed. He had a lot of years on him and a term for murder might not fit in the frame of his life."

Birukov took Kholodova's purse out of the safe and put it on the table. "Here's what we found in your mother's apartment."

"Wha-a-at?" Sipeniatin drawled in astonishment and rose from his chair. "Let me see that!"

Anton raised a warning hand. "We've already gotten your fingerprints from the purse. To save time I'll tell you that the woman who owned this purse is dead."

Squinting as though in intolerable pain, Vasya gritted his teeth. "Is he crazy or what, the stupid jerk!" And he stared into Anton's eyes. "Citizen inspector, tell me, who dumped the purse there? I'll tear out his face with my own hands!"

"Your 'pals' did."

"Who was at my mother's?"

"After you, Zvonkova."

"Sweetheart? What did she come over for?"

"You called her."

For a minute Sipeniatin sat in stunned silence. Then, swallowing hard, he smiled crookedly. "Are you trying to trap me, inspector?"

"I can suggest a meeting. Shall I call in Zvonkova?" Anton asked calmly.

Sipeniatin's eyes darted about nervously, but he answered with a challenge. "Go ahead!"

"I will, but first let's find out how your fingerprints got on that purse."

Vasya's full-lipped round face spread in a smile. "Negligence . . . I won't lie, I know that purse. On August twenty-first I was in need, I had to take care of a hangover. I went to see what I could find at the train station. The Adler train came in. I see a fancy lady in a pink dress paying no attention, waiting for someone. There was a red suitcase at her feet and on it, this purse. I walk past, drop my handkerchief, bend over . . . The lady has a mouth like a crocodile: 'Stop, thief!' Obviously I had to drop it and run . . ."

"Then you met Kholodova at the station?" Anton asked quickly.

Vasya laughed. "Don't jump to conclusions, inspector. I don't know any Kholodova. Call in Zvonkova, you'll hear her song."

Frosya came into the office, feeling "not herself." Looking quickly at Sipeniatin, she asked in a rebuke, "Got caught again?"

"Nah," Sipeniatin said happily. "The inspector is trying to talk me into taking a rap for murder. Did you already bring me a parcel?"

Zvonkova's beautiful face took on a childishly stupid expression. She had not understood a word of Vasya's humor, and stared at his scabs. "Why are you all scratched up?"

Vasya winked at Anton and laughed. "I was testing the hardness of the concrete on the Toguchin platform." But the laughter was unnatural, strained.

Having completed the necessary formalities, Birukov read back Zvonkova's statement about the phone call and asked Frosya, "Do you confirm your statement?"

"I do," Zvonkova said in a barely audible voice.

Birukov turned to Sipeniatin. "What do you have to say about this?"

"I didn't call anyone, inspector! May I become the lowest of the low, I didn't call!" As though only now seeing Kholodova's purse on the table, he pointed at it harshly. "A broad was tossed from a third floor for that reticule! You stupid doll! You want to stick me with murder? . . . You tell the inspector right now who gave you the purse in order to screw me . . . Come on! Well?"

Frosya, pleading for mercy, said, "A man dropped by Maria Anisimovna's while I was there. Maybe he left it . . ."

"What man?" Sipeniatin asked quickly.

"I was in the room, Vasya, and he was in the foyer." Zvonkova crossed her hands over her chest. "Honest, Vasya, I never laid eyes on him!"

"Lying again?"

"It's the truth," Anton interjected on Zvonkova's behalf. "The man was distinguished, with a briefcase, in mirrored sunglasses."

Sipeniatin was stopped for a second. "I don't know anyone like that . . ."

The phone rang. Birukov answered and heard the voice of forensics expert Dymokurov.

"Anton Ignatievich, shall I bring over the final analysis of the contents of the purse?"

"A bit later, Arkady Ivanovich. Just tell me now who held the purse besides Sipeniatin and Kholodova?"

"The prints of the scarred fingers are identical to the ones left on the balcony door in Demensky's apartment."

"What did the analysis show?"

"The spots are traces of evaporated turpentine. We can assume that it destroyed some of the prints."

"Thanks, Arkady Ivanovich." Anton hung up and looked at Sipeniatin. Vasya, who was listening intently to the conversation, even had his mouth open. When he saw Anton looking at him, he jerked his head in Zvonkova's direction.

"The guy who came to my mother's is a pal of Frosya—"

"Vasya!" Zvonkova cried out. "Why are you blaming others? They'll put you in jail anyway . . ."

Sipeniatin, turning purple, made a rude gesture. "See that? Before they put me away, I'll put your whole gang where it belongs!" Sipeniatin's bloodshot eyes narrowed threateningly. "You tell them what I said. Got it, sweetheart?"

Zvonkova covered her face with her hands, and her shoulders shook.

Anton called the guard and said dryly, "Take away the prisoner."

Sipeniatin, giving Zvonkova a vicious look, rose abruptly, put his hands behind his back, and strode toward the door. From the corridor came his rollicking voice:

"Ladies kissed my feet like crazy,
With a chic widow I drank away my father's house . . ."

17

Exactly at nine a tall, elderly man with four ribbons on his military coat without shoulder boards walked into Anton's office.

Stopping in the doorway, he seemed to be reporting for duty out of habit as he said in a quiet, tired voice, "Fedor Fedorovich Kholodov, major retired. May I?"

"Come in, Fedor Fedorovich." Anton stood up from his desk and came out to meet the man, offering his hand. "Senior Inspector Birukov. Forgive me for asking you to come in so early. I know you're not in the mood for chats right now, but circumstances are such . . ."

Kholodov bent his gray head. After he took his chair, Anton went back to his own seat.

"The sergeant told me that you are staying at Demensky's . . ."

"Yes, he helped us find Yuri Pavlovich's apartment." Kholodov rubbed the bags under his eyes caused by a sleepless night. "My wife and I came straight from the airport late last night to detective headquarters. We were taken to—the morgue, to identify Sanya . . . It's her . . . Mother felt sick, they called for an ambulance in the night. Yura is stunned by the death. He says that he had spoken to the doctor the day before and was told that she would recover . . ."

"Demensky wasn't told on purpose," Anton said and added after a pause, "They didn't want to upset him before it was necessary."

Kholodov shut his eyes. "We'll probably have to stay on here a bit. The funeral is set for tomorrow at three. I don't know how

my wife and I will bear all this . . ." After a silence he looked at
Anton. "We've not long to live, she and I. We'll have to leave
Seryozha with Yuri Pavlovich. He wants to adopt him."

"Do you believe Demensky?"

"Completely. Yuri is a marvelous man. Their domestic problems were caused by Sanya, I have to say, even though she is our
daughter."

"Tell me about her."

"Sanya was born under an unlucky star . . ." Kholodov
squeezed the bridge of his nose between two fingers, as if trying
to get rid of the tears that were choking him, and after a brief
period of silence, spoke in a faraway voice.

His story, which Birukov followed closely, made Anton think
grimly about how many tragic moments and coincidences had
filled the life of Aleksandra Fedorovna Kholodova. At the age of
ten, coming home from her grandmother's house, Sanya miracu-
lously survived an automobile crash. At sixteen she almost
drowned while swimming across the Irtysh river on a dare. At
twenty-two, defending a girlfriend from some drunken hooligans, she was knifed in the stomach. At twenty-six she decided
to marry a fellow she had known for three years. They applied,
prepared a wedding, and the night before they were to go to the
registry office, he was run over and killed by a bus.

Kholodov, pressing the bridge of his nose again, stopped talking, and then continued. "And Seryozha is a memento of the
wedding that never took place . . ."

"Does Demensky know all this?" Anton asked.

"No. Sanya didn't like bringing up her past. I told Yuri Pavlovich about Seryozha's father this morning. He was amazed. It
turned out that Sanya had made up all kinds of unbelievable
stories. She didn't know how to lie, and these falsehoods merely
diminished her in Yuri's eyes."

"Have you heard the name Stepnadze from your daughter?"

Kholodov grimaced nervously. "Stepnadze is another painful
chapter in Sanya's life. In 1970—we were living in Omsk then—
Sanya took over a bookstore. I don't know how it happened, but

in the very first audit there was a discrepancy of twenty-five hundred rubles. You might say that an entire packing case of books had disappeared—it's no joking matter. And just then Stepnadze appeared on the horizon. He offered Sanya the money to cover the discrepancy and talked the auditor into hushing up the case. I don't know what his motive was: generosity or vileness. I think it was the latter because then Stepnadze gave Sanya the choice of repaying her debt either by marrying him or paying him back with rare books. Sanya refused marriage . . . Can you imagine what a long-term business she had gotten herself into?"

"She did it without asking your advice?"

"Yes. She told mother and me about it only in 1974, when she had paid Stepnadze back in full."

"Do you know anything about the last period of Sanya's life?" Anton waited a bit. "You see, Fedor Fedorovich, just before the incident Sanya started writing a statement for the prosecutor and never finished it . . ."

Kholodov took out a handkerchief and wiped his brow. "In the last year everything seemed to be going well. Seryozha was living with us, Sanya wrote letters frequently, sent packages with sweets and clothing. Last week we received a telegram that she was coming to spend her vacation with us, and then . . ."

"What could have brought Sanya so suddenly to Novosibirsk?"

"Yuri Pavlovich and I were racking our brains over it last night," Kholodov said slowly, putting away his handkerchief. "Probably it was an unbalanced act. When they broke up, she was beside herself. She would fly off suddenly to visit us from Cheliabinsk, or suddenly take a vacation and go south in winter, and once she almost signed up to go north along the Ob River, to work in Nadym. She was in a frenzy, as though sensing misfortune and trying to get away from it, but . . . she didn't get away."

"Did Demensky ever complain about Sanya?"

"Never. Nor Sanya about him."

The conversation lasted about an hour.

When Kholodov, stoop-shouldered, left the office, Anton felt that the self-controlled man, tormented with grief, had handed him the full enormity of his sorrow.

At ten in the morning the division chief called and asked Anton to see him. As he came into the spacious office, Birukov could tell from the lieutenant colonel's grim expression that something was worrying him. Seating Anton in the chair at his desk, the lieutenant colonel said, "What's new in the Kholodova case?"

"A lot is new," Anton said, untying the folder he had brought with him, "but unfortunately, there's nothing concrete."

"What's the information on Stepnadze?"

Anton took two telegrams out of the file and handed them to the lieutenant colonel.

"Stepnadze flew out of Rostov on flight 6129 to Omsk with a changeover in Cheliabinsk. Cheliabinsk confirms checking the ticket through to Omsk."

"Then Revaz Davidovich wasn't in Novosibirsk when Priazhkina was riding around in his Volga?"

"If you believe the airport documents, no."

"You don't?" the lieutenant colonel asked, examining the telegrams closely.

"I do, but I want to double-check them thoroughly. The Adler train comes in today. Let's see if Stepnadze is on it."

"What if he isn't?"

"We'll put out a bulletin."

"Yes," the division chief said grimly, returning the telegrams. "What does Lusya Priazhkina say?"

"Absolutely nothing. She says that she got a ride to the Motodrom stop with a passing private car and wanted to get a taxi there."

"What was she doing at the Aurora?"

"Checking to see with whom Ovchinnikov was 'fooling around.' "

"Have they released her from the hospital?"

"The doctors are worried about complications; they want to keep her two more days."

"What's your impression of Kholodova? How do you explain her behavior?"

Birukov thought.

"A lot depends on character. But it seems that Kholodova was unbalanced."

"The prosecutor just called me. Rebuking me for dragging out the investigation."

"We're allowed three more days by law."

18

The light gray Volga with license number 31-42 NSU rolled up to the Novosibirsk Central Station ten minutes before the loudspeaker announced the arrival of the Adler–Novosibirsk passenger train, and Anton Birukov saw Nina Stepnadze. She was a tall, slightly plump woman of thirty-five, with a complicated golden blond hairdo. The bell-bottom pantsuit boldly revealed her striking figure. Checking the Volga from all sides, she took a book from the backseat, looked at her shiny gold watch, and, getting behind the wheel, yawned and started reading.

The Highway Patrol car passed the Volga and parked in the shade of the viaduct. Anton recognized the driver, the fat-cheeked lieutenant who was first on the scene of Priazhkina's accident at the Motodrom stop, and hunched in the backseat was the auxiliary car inspector, Little Kolya.

The electric locomotive, slowing down, pulled into the station. Figuring out where car number 8 would stop, Birukov, trying not to push people meeting the train and staring hypnotized at the windows, hurriedly made his way through the crowd. Suddenly he was shoulder to shoulder with Demensky. For a second Yuri Pavlovich was struck dumb; then he distractedly said hello.

"Meeting Revaz Davidovich?" Anton asked quickly after responding to his greeting.

"Ye-yes," Demensky stuttered. "I want to know what happened to Sanya. You know that Sanya—is dead?"

"I know everything and I don't recommend meeting Stepnadze now."

Yuri Pavlovich's eyes began to turn red. "Revaz Davidovich will be more frank with me than with CID."

"He won't tell you a thing," Anton said dryly. "Please, stay out of this business."

"Have it your own way," Demensky said angrily and melted into the crowd.

Birukov saw Stepnadze's distinguished figure from afar. Revaz Davidovich was wearing the gray uniform and cap with the yellow railroad symbol—wings. As soon as the train stopped, he carefully dusted the railings and started letting out the passengers.

Slava Golubyov was practically the first to jump down to the platform and make his way through the crowd. Understanding where he was headed, Anton went to the terminal, where they could talk without witnesses.

"Why no flowers or band?" Slava asked as he shook hands with Anton.

"The orchestra is getting ready for Kholodova's funeral," Anton replied grimly.

Golubyov's good mood dissipated instantly. "She's dead?"

"Night before last. Tell me fast: how did you lose Stepnadze?"

The passenger disembarkation took about twenty minutes. In that time Golubyov, in his usual fast-paced chatter, had time to tell Birukov about Revaz Davidovich's travels in Adler and Rostov, ending with how Stepnadze, whom he had lost in Rostov, met the train in Omsk and took it to Novosibirsk.

"Where was he for two and a half days?" Anton asked.

"He says he was visiting his cousin in Omsk."

"Did you learn the cousin's name?"

"No, I tried to keep out of Stepnadze's sight." Golubyov looked around. "Which hotel would have two beds now? I met a work supervisor from Adler and his wife on the train. They've come to help their son get into NETI. Stepnadze promised them pull at the institute, and I blurted out that I would help them with a hotel. They're waiting for me at the taxi stand."

"Go to the Ob Hotel, they almost always have room. As soon

as you get them settled, go to NETI. I think Stepnadze's 'pull' smells of a bribe."

"That's what I think, too. Revaz Davidovich seems to have too many friends in colleges. Could he be setting up a major bribery ring? I have to get in touch with the institutes in Sukhumi and Rostov today."

"Right."

Golubyov shifted his simple briefcase from hand to hand. "We also have to find out what Stepnadze was doing in Omsk."

"First we have to determine whether he was there at all," Anton said. "There is reason to suppose that Stepnadze flew to Novosibirsk from Rostov and then flew back to Omsk from here to meet his train."

"Why bother with so much flying?" Slava said in surprise. "It's like going to Arkhangelsk from Moscow via Sukhumi."

Anton prodded Slava's shoulder. "All right, go to your fellow passengers, get them into a hotel. They may be invaluable to us."

After he had unloaded the passengers and apparently turned over the car to his partner, Stepnadze went out on the platform, approached the flower vendors, bought an enormous bouquet of gladioli, and, thoughtfully lowering his head of white hair that pushed out from his cap, headed for the light gray Volga with the license number 31-42 NSU.

Seeing her husband approaching, Nina ran out of the car joyfully. Gently kissing her on the temple, Revaz Davidovich gallantly handed her the flowers. Then, putting his briefcase on the backseat, he slumped heavily in the front seat next to the driver. The Volga left the parking lot and easily started up the road that led from the station.

At that same moment the Highway Patrol car pulled out of the viaduct's shade and stopped near Birukov. Anton got in quickly next to the fat-cheeked lieutenant and, turning to Little Kolya, asked, "Did you recognize the railroad man?"

"I think the other one was thinner and younger," the auxiliary auto inspector replied.

Just when the patrol car started moving, the Volga, in the

middle of the ramp, stopped so suddenly you might have thought its engine had died.

"Let's wait," Anton said curtly to the lieutenant.

Its warning lights blinking, the Volga backed up and jerked. The signals blinked and the car jerked again. Stepnadze got out of the car, opened the hood, and bent over the engine. Nina joined him on the other side of the car. Several minutes passed.

"Let's drive up to them," Anton said and turned to Little Kolya. "Don't get out of the car. I don't want the Stepnadzes to see you."

"I understand," Kolya boomed in his deep voice.

As they pulled up to the Volga, the lieutenant stuck his head out of the car. "What's the matter here? Why are we stopped in an illegal spot? Don't we know the rules?"

"My hood is raised," Stepnadze replied quickly. "The spark is gone, I think . . ." And he showed the lieutenant a spark plug he had removed.

The lieutenant and Anton approached the Volga. Seeing Stepnadze's hands, Anton grew wary—the skin of Revaz Davidovich's fingers was pale blue and scarred. Fingers like that could have left the mutilated prints found on the unfinished bottle of cognac and the balcony door in Demensky's apartment.

The lieutenant took the spark plug, worked on it briefly until a light blue electric discharge crackled dryly.

"The spark is fine, pops."

Revaz Davidovich looked at his wife. "What's the matter, mama?"

Nina made a puzzled face. "It was fine on the way over."

The lieutenant checked the carburetor and leaned over the fuel pump. An ironic smile played on his lips. He took a handkerchief from his pocket and wiped his hands. Jokingly he said, "Volgas don't run without gas. Your fuel tank is empty."

"Impossible!" Nina said in genuine surprise. "I had it filled up just two days ago."

"You can burn up a lot of gas in two days," Anton said.

"I only made one trip to Shelkovichikha!" Nina said in outrage.

Pretending to know nothing, Anton looked at Stepnadze.
"You didn't use the car, either?"

"I haven't been home the last few days," Revaz Davidovich
said with a smile and, apparently taking Anton for the senior
officer, asked, "Dear fellow, could you lend us enough gas to get
to the gas station?"

Anton felt that Revaz Davidovich's calm was put on and decided he wanted a closer look. He asked the lieutenant, "How's
your gas situation?"

"Fine," the lieutenant replied.

"We'll help you out," Anton said to Stepnadze. "But we'll
have to take a look at your garage. I think someone used your
Volga. Teenagers, you know, sometimes act like hooligans: they
open garages while the owners are away."

Stepnadze smiled and said, "My garage has dependable locks.
There's nothing there for teenagers."

"When the cat's away, mice will play," Anton said worriedly.
"You might realize a loss later, and it'll be too late."

Getting some gas in the tank took a short time. Revaz Davidovich took the wheel, turned the ignition, and pushed the starter.
The engine revved. Birukov, without waiting for an invitation,
opened the Volga's back door.

"I'll ride with you."

"Please do, dear fellow!" Stepnadze said with a large smile,
but his wife, it seemed to Anton, frowned with dissatisfaction.

Stepnadze drove easily, even with a certain devil-may-care ca-
sualness. Stopping for only a few seconds at the first light, the
Volga sped merrily through green lights, and Anton suddenly
thought that the driver who had taken Lusya Priazhkina out
from under his nose had driven the same way. The Highway
Patrol car, as though tied to them, followed behind at a steady
distance. Turning into the first gas station they came to, Revaz
Davidovich had the car filled up.

The fuel tank was full in minutes. Revaz Davidovich got back in, and the Volga sped on. In order to break the long silence, Anton was about to start on an extraneous topic when Revaz Davidovich turned to his wife.

"Mama, Givi is completely well."

"What's so special about that?" Nina said in surprise.

"Nothing."

"That's what I think."

"Oh, yes?" Stepnadze laughed vaguely and, as if chastising his wife, warned jokingly, "Oh, Nina-Nina-Nina!"

Nina turned away petulantly. Anton gazed distractedly out his window, trying to convey the impression that he wasn't in the least interested in the conversation between the Stepnadzes.

The sun struck the windshield. Stepnadze leaned back in his seat and asked his wife, "Please give me my glasses from the glove compartment."

Nina opened it. "There are no glasses in here."

"Where are they?"

"How am I supposed to know!"

Revaz Davidovich smiled. "Why is mama out of sorts today?"

"Oh . . . I don't understand about the gas."

The rest of the way was traveled in silence, as though the Stepnadzes had read their lines according to the script and now were through.

Revaz Davidovich's garage was a fine one: made of silicate brick with heat and electricity. It stood not far from the house in a row of other garages, most of them low metal sheds. Nearby was a large playground with castles, sandboxes, and concrete mushrooms painted in different colors. There was also an open gazebo with a playful plywood sign: "THE ZATULA GOATS DOMINO CLUB." Dominoes could be heard being slapped down wildly inside.

Revaz Davidovich kept his garage in ideal order. The walls of the maintenance pit glowed with multicolored tiles, there were spare parts and instruments on the shelves, two roomy metal canisters in the corners, and at the door hung an almost-new railroad conductor's jacket and a cap with the wings emblem.

Looking over the garage with practiced eyes, Revaz Davidovich calmly went through the pockets of the jacket hanging by the door and stared angrily at his wife.

"Mama, where are my glasses?"

Nina glowered at him. "What's the matter with you? You'd think the sun rises and sets on your glasses . . ."

Stepnadze looked embarrassed. "Did you fill up the car?"

"Naturally," she replied.

Of course, no trace of car theft was found in the garage. Actually Birukov hadn't hoped to find any. He was very interested in the scenario with the gas. At first Anton didn't have an iota of doubt that it was put on for his benefit, but the more he watched Revaz Davidovich and his "mama," the more he hesitated—the Stepnadzes were behaving so naturally.

Finally Anton decided to move from passive observation to action. Looking at Revaz Davidovich's bluish, scabbed fingers, he asked curiously, "What happened to your hand?"

Stepnadze was taken aback. "I was mixing electrolyte for the battery and got my fingers in it by accident."

"May I see your driver's license?"

Revaz Davidovich calmly took a thin folder carefully sealed with plastic out of his uniform chest pocket and handed it to Anton without a glimmer of anxiety.

Opening the license, Anton asked, "You bought the car last year?"

"Dear fellow, I've had the car for five years."

"Then why did you only get a driver's license last year?"

"Just happened," Stepnadze replied uninformatively.

The answer didn't satisfy Anton. It looked as if Revaz Davidovich had been tripped up and gave the first answer that came to mind. However, Anton did not reveal any dissatisfaction. Looking like a man who was tired of his official duties, he returned the license to Revaz Davidovich and asked indifferently, "Shall we consider then that no one touched your car?"

"My glasses are missing," Stepnadze announced suddenly.

"Where were they?"

"In the car."

"Oh, my God," Nina sighed dramatically, "who needs your lousy glasses?"

"Keep out of this," Revaz Davidovich put her in her place sharply. "Needed or not, they're missing!"

"Fill out a statement," Anton said to the lieutenant and pointed to the gazebo from which came the fevered click of dominoes. "I'll have a chat with the club members."

Under the main sign hung a smaller one. In oil paints it read:

NO DRUNKS MAY PLAY!
ACCORDING TO THE
ORAL DECREE OF THE PRESIDENT
OF THE ZATULA GOATS DOMINO CLUB

In the gazebo four men stripped to the waist ruthlessly slammed dominoes onto the table surface. A fifth man, seemingly pumped up with air, with a disproportionately large head and lilliputian arms, watched the game with concentration. All five mumbled a hello and went on slapping the table. Patiently waiting until one of the players jumped up from the table with a cry of "Cod's also a fish!", Anton turned the conversation to the topic that interested him.

"What happened at Revaz Davidovich's?" the large-headed man asked curiously.

"Someone siphoned the gas out of his car," Anton said.

"You don't say!" The man waved his short arms in surprise and turned to the players. "Did you hear that? Maybe our motorcycles are standing around empty?"

"Your antedeluvian Kovrovets doesn't have enough in it for a cigarette lighter," said the fellow who had managed to make a "fish."

"Watch your mouth!" the little man said, wagging his finger meaningfully. "I'll give orders that you can't play even when you're sober."

"That's not fair, comrade president."

"And mocking the president is?" The man pretended to be in

a huff and then suggested to Anton, "Let's walk over to my garage."

The players teasing the president started mixing up the dominoes for a new game, and the president, as soon as he and Anton had walked away from the gazebo, said in a conspiratorial whisper, "My name is Semechkin. Andrei Andreevich. I work as the elevator operator in the building where Stepnadze lives. I want to report this to you. At the request of Revaz Davidovich, a year ago I outfitted his garage with an alarm. So there's no way you can get in there secretly. Who could have managed to siphon gas with a system like that?"

The elevator operator's "report" strengthened Anton's wavering belief that the Stepnadze couple was acting out a prepared scenario and that the sincerity of the acting was due to the fact that one of the actors wasn't in the confidence of the scenario's author. Unfortunately the elevator operator couldn't help him decide which spouse was playing the rehearsed part and which one was improvising with such talent. Anton was inclined to believe that Revaz Davidovich was in charge, but then Semechkin followed his first statement with another one.

"Here's what I think: Revaz Davidovich's wife used up the gas with her lover and now she's trying to get out of the water dry, so to speak."

"She has a lover?"

"I think so. Last week our elevator was acting up, getting stuck between floors. And at midnight I hear a voice over the intercom that sounds like Revaz Davidovich: 'Dear fellow, why is this happening?' Naturally I got them down immediately. Mrs. Stepnadze came out with some railroad man. They got in the Volga and drove off."

"Revaz Davidovich is a railroad man, too."

Semechkin squinted slyly. "No. Wrong bearing."

"Do you remember what that man looked like?"

"From his walk, I'd say under forty. Trim and tall. The railroad jacket was baggy on him."

"Did you see him only that one time?"

"One time and then only because of the elevator."

As they talked they reached Semechkin's garage. Anton looked into the metal shed that held the Kovrovets, asked a few more questions about the Stepnadzes and, receiving nothing substantial in response, bid the club president farewell.

"What did you find there?" the lieutenant asked Anton.

"As the domino players say, double blank. But there is a supposition that someone's hanging around the garages," Anton replied with feigned indifference and then asked, "Have you written up the report?"

"It just has to be signed."

While the lieutenant signed his name, Anton surreptitiously wiped a ballpoint pen in his pocket with a handkerchief so that there would be no old fingerprints on it and handed it to Revaz Davidovich.

19

"To Tolmachevo airport," Birukov said softly.

The lieutenant turned the key and stepped on the gas. They drove in silence for a while. Anton was concentrating on an analysis of Revaz Davidovich's behavior from the moment he saw him in the railroad car to the frankly confused look with which Stepnadze had followed the retreating patrol car. He remembered how Revaz Davidovich had bought gladioli at the station entrance. Anton had seen similar bouquets in Demensky's apartment and in Dr. Shirokov's clinic and at the building administration office. Mentally dressing Stepnadze in a blue shirt with rolled-up sleeves and plopping a sombrero on his white hair, Anton pictured Revaz Davidovich talking with nurse's aide Renata Petrovna.

Little Kolya coughed in the backseat; the Stepnadzes never did see him. Anton turned to him.

"So who was driving the Volga when you stopped it?"

"Ninety-nine percent sure, it wasn't that railroad man."

"In our work we need at least a hundred."

Kolya sighed deeply. "I can't give you a hundred. The uniform is confusing me and the face . . . tanned, large nose . . . In brief, I was remiss in my duty. Did he show you his license?"

"He has a new license," Anton said and looked at the lieutenant. "He got it last May in your precinct. Let me talk to your desk."

The lieutenant used the radio. The desk man responded so fast it seemed he had been waiting for their call. Anton gave him the date and asked him to look up the minutes of the qualifying commission's meeting. A few minutes later the desk man called back.

"Stepnadze, Revaz Davidovich, passed with excellent marks the test for reissuing a license after losing it."

"Thank you," Anton said and, turning off the radio, spoke to the lieutenant. "So that's it."

The airport building came into view as the greenery suddenly parted. Anton Birukov found the duty officer—a young, lively fellow in a summer uniform—showed him his ID, and explained the purpose of his visit. The duty officer tugged at the visor of the cap that sat jauntily on his curly hair.

"That will take a long time to find. Could you give me an approximate idea of when this Stepnadze could have left from here?"

"Approximately two days ago on the last flight," Anton said.

"The last flight stopping in Omsk is 5468 to Kazan. It leaves at twenty-three fifteen local time. How's that?"

"Perfect."

The officer left his office and returned in a few minutes with the boarding passes from flight 5468. Before he got halfway through, Anton felt his heart jump—number forty-seven was STEPNADZE, R. D. However, that line was neatly crossed out and BRAZHNIKOV, A. E., was written in. Anton called the duty officer over.

"What's this?" he asked.

"Everything's in order," he quickly replied. "Brazhnikov took off instead of Stepnadze."

"How could that happen?"

"Elementary. Probably Stepnadze had a reservation but didn't appear for boarding, and his seat was sold to someone else."

"Does that happen often?"

"Not often, but it happens." The officer thought a bit and tugged at his jaunty cap again. "Wait! That happened when I was on duty. So . . . well . . . I remember! Passenger Brazhnikov came to the counter with Stepnadze's passport and ticket and asked us to make the ticket over to him because he said

Stepnadze had changed his mind about the trip. Naturally the clerk wanted to see the ticket owner himself. Some man who didn't look at all like the picture in the passport came over. The clerk called me. When I turned up to see what was what, the men were gone without a trace, but the passport and ticket were left behind." He opened his desk drawer and took out the dog-eared passport and handed it to Anton. "Here, take a look."

Anton opened the scruffy cover and saw a photo of Revaz Davidovich that was about ten years old.

Looking up at the duty officer, he asked, "Then what?"

"We made out a ticket to Brazhnikov, and Stepnadze just disappeared."

"Did you ask who this Brazhnikov was?"

"A journalist from Omsk, here on an assignment." The duty officer peeked into the desk again and gave Anton a modest calling card. "He left this for me because I helped him."

"Brazhnikov Alexander Egorovich—senior editor of *Siberian Land, Far Eastern Land Magazine,* member of the Journalists' Union of the U.S.S.R.," Anton read. On the reverse side was the magazine's address and telephone.

"Can I put in a long-distance call to Omsk from here?" Anton asked.

"We don't need the long-distance operator. We have our own lines to any city in the U.S.S.R." The duty officer dialed a number. "Omsk? . . . George? Hi . . . Of course, it's me . . . Flying away . . . Listen, plug me into the city lines. I have to talk to someone . . . The number? Just a second."

Anton gave him the calling card.

"Two two five four three one," he said quickly. "Are you getting it? . . . Thanks, George." He passed the phone to Anton.

After two long rings there was a click, and a woman answered. "Editorial."

"Is this *Siberian Land, Far Eastern Land?*" Anton asked. "Does Brazhnikov work for you? Can he come to the phone, please?"

"Just a minute." The receiver must have been placed on the desk, for the door creaked and the woman's voice, now muffled, called: "Boris Ivanovich! Is Sasha Brazhnikov in your office?"

In a few seconds a deep male voice got on the line. "Brazhnikov here."

"Alexander Egorovich?" Anton persisted.

"The same."

"This is Novosibirsk airport. Stepnadze, in whose place you flew, never has shown up."

"I don't know how I can help you," Brazhnikov replied after a bit.

"How did you meet him?"

"I arrived at Tolmachevo airport when they were boarding for the last flight. I went to the counter—no seats left. I went to the boarding section. Sometimes passengers are late . . . I was on standby, just in case there was a free seat. A tipsy man came over to me and asked: 'Where are you going?' 'I have to get to Omsk,' I said, 'but there are no tickets left.' 'Buy mine. I have a reservation, but I don't feel like going.' And he handed me the ticket. I looked—it was a regular ticket, but the name wasn't mine. I said: 'My office won't accept this on my expense account.' He pointed to the counter. 'Let's go reissue this ticket in your name.' For some reason the clerk had some doubts, took the ticket and passport, and went to the duty officer, and the man went out for a smoke. I never saw him again . . ."

"What did he look like?"

"Big, typical Russian face, long white hair."

"Vasya Sipeniatin!" Anton guessed, and he asked Brazhnikov, "How old?"

"Around thirty."

"Any other characteristics?"

"No, I can't tell you anything else."

"Thanks for what you have told us."

As soon as he hung up, the duty officer said, "Before selling Brazhnikov the ticket, we paged Stepnadze several times. In vain."

Anton showed the officer Sipeniatin's photograph. "Has this citizen shown up around here?"

"No," the officer replied with certainty.

Back at CID, Birukov first went to forensics. He left the three-sided ballpoint pen that Stepnadze had used in the garage and the passport and ticket he had gotten at the airport. He decided to wait for their results. On the way to his office, he saw Slava Golubyov walking up the stairs. He asked him, "Have you settled in your fellow passengers?"

"Fine," Slava said. "The Ob had a separate room with a telephone and all sorts of conveniences."

"What's up at NETI?"

"Almost nothing and yet quite a bit . . ."

They had reached the office by then and both sank down wearily: Anton at his place behind the desk, Golubyov on a chair near the window. Pushing back an unruly lock of hair from his brow, Anton looked at Slava.

"Give me the details."

Slava sighed. "There are no details, so to speak. While the Yarko parents were jostling in the train, the son was registered for the first term. It turns out that he had one point more than necessary for admission to NETI."

"When was he registered?"

"The order was signed yesterday."

"Then he managed without help from Revaz Davidovich?"

"Looks that way. And you know, Anton, as far as I can determine, no one from NETI who has anything to do with admissions even knows Stepnadze."

Birukov digested this information.

"In a case like this, you can't figure anything out at first glance."

"I know. But as for the Yarkos' son, we know one hundred percent: the fellow was registered at the institute without any help. Twenty-seven students were accepted with a lower score than his."

"Do the parents know about this?"

"They know their son was accepted but not how it happened. Taras Tarasovich told me in secret that Evdokia Nilovna is certain that it couldn't have been managed without Revaz Davidovich. It seems that Stepnadze assured her after Omsk that her son would be accepted."

"Did he tell Evdokia Nilovna that he had been in Novosibirsk?"

"Not a word about Novosibirsk, but he did tell her about her son."

"How much did he ask for his 'service'?"

"Not a cent." Golubyov took out his notebook and after some digging pulled out a small rectangle of yellowed paper. "He just gave them his calling card."

"Stepnadze Revaz Davidovich. Novosibirsk. General Delivery." Anton recognized the letters of the old typewriter at the building maintenance office and asked Golubyov, "What's this for?"

"Evdokia Nilovna immediately offered Revaz Davidovich five hundred rubles for the 'service.' He refused categorically and, giving her his card, joked, 'When your son graduates, have him send a case of American cognac to this address.' "

"When are the Yarkos leaving Novosibirsk?"

"They're planning on spending a week here."

"Keep up your relationship with them and get Taras Tarasovich to tell you if Evdokia Nilovna begins seeing Revaz Davidovich."

"I already have." Golubyov put his notebook back in his pocket. "Anton, do you think Revaz Davidovich really flew from Rostov to Novosibirsk? Let's say he wanted to arrange things for the Yarko boy, but it worked out without him. Maybe that's why he refused the bribe?"

"The evidence indicates that Stepnadze was in Novosibirsk. However, we haven't a clue as to what he was doing here . . ." Anton stopped to think. "No, Slava. He didn't come just to help the Yarko boy. I can't believe that a bribe-taker who made a round trip like that would nobly refuse money offered him for nothing. That's out of *Believe It Or Not.* There's something else here, Slava . . ."

"Sanya Kholodova?"

"Most likely."

Arkady Ivanovich Dymokurov came in and gave Anton the results of the tests he had just run. The forensics expert had determined that the boarding pass of the airplane ticket made out to Stepnadze had been filled in by Sipeniatin. But an even greater surprise came from the fingerprint people—Revaz Davidovich's prints on the three-sided pen were identical to the prints left on the unfinished cognac bottle and the balcony door in Demensky's apartment. They had an answer to one of their key questions: Kholodova had drunk cognac with Revaz Davidovich.

Immediately sending a summons to the desk for Stepnadze to come to CID the next morning, Anton, despite the late hour, called Sipeniatin in for questioning.

"We didn't finish last time," Anton said.

Sipeniatin's thick lips smiled crookedly. "Even a fool can see that it's as easy as pie to put Vasya Sivy away: his fingerprints were left on the bell; the victim's purse was found at his mother's; he tried to run when his papers were examined; in his pocket, almost three thousand rubles; he was threatening the doctor . . ."

"What do you think—that the evidence isn't enough to detain you?" Anton interrupted.

"What am I—a stupid jerk to think that?" Sipeniatin smirked again. "You're holding me legally, but I'll tell you something, citizen inspector, you're wasting your time holding me. I'm an honest thief. I steal the way my ancestors stole. And now there are vipers that steal the modern way. They don't leave fingerprints and don't eye cheap ladies' purses, but like vacuum cleaners they suck up big money that wasn't earned through hard labor. Instead of wasting time on me, citizen inspector, you'd be better off taking care of them. Then you'd have a haul."

"Help us take care of them," Anton said calmly when Sipeniatin was finished.

Vasya was taken aback. "Sivy is no snitch."

"In that case, let's take care of you. Why did you want to fly to Omsk on someone else's ticket?"

Sipeniatin's face hardened in bewilderment for a few seconds, but then melted in a smile, as though Vasya had figured out Birukov's lame joke and wanted to joke along with him. "I wanted an airplane ride."

Anton showed him the boarding pass filled out in a clumsy scrawl. "The handwriting experts say you wrote this . . ."

The smile disappeared immediately from Vasya's face. He sighed, stroked a scab on his chin, and looked away in embarrassment.

"Out of habit I stuck my hand into some guy's pocket on the bus. I thought there'd be a tenner in his passport, but there was a ticket instead. I had been drinking and decided to hop over to Omsk. When I registered in the crowd I suddenly got scared: the militia could find me in a plane as easily as a blind puppy! I looked around to see if there was a tail. It seemed quiet, but there was a fellow hanging around the counter looking like he had to take a leak. We talked—he was desperate for a ticket to Omsk. I wanted to help him out, but the clerk saw it was phony, went to the authorities. I went out for a smoke and took a taxi . . ."

Sipeniatin's reply, even though it sounded sincere, didn't ring true to Anton. Opening Stepnadze's passport so that Vasya could see the picture of Revaz Davidovich, Anton asked, "Did you pick his pocket?"

"I didn't notice in the bus crowd."

"Is he the one who gave you the three thousand?"

"What?" Sipeniatin rose from his chair and immediately sat back down. "That guy was older."

"This passport was issued ten years ago."

Vasya stared hard at Stepnadze's picture. For almost a minute he contorted his face, furrowed his brow, thoughtfully stroked his scabbed chin, and moved his thick lips. Finally, as though unable to believe his own eyes, he exclaimed, "That's the musk-ox! . . . Frosya's sister's husband." His laugh was unnaturally loud. "Did I find a mark!"

"Ripped off an acquaintance?"

"Acquaintances like that reach from here to Moscow. I saw the guy once at the sweetheart's place, when my mother lived next door to her."

"You mean this man doesn't leave his fingerprints around?" Anton asked casually.

"Don't try to trip me up, citizen inspector." Vasya's merriment was gone. "I'm no snitch."

"Then why were you so upset before?"

"Nerves acting up."

"Well, go calm down."

Birukov called the guard. Hands behind his back, Sipeniatin left the office with relief.

"An actor," Golubyov said, watching the door close.

"From a bankrupt theater," Anton added grimly.

At the end of the day an urgent telegram from Sukhumi reached CID. The head of the city's embezzlement squad replied to Golubyov's question, reporting that he knew of no relatives of Revaz Davidovich Stepnadze working at the Sukhumi Pedagogical Institute.

20

Revaz Davidovich calmly sat right at the edge of the desk, looked sideways at the nickel-plated microphone, and, putting his railroad cap on his lap, froze in concentration. His tanned large-nosed face was tired, as if he hadn't slept at all.

"Nothing new with the gas?" Anton asked as he filled out the top part of the statement form.

Stepnadze smoothed his gray hair. "No, you see—"

"Do you have any objections to taping this interview?"

"Please do!"

Birukov pushed the button.

"Revaz Davidovich, tell me what you know about Sanya Kholodova."

Bewilderment appeared on Stepnadze's face. "Sanya is a very beautiful and decent woman. A rare combination, you know . . ."

"When and under what circumstances did you meet?"

"In the early seventies—I don't remember exactly."

"Try to remember."

Stepnadze cleared his throat and squinted at the microphone with a charming smile.

"You see, I'm not used to speaking when I know that every word is being recorded by technology."

"Don't pay any attention to the technology. At the end of our talk you will be given a taped statement which will not contain anything superfluous."

"Yes?" Revaz Davidovich asked with the most natural surprise. "Just think what a help that is for investigators! It wasn't like that before, I remember."

"You are referring to 1961, when you were under investigation in the case of bribery of the Tomsk lumbermen?" Anton asked.

"Dear fellow, I almost have a law degree," Stepnadze said with a note of injury and then smiled again. "And the Tomsk lumbermen really did almost land me in prison. I was saved, you see, by more foresight and careful documentation. In our times a document is power! At the trial I had those grabbers flat on their backs, and they got what they deserved."

"I believe many of them were rehabilitated in an appeal?"

Revaz Davidovich sighed deeply. "We have humane laws; we like to forgive."

There wasn't a trace of anxiety on Stepnadze's face, and Birukov turned the conversation back to their interrupted theme. After several clarifying questions, Revaz Davidovich recalled that he had met Sanya Kholodova in early 1970, when she took over a bookstore from his cousin Givi Razhdenovich Kharebashvili, who retired that year and now lived in Omsk. "So that's the Givi who's completely well," thought Anton, recalling Stepnadze's conversation with his "mama," and wrote down Kharebashvili's address.

"What was the problem Kholodova had the first year she was managing the store?"

Revaz Davidovich slowly took a handkerchief out of his pocket, carefully licked his lips, and seemed a bit embarrassed.

"Dear fellow, I don't know the details. There was a shortage in the audit, but Sanya managed to cover it."

"With your help?"

Stepnadze noisily blew his nose, neatly refolded his handkerchief, put it back in his pocket, and only then answered the question.

"It may seem strange to you, dear fellow, that I handed over a large amount of money to an almost complete stranger. I'll try to explain. The deficit occurred in the first audit after Sanya took the store over from Givi . . . Can you see the psychological problem? My cousin was under a certain amount of suspicion, and in giving Sanya the money, I was concerned not so much with her reputation as with my cousin's good name."

"What were the terms on which you gave Kholodova the money?"

"Very easy ones, you might say. I am an inveterate bibliophile, you see, and so I asked Sanya to repay me gradually in books. I might add that she paid me back a long time ago."

"Did you ask her to marry you?"

"Of course not!" Stepnadze exploded. "Sanya could be my daughter."

"Your present wife is Kholodova's age . . ."

Revaz Davidovich narrowed his brown eyes. "Do you see . . . My present wife and Sanya are complete opposites. Nina is an earthy woman. She's not interested in a man so much as in a master of the house behind whose back she can live as safely as behind a stone wall. Sanya is a berry from a different field. She believes in the Russian proverb: As long as I'm with my love, a tent will fit like a glove." Revaz Davidovich laughed disarmingly. "Of course I'm too old to play the part of the 'love.' "

Listening to his replies, Anton tried to detect false notes, but Stepnadze spoke as calmly and convincingly as only a man with a clean conscience could. Of all the emotional shades in his voice, the only prominent one was didacticism, typical of very self-confident elderly people talking to youngsters starting out in life. With the age difference between Anton and Revaz Davidovich, there was nothing strange about it.

In recounting the parts he knew of the complex relationship between Kholodova and Demensky when they lived in Omsk and Cheliabinsk, Stepnadze did not hide the fact that Yuri Pavlovich had called him from Sverdlovsk and asked him to buy four skeins of good mohair in Adler. Yuri had told him that he would meet Revaz Davidovich in Novosibirsk and repay him. However, instead of Demensky, it was Kholodova at the train station. She had a black purse and a heavy red suitcase. As Stepnadze learned, Sanya had planned to drop off Demensky's laundry but the laundry was closed, and in order not to be late for the Adler train, Sanya had to take the suitcase with the laundry to the station.

"So, you see, I unexpectedly saw Sanya again." Revaz Davidovich gave the microphone another sidelong glance, as if it was still bothering him, and took a breath. "I gave her the mohair, got the money, and helped her carry the suitcase to Yuri Demensky's apartment."

"So you and Sanya arrived at the apartment—" Anton began, but Stepnadze didn't let him finish.

"Yes, we went to Yuri Pavlovich's apartment. Sanya was as pleased as a child with the mohair. She began setting out some food, but there was no wine in the house. So, you see, in the name of our old friendship, I had to take a bottle of cognac from my briefcase. We had a glass, talked."

"And that's all?"

"I understand you, dear fellow . . . Sanya is a beautiful woman, but, as you see, I'm not sowing wild oats anymore."

"I wanted to ask you who brought the bouquet of gladioli to Demensky's apartment."

"I gave the flowers to Sanya to mark our friendship," Revaz Davidovich said without a shadow of embarrassment.

"What do you know of the recent relationship between Kholodova and Demensky?"

"I can't understand them, dear fellow. Sanya seemed to have made up with Yuri and yet was complaining about him. She had found some old letter and said: 'If Demensky deceives me again, I'll kill myself!' "

"Had Yuri Pavlovich deceived Kholodova before?"

"A clever one, you see. Sanya has a son by Yuri, but Yuri won't admit paternity; he doesn't want to pay alimony."

"Kholodova had the child before she met Demensky," Anton countered.

Stepnadze's eyes narrowed slyly. "Who besides Yuri and Sanya really knows when they became close friends? Friendship in young people is a subtle thing . . ."

Anton thought, as soon as he started talking about Kholodova and Demensky, that Revaz Davidovich was exaggerating things. At least he talked about himself in a different tone. Both the reason for his appearance in Demensky's apartment with Kholodova and the unfinished bottle of cognac in the kitchen were explained in a way that did not give Anton any reason to accuse Stepnadze of anything reprehensible. The only unexplained matter was the most serious clue—the scarred fingerprints on the balcony door—and Anton suddenly asked, "Revaz Davidovich, why did Kholodova jump from the balcony?"

"Are you trying to scare me, dear fellow?"

"Unfortunately not. Two hours after the Adler train came in, Kholodova fell from the balcony; she died just recently. When the detectives arrived at the scene, the balcony door in Demensky's apartment was shut. Besides Kholodova's fingerprints, the door had your prints on it." Anton showed Revaz Davidovich several enlarged dactyloscopic photographs. "You see how the papillary lines are mutilated?"

Leaning forward with his entire body, Stepnadze stared intently at the pictures. For a few seconds he was still. Then he rubbed his chest with his right hand, as if his heart was troubling him, and started talking in broken sentences.

"I, dear fellow, did not shut the door . . . I opened it . . . You see, after the cognac, Sanya was smoking . . . cigarette after cigarette . . . I opened it to air out the room . . . Understand?"

Anton, hiding his disappointment, nodded. An important thread was gone: if Revaz Davidovich's fingerprints were left opening the door, then the one who shut it might not have used a hand at all but, say, a foot.

"Why was Kholodova smoking so much?" Anton asked.

"Sanya was upset. She said she adored Yuri like a devoted dog and ran whenever he called, and Yuri was jealous and tormented her . . ."

"What did she want to write to the prosecutor about?"

"I don't know, dear fellow!" Stepnadze cried out.

When Anton showed him the purse and the mohair, he identified them without hesitation and asked anxiously, "Was Sanya accusing me of speculation?" Without waiting for an answer, he hurried on. "I took one hundred eight rubles from Sanya. I swear that's how much I paid of my own money at the market in Adler!"

"Did you hold Kholodova's purse in your hands?"

"Of course! I helped her put in the mohair." The didacticism was back in his voice. "You were misinformed, dear fellow. As a former lawyer, I know that criminals are inventive in covering up their tracks, but you can't take their bait. Accusing me of the misfortune that befell Sanya is, to put it mildly, a blatant absurdity."

"There are many absurdities surrounding Kholodova's death and they are all connected to your name."

"My name!"

"Yes, Revaz Davidovich," Anton repeated calmly and gave a brief account of the last few days, beginning with the unknown man who had visited the clinic and ending with the adventure at the Aurora, in which Stepnadze's Volga played a part.

Revaz Davidovich listened the way children do to a scary story. When Anton had finished, he wiped his brow and said softly, "Dear fellow, I couldn't have done all those stupid things. First, I am a former lawyer, and second, I was far from Novosibirsk, on a trip."

"Why did you leave so suddenly?"

"You see, it's almost September. I have a large orchard—it's harvest time. I took two trips in a row so that I could have two weeks to tend to the harvest."

"Two days ago did you fly into Novosibirsk?"

"No, dear fellow."

Anton took the transcript of his visit to Tolmachev airport and handed it without a word to Revaz Davidovich, along with the boarding pass filled out by Sipeniatin.

The reaction was unexpected. After reading the transcript

with a frown, Stepnadze looked at the pass and said with a laugh,
"That's not my handwriting."

"However, the ticket is made out in your name and the number on the boarding pass comes from your passport," Anton
replied, also with a laugh.

Revaz Davidovich took out a plump wallet from his inside
pocket. Opening it, he pulled out a new red booklet with the
state seal and calmly handed it to Anton.

"Here's my passport."

Anton looked at the clear, large photograph and then flipped
through a few of the pages. When he returned the document, he
took out the old passport with scuffed covers from his desk. He
opened it and showed it to Revaz Davidovich.

"How do you explain this?"

Stepnadze gave Anton the reproachful look that a kindly old
teacher might bestow on a talented but overeager pupil. "I lost
that last spring."

"With your driver's license?" Anton asked, almost automatically.

"Absolutely correct, dear fellow. I forgot my jacket with the
documents in my own garden at the dacha in Shelkovichikha. In
the morning I went to look—the jacket and the documents were
gone. I reported it to the militia precinct, but they couldn't find
them. I had to pay the fine and get new documents."

The black storm cloud of apparently incontrovertible evidence
hovering over Stepnadze's head turned with every one of his
answers into a harmless, fluffy one. Meeting the calm gaze of the
slyly squinting brown eyes, Anton decided to change the subject.

"Revaz Davidovich, do you have any enemies?"

Stepnadze spread his hands in bewilderment. "I can't imagine
whose path I've crossed."

"I hope you realize that someone is trying to blame you for
Kholodova's death?"

"I'm not a boy; of course, I understand." After some hesitation he took a folded telegram out of his wallet and handed it to
Anton. "Here, dear fellow, another puzzle for you."

The urgent telegram was sent from Novosibirsk to Rostov-on-Don and addressed to the stationmaster, "To be forwarded to conductor Stepnadze of car number 8, train number 112. "GIVI CALLED STOP VERY ILL STOP ASKS YOU FLY TO OMSK IMMEDIATELY STOP LOVE YOUR NINA." Anton read it and looked up questioningly at Revaz Davidovich.

"This was a hoax," he replied. "When I reached my cousin, Givi was in perfect health. He hasn't called my wife, and Nina didn't send this telegram."

"Who could have sent it?"

"I have no idea."

Anton spread out several photographs on his desk. "Revaz Davidovich, tell me about these people."

Stepnadze looked at the pictures with the concentration of a card player who holds the pot. After a lot of thought he set aside Demensky's photograph.

"I can't add anything to what I've already said about Yuri."

Anton pushed the picture of Ovchinnikov toward him. "What about him?"

"Anatoly Nikolaevich helps me find workmen for my apartment every year. You know, whitewashing, painting, and so on. He's a sociable and eternally optimistic man, but I think he drinks too much. He was at school with my nephew . . ." Stepnadze pointed to Zarvantsev's picture and smiled. "Well, do you think I could say anything bad about my own nephew?"

"I need objectivity."

"I understand you, dear fellow." Revaz Davidovich's face grew sad. "Alik is the victim of his own character. Nature endowed him with painting talent but did not give him any confidence in his powers or any courage. After school he made a good start as a portraitist, but he was crowded out by pushier artists. You won't impress anyone with modesty in art; you have to clear a path for your work. Alik isn't terribly aggressive; he has no confidence; therefore he wisely took up work that would guarantee a comfortable existence. I think that's all . . ."

Anton pushed Sipeniatin's picture over. Stepnadze shrugged.

"I don't know that man." And then Revaz pointed to Priazh-kina: "Now this girl works at the station barbershop. I've had a haircut from her several times."

"Then you know Lusya Priazhkina?" Anton pressed.

"Briazhkina? . . . What Briazhkina?" Revaz Davidovich had gotten the name wrong, perhaps on purpose. "A barber? I told you, she cuts my hair. She's good at it."

Anton had at least a dozen more questions for Revaz Davido-vich, but they were premature. Gathering the photographs, An-ton asked, as if out of sheer curiosity, "How's the weather in Rostov, Revaz Davidovich?"

"Terribly hot."

"Were you there long?"

"I spent a whole day in the airport," Stepnadze replied with-out blinking an eye and added for further conviction, "I barely got a ticket, you see. I had to travel with a changeover in Chelia-binsk."

"I see," Anton said dryly.

21

Anton put Revaz Davidovich's signed statement in a folder, pushed a button, and asked for a playback of the interrogation.

Just when he was told it was ready, Slava Golubyov burst into the office and demanded on the run, "So, how was Stepnadze?"

"Sit down and listen," Anton replied grimly.

The recording was excellent, capturing all the intonations. Exchanging glances now and then, Anton and Slava listened to the end. When he heard Revaz Davidovich's answer about Rostov, Golubyov seemed disappointed.

"Why did he do that? He answered everything convincingly, and at the end he told a blatant lie. Why didn't you take him to task?"

Anton laughed. "Why pull the tiger by the tail before it's necessary?"

Slava abruptly paced the room. "To keep from bumping into Revaz Davidovich around here, I went over to the embezzlement squad. I told the fellows about Stepnadze's business in Adler and Rostov. They all agree: 'This smells of book speculation and bribery.' "

"Everyone thinks he's a strategist when he's observing the battle," Anton joked without merriment. "Perhaps the fellows from embezzlement are right, but I don't think that Kholodova's death has anything to do with speculation or bribery, and Stepnadze had no idea of what had happened to Sanya until I told him."

Golubyov stopped dead in his tracks. "Why?"

"Because after committing a murder, even the most hardened

criminal starts worrying about his own skin. And Stepnadze behaved down south as if nothing had happened."

"Maybe he thinks that's his ace in the hole!"

"No, Slava, there's something else here." Anton gave Golubyov the telegram Revaz Davidovich had received in Rostov and an order for confiscating correspondence. "Here's an urgent mission. You have to find the original of this telegram. Start at the Main Telegraph Office. Incidentally, find out if there's anything 'resting' for Stepnadze. He can only pick up mail at the Main Post Office."

"Do I have to stop at the prosecutor's for a warrant?"

"Absolutely. I've already talked to him; it will be ready."

The phone rang sharply. Birukov picked it up and immediately recognized the voice of the fat-cheeked lieutenant from Highway Patrol.

"Comrade captain, Mrs. Stepnadze is here, complaining about her husband."

"Why is she complaining to Highway Patrol?"

"They can't resolve the Volga problem."

"Send her to me right away."

Nina Stepnadze entered his office with the independent air of a pretty secretary, used to adoration, entering her boss's office. However, when she saw Anton she blushed and said hello in bewilderment.

Like yesterday, she was wearing the light blue pantsuit, but instead of the fancy hairdo, her golden hair was swept back by two simple combs.

Returning her greeting, Anton asked his unexpected visitor to sit down and said sympathetically, "What happened, Nina Vladimirovna?"

She batted her luxurious false eyelashes. "Really, nothing . . . I went to the auto inspection headquarters, and they brought me to criminal investigation. Why?"

"Highway Patrol doesn't handle complaints of this nature."

"Oh?"

"Yes. So tell me your problem."

"Revaz Stepnadze is mad with jealousy." Nina casually removed her jacket and, remaining in a guipure blouse that showed her pink bra, turned her back to Anton. "Look at the bruises he gave me . . ."

The tanned, sleek body did have large bruises. Assured that Anton had seen them, Nina put on her jacket without buttoning it and seemed about to cry, but apparently remembered her eyelashes and changed her mind.

"I want to take him to court. What do you think—should I?"

"Button your jacket," Anton suggested in lieu of an answer, trying to decide whether Revaz Davidovich's wife was playacting or had really been hurt by her husband.

Running her long, beautiful fingers with perfectly manicured nails over the buttons, Nina spoke with frank outrage. "The old man's become impossible! First he demanded to know what I did with the gas in the Volga, then he looked for his glasses—as if I had sold them or something . . . Then he starts shoving a telegram at me! Can you imagine the horrible night I had?"

"Yet Revaz Davidovich this morning appeared quite calm," thought Anton and asked, "You really didn't send a telegram to your husband in Rostov?"

Nina lifted her eyelashes in astonishment. "What do you take me for? Naturally, I didn't."

"Who could have?"

"Many of Revaz's co-workers are envious of him. It might have been a mean joke and nothing more. He's turning it into a tragedy." Nina, like a good actress, switched to a tragic whisper. "I understand what Revaz is doing. He wants to get rid of me and is starting to make up all kinds of filth about me. Judge for yourself: if we get an amicable divorce, half his property becomes mine. That doesn't suit Revaz. He knows all the laws and he probably has come up with something so that the courts won't give me a penny . . ."

Anton tried to catch something hidden behind Nina's words. If an ugly old woman were sitting in her place, then Revaz

Davidovich's desire to get rid of his wife might be understandable. The criminal records contained many instances of playboys who wanted to get rid of elderly wives, resorting to a variety of vile tricks, up to and including murder. However, Nina, glowing with health, was far from old age. Why would Stepnadze want to be rid of her? What had she done to him?

Nina continued without stopping.

"That missing gas—that's Revaz's handiwork. Just think about it: only he and I have keys to the garage. Who could have unlocked it besides us? The previous two nights I stayed at home all the time—everything was fine. As soon as I go to the opera one night—the gas is gone! Apparently while I was listening to Prince Igor, Revaz took care of it . . ."

"But he was on a train then," Anton reminded her, as if he knew nothing.

"Oh yes?" Nina's face was contorted with a smirk. "It's easier for Revaz to fly in to Novosibirsk from a trip than for me to go have my hair done."

"He flies in often?"

"Not often, but it's happened. I think this time the old man dropped in at home instead of Omsk."

"You think so?"

"When I got home from the opera, someone had been fooling around with the lock, trying to get into the apartment. Who else but Revaz?"

"You went to the opera alone?" Anton asked suddenly.

"Naturally," Nina said and took out a ticket stub from her jacket pocket. "I even kept this."

"Why?"

"To show Revaz, there's only one ticket."

"Very naïve proof."

"What do you take me for?"

"You were in row thirteen, seat twenty . . ." Anton said, examining the stub.

Nina looked wary. "What of it?"

"Nothing." Anton put the stub in front of him on the desk.

"Nina Vladimirovna, you know you are to blame before your husband; you owe him an apology."

Nina's curled lashes trembled. "The old man's been here already? How can you believe him! He's ready to swallow me alive, he's—"

"What business were you discussing with Ovchinnikov until three A.M. after you returned from the opera?" Anton interrupted.

Nina's beautiful, slightly tired face did not reveal the slightest hint of fear or confusion. Shrugging her shoulders, she responded casually, "Anatoly Ovchinnikov asked to take me home after the opera. When the taxi reached the house, he suddenly had to have a drink. I naïvely let him into the apartment and couldn't get him out until three. He's so obnoxious I don't even want to think about it!"

Anton decided to dig a little deeper.

"Ovchinnikov says otherwise . . ."

"Naturally. Do you think he'd admit he was barking up the wrong tree? Never!" Nina smiled disdainfully. "To think Tolya Ovchinnikov was my lover . . . That would make chickens laugh!"

"Why did you have him take you home?"

"I was afraid to go to Zatula at midnight."

"Nina Vladimirovna, tell the truth: why did Ovchinnikov leave your place so late?"

"It's all rather awkward, but honestly, there was nothing—like that between us."

"I'm not interested in anything 'like that,'" Anton said. "I need to know something else. Was Stepnadze in Novosibirsk that night or not?"

Nina shrugged. "I didn't see him, but judge for yourself: who else would have been digging around in the lock?"

Every answer made Anton more certain that Nina was ruthlessly trying to compromise her husband, but he couldn't understand why. Trying out various versions, Birukov asked Nina's opinion about everyone involved in the case. Nina "had no idea" about Sipeniatin and Lusya Priazhkina, called Ovchinnikov "an obnoxious bum," defined Alik Zarvantsev as "neither fish nor fowl," and when it came to Demensky, smiled playfully.

"Yuri is a weakling. He can't handle his hot tomato."

"Who?"

"There's a chickie in Cheliabinsk. Kholodova, Revaz's former mistress."

"Former?" Anton asked.

"Naturally." Nina grimaced. "Do you think Revaz would do such things with me around?"

"But before you, then, he did?"

"It's not out of civic spirit that Kholodova sends him book parcels."

"They say Revaz Davidovich is a real bibliophile."

"The old man is nuts about books. He spends his whole salary on them."

"Then what do you live on?"

"What do you mean?" Nina seemed frightened. "Revaz gets a pension of a hundred twenty a month, plus every fall our orchard brings us about five thousand."

"Aren't you uncomfortable selling produce at the market like an old woman?" Anton asked.

Nina frowned, insulted. "I'm uncomfortable putting on trousers over my head. What do you think, we're selling stolen goods or something?"

She left the office with the haughty demeanor of an overly proud person who had been insulted by undeserved suspicion.

22

The interrogation of Stepnadze and the unforeseen conversation with his wife took more than three hours of Birukov's time. The bright August sun was high in the blue sky. Young sparrows twittered away in the poplars under the CID windows. Anton watched the hopping gray bits of fluff as he reflected. He was left with complex and contradictory thoughts after his talk with Revaz Davidovich's wife. It seemed that throughout the conversation two emotions had struggled in Nina: a deep anger with her husband for the beating and a fear of losing him and, with him, a comfortable life. Anton suddenly found himself thinking about Alik Zarvantsev. Of all the people involved, only Albert Evgenievich could shed some light on the relationship of the Stepnadzes and explain its paradoxes. Picking up the phone, Anton called Zarvantsev; his line was busy. You have to strike while the iron is hot, and since Zarvantsev was home, Birukov set off for the familiar address.

After the first ring the dog started yapping on the other side of the door. Steps soon followed, and Zarvantsev opened the door. This time he was wearing an old, full-length robe tied at the waist by a broad belt with mangy tassels. Albert Evgenievich was not in the least surprised to see Birukov; it was almost as if he had been expecting him.

"Come in," he said, letting Anton pass.

Everything was the same. The modest furniture was in place and on the walls the nude beauties laughed and wept, bosomy mermaids frolicked in the waves, and muscled gladiators fought sea monsters. As before, Zarvantsev put Anton in the old armchair and sat on the couch, but this time instead of the white-toothed, charming smile, his tanned, large-nosed face showed anxiety.

"My uncle's wife just called," he suddenly said. "She said that uncle had beaten her and that she had made a formal complaint at CID. Apparently Nina saw you?"

Birukov hadn't expected that turn of events, but he answered calmly without taking time to think.

"She did."

"What happened between them?"

Anton smiled. "That was just what I was going to ask you, Albert Evgenievich. Really, what could have happened between Nina and Revaz Davidovich?"

Zarvantsev lowered his eyes and frowned. He ruffled the tassels on his belt as though he was embarrassed, and then said, "Apparently, uncle is mad with jealousy. Just imagine, Nina is thirty years younger than he! How can you be calm in that case?"

"Perhaps Revaz Davidovich has cause for his anxiety?"

"That's a tricky question, Comrade Birukov. Women are complex creatures—sometimes they pull tricks that are impossible to believe."

"I believe you've known Nina a long time?"

"Fairly long."

"They say you wanted to marry her?"

Albert Evgenievich's swarthy face displayed a range of emotions with kaleidoscopic speed, from fleeting fear to open disbelief.

"Who told you something like that?"

"What difference does it make?"

"I'd like to know which of my friends is an imaginative gossip," Zarvantsev said with a bitter laugh. "I won't hide the fact that for a time Nina and I dated, but our relationship didn't get that far. Nina posed for me. She's a striking model, but you know, she's boring. And I wasn't in the least surprised when

Nina chose to marry my uncle. A comfortable life is the height of her dreams."

"What is Nina's relationship with Ovchinnikov?"

"With Ovchinnikov?" Zarvantsev repeated the question. "Sometimes they see each other, I think, but I doubt that Nina would seriously consider replacing her wealthy husband with a poor loudmouth."

"Then why do they meet?"

"I don't know, Comrade Birukov." Albert Evgenievich seemed to feel a chill and pulled his tassled belt tighter and then, as if apologizing for his lack of information, added guiltily, "I only saw them together once, when Anatoly met Nina at the opera and left in a taxi with her."

"Was this two nights ago?" Anton asked.

"Right, Comrade Birukov."

"Tell me more about it."

Zarvantsev seemed to be collecting his thoughts and hesitated for a while. Then, while his long, tanned fingers played with the tassels, he began telling Anton the story he already knew from Ovchinnikov—about Lusya Priazhkina appearing suddenly with tickets for the eight o'clock show at the Aurora, how Ovchinnikov took two tickets, posed a little longer, and headed for the movies, saying that he would take Frosya Zvonkova.

"You haven't seen Priazhkina since?" Anton asked.

"No. The earth swallowed her up, it seems."

"Did she offer you a ticket, too?"

"She did. But I refused. I've seen *Esenia*, and besides I had other plans for that evening . . . I was going to the opera."

Anton had to work at hiding his surprise; however, he managed. He asked with perhaps more irony than necessary, "Planning to spend the evening with Nina Vladimirovna?"

The irony or something else embarrassed Albert Evgenievich.

"Not quite like that, Comrade Birukov. That morning Nina called and asked me to get her a ticket to the Moscow opera. The Muscovites have been guest starring here for a month now. The request seemed strange—Nina was never interested in the opera before—and out of sheer curiosity, when I was buying a ticket through an administrator friend of mine, I decided to go to the evening performance of *Prince Igor*."

"Did you save the ticket?" Anton asked.

"I don't know . . ."

Zarvantsev opened the cracked wardrobe door, searched in the pockets of his white jacket, and exclaimed happily, "Here it is!"

The neatly torn stub showed row 30, seat 21, and the date stamped on back corresponded with the date on Nina's ticket. Anton pocketed the ticket, to Zarvantsev's anxiety.

"Excuse me, why are you doing that?"

"In case you have to prove your alibi."

A pleading look crossed Zarvantsev's face. "Comrade Birukov, I beg you not to advertise that fact."

"Don't worry. The CID isn't an advertising agency," Anton said soothingly and immediately asked, "Did you see Nina in the theater?"

"No, I tried to avoid her."

"Was she alone?"

"Yes, but after the performance, as I told you, she was met by Anatoly Ovchinnikov."

"Do you know anything else about them?"

"No, Comrade Birukov."

As he talked with Zarvantsev, Birukov felt his head pounding from the protracted concentration. The dull, nagging pain added to his frustration, making him feel he had missed something important in the conversation. With stubborn persistence Anton sought what he missed, but Zarvantsev, as if purposely trying to distract him, started musing aloud.

"Just imagine, Comrade Birukov, at first I suspected Anatoly Ovchinnikov or Yuri Demensky in what happened to Sanya Kholodova. One of them. But when Nina told me on the phone about what Revaz did to her, I felt horrible. I'm more than convinced: it didn't happen without my uncle's participation . . ."

"What?" Anton asked mechanically.

"Yes, Comrade Birukov, yes! Revaz Davidovich is uncontrollable in his desire to fool around with pretty young women, and if he was left alone with Sanya in Yuri's apartment . . ." Albert Evgenievich frowned. "It will be a great shame if my revered uncle is tried for attempted rape."

"You think that's it?"

"Does any other statute of the law apply?"

"One hundred seven might apply—driving someone to suicide."

Bewilderment flashed across Zarvantsev's face. Albert Evgenievich seemed upset that there was another explanation besides the one he believed in.

23

Medical forensics expert Karpenko, clutching his professorial beard, was working on a crossword puzzle. Nodding briefly to Birukov, he said without preamble, "Japanese island, four letters."

"Kusu," Anton replied.

"Is there really one?"

"There must be. Give me something for a headache."

"Two more words. Across. Endless work with attention to detail." Karpenko used his fingers to count. "Six letters."

"Murder," Anton said after some thought. "Give me an aspirin or I'll solve the whole puzzle for you."

He swallowed two aspirins with a glass of water and headed for his office. Hearing Slava Golubyov's lively voice through the half-open door of the forensics lab, he dropped in. Slava was excitedly telling something to Dymokurov, seated at his desk. Seeing Anton, he stopped short and blurted out, "Lusya Priazhkina has escaped."

Anton, feeling the throbbing in his temples increase, sat down next to Dymokurov.

"Can you tell me a little more about it?"

"I can. When I returned from the Main Post Office, there was a call for you as I came into your office. 'Where's Birukov? There's another problem at the clinic—Priazhkina has disappeared.' It goes without saying I rushed over there. When I got there, prosecutor's investigator Makovkina was already questioning Renata Petrovna, the nurse's aide. According to Renata Petrovna, here's what happened." Golubyov took a breath. "Lusya was in a private room, as we wanted, and wearing a hospital robe. In the morning she demanded her blouse and jeans, supposedly to make sure that her ten rubles hadn't been stolen. Renata Petrovna tried to calm her down, but Lusya made a stink, broke a glass, and tried to cut her wrist with a shard. The aide had to bring her the clothes and money. Priazhkina seemed to calm down but refused to eat her lunch and said she would be on a hunger strike until they let her out of the clinic. The aide talked Lusya into taking a tranquilizer. After the shot Lusya calmed down and even began complaining that she had been dragged into a terrible situation that she'll probably never get out of. Apparently a friend who's a conductor on the Adler train fed her cognac and then gave her three tickets to the Aurora. He asked her to put one in Dr. Shirokov's mailbox and to give the other two to Ovchinnikov. Then he took Lusya to his dacha in Shelkovichikha, gave her more cognac, and in the evening brought her to the movie theater and asked her to see if the doctor came to the movies or not. When Lusya told the conductor that Shirokov had given away his ticket to some Gypsy woman, he got very frightened. He gave Lusya ten rubles to keep her from telling anyone about it, brought her in his Volga to the Motodrom stop, and let her out, saying that he was late for the airport." Golubyov was silent for a minute. "Having confessed all this to the nurse's aide, Priazhkina seemed to fall asleep. Renata Petrovna left the room, and when she peeked in half an hour later, Lusya's clothes and Lusya herself were gone."

"Is that it?" Birukov asked grimly.

"No, it's not. Renata Petrovna says that the way Priazhkina described the conductor, he sounded just like the man who tried to pass the note to Kholodova."

"Curious," Anton said, rubbing his throbbing temples. "Did you find the original of the telegram to Rostov?"

"Naturally. You know where it was sent? From the post office at the railroad station."

"Whose handwriting?"

Dymokurov spoke up. "The same handwriting—it was typed at the building management office."

Birukov drummed his fingers on the table. Golubyov quickly pulled out a piece of paper from his pocket.

"Here are some amazing facts!"

The paper had about a dozen dates written on it. Next to one was written "300," next to three, "400," and the rest had "500." Cities were also noted here. Rostov-on-Don and Adler were mentioned twice, and Azov, Taganrog, Bataisk, Shakhty, and Sukhumi once.

Without waiting for questions, Golubyov began explaining. It seemed that in the last twenty-four hours Revaz Davidovich Stepnadze had received two wires of 500 rubles each, one from Sukhumi, one from Rostov. He hadn't picked up the money yet. In the little time he had, Slava had checked the register for "general delivery" transfers in the last two weeks and had discovered that on the day he left Novosibirsk on the train journey, Revaz Davidovich had received six orders totaling 2,500 rubles.

"There they are—the bribes!" Golubyov pointed at the piece of paper. "Look, a money order from Sukhumi . . . That must be from the mother of the girl who had to pass her Russian exam for the Pedagogical Institute where Revaz Davidovich's uncle works."

"But we were told from Sukhumi that there are no relatives of Stepnadze's working at the institute."

"Who would admit it if he's mixed up in this?" Golubyov met Anton's gaze. "Why isn't Revaz Davidovich in a hurry to pick up the money? I think it came by wire for a reason."

"He can't think of money right now." Anton picked up the phone and asked the desk sergeant, "Where's Stepnadze?"

"With his wife at the dacha in Shelkovichikha."

"With his wife?"

"Yessir."

"How are they behaving?"

"Looks peaceful, but we don't know what they're saying."

Anton hung up and turned to Dymokurov.

"Arkady Ivanovich, do you remember there were turpentine traces on Kholodova's purse? Could it have been used to obliterate fingerprints?"

"Perhaps, but it would have been easier to use cologne," Dymokurov replied. "Why?"

"I think that Alik Zarvantsev is mixed up in this."

"Is that logical? Using turpentine when you're an artist is like signing a confession."

"Zarvantsev is an amateur in crime."

"You continue to believe in your theory?"

"I do, Arkady Ivanovich."

"But we saw a flask of turpentine in Demensky's apartment, too."

"Yes, we did," Anton said musingly and turned to Golubyov, who was listening in silence. "Slava, we must find Lusya Priazhkina urgently. If she's not home, check the railroad station barbershop, Zarvantsev's place, all the bars and cafés that sell liquor by the glass. If you have any questions, call the prosecutor's office —I'll be with Makovkina."

Silence reigned in the empty hallways of the prosecutor's office, as it usually does in any office at the end of a workday. Makovkina was reading when Birukov came in. Tearing herself away from the papers, she greeted Anton happily and immediately handed him the transcript of Renata Petrovna's statement —two pages written in a schoolchild's neat hand. There was nothing new in it for Anton, and he asked as he returned it, "Is Renata Petrovna lying?"

Makovkina shook her head. "No. The nurse's aide is frightened out of her wits by what happened."

Anton rubbed his temples—the pain was gone, but his head still felt heavy. He looked at Makovkina as he mused aloud.

"A very interesting situation is developing. Working out of considerations unknown to us, all the people involved in the Kholodova case are leading us to their trails in the most blatant manner. Stepnadze drags Lusya Priazhkina into a wild adventure; the notes are all typed on the machine in the building management office where Ovchinnikov works; the turpentine that left traces on Kholodova's purse in all probability belongs to Zarvantsev; and Sipeniatin . . . Vasya has lost his mind completely: he brought the purse from the scene of the crime to his mother's house for no reason at all."

"Is Demensky the only one above suspicion?" Makovkina asked.

"No. Remember how Kholodova's purse was found. A man called zero-two and said that Vasya was hiding out at his mother's. Ilynykh arrived at Maria Anisimovna's and instead of Vasya found the purse."

"What does Demensky have to do with it?"

"When the call concerning Sipeniatin came, Yuri Pavlovich was in a phone booth and had just talked to Dr. Shirokov. And then I saw a half-empty bottle of turpentine in his oil paints box."

Makovkina thought.

"I can't understand why they wanted Shirokov to go to the movies."

"I imagine they were planning to hand him the bribe there, but someone mixed up the cards. Of course all this is so obviously amateurish."

There was a silence. Smoothing out the papers, Makovkina said unhappily, "Kholodova's funeral is tomorrow at three."

"We have to be at the cemetery. Let's see who attends." Birukov turned the page on the desk calendar. "By the way, Natalya Mikhailovna, tomorrow is Saturday. The book market runs from early morning. Would you like to accompany me? We might run into a few acquaintances."

"All right."

Anton looked at his watch.

"And now to celebrate the end of the workday, may I suggest we have dinner at some nice café? I was so busy today that I didn't have time to eat lunch."

Makovkina looked shy, but replied pertly, "Suggestion accepted."

Without discussion they both automatically headed for the Snowflake. Taking a table near the decorative fireplace under a broad-leafed palm tree stretching to the ceiling from a pot-bellied tub, they gave their order to the stiff and formal waitress and smiled as their eyes met unexpectedly.

Makovkina asked, "Have you been a detective long?"

"In the regional division, over two years, and before that I worked for the district force."

"Did you ask to be transferred?"

"No. I try to serve according to the rule of Andrei Petrovich Grinyov from Pushkin's *Captain's Daughter*. Remember how he told his son: 'Listen to your superiors, don't pursue their kindness, don't ask for work, don't turn it down.' "

"And remember the saying: Preserve your clothing when it's new and your honor when it's young," Makovkina quickly added.

"Right. It's a wise saying, don't you think?"

"I do. Too bad not everyone remembers it." Makovkina toyed with the menu thoughtfully. "There's a lot I don't understand in Kholodova's behavior. Having paid off her debt to Stepnadze for the store deficit, she meets him again. Is that Sanya's evil fate or the notorious difficulty of breaking with the past?"

Anton replied, "It's easy to trip and hard to mend a sprained limb, Natalya Mikhailovna. It's a cliché, of course; maybe that's why it's so often forgotten."

"I don't understand Priazhkina, either. What does Lusya hope to gain by running away from the clinic?"

"It's easier with Lusya. She's alive, and we'll learn her motives as soon as Golubyov locates her."

However, Slava Golubyov didn't find Lusya that night. She didn't go home or to the barbershop or to Alik Zarvantsev's. After a quick survey of dozens of bars called the Breeze, the Sail, and other lyrically named spots where one could quaff a glass of wine, Golubyov dropped in at Zarvantsev's again, but this time Alik himself was out. He learned from the neighbors that Albert Evgenievich had driven off in his Zaporozhets to go fishing for the weekend.

24

Birukov and Makovkina met at seven in the morning at the House of Culture of Railroad Workers, because on Saturdays the park near it was the site of the lively book market.

Soon the first bibliophile showed up. Looking like an Odessa longshoreman, a man with a beret pushed down over his eyes and two books with bright red bindings tucked under his arm strolled down the path through the park and, looking around, sat on the far bench. Some ten minutes later he was joined by an intellectual-looking man in glasses with a full canvas bag. Then two hairy fellows with wide cowboy belts came rambling over. Each had a full briefcase. The cases were obviously heavy, judging by the alacrity with which they set them down. The regulars smoked and chatted lazily.

Looking like interested buyers, Birukov and Makovkina approached the bench.

The bibliophile who looked like a longshoreman, his round eyes focused on one of the hairy men, was saying, "Don't tell me about Shukshin's cheap boots. Vasily Makarovich managed to do in Soviet-made boots what thousands of dandies in foreign boots will never manage. Right?"

The cowboy tossed his yellow filter stub into the bushes and laughed with condescension.

"Literature, pops, is first and foremost graceful language."

"I'm a philologist."

The longshoreman's eyes flashed angrily. "You're a horse trader, is what you are, sonny! A philologist couldn't ask fifty rubles for a two-volume set."

The fellow bent down, picked up his briefcase, nodded to his pal, and they headed in silence to the next bench. Watching their retreating backs, the longshoreman added, "Philologists . . ." And looked up at Anton. "Do you know anyone who would trade the two-volume Shukshin for Pikulya's *Word and Deed?*"

"I don't," Anton said.

The longshoreman squinted at the fellows again. "The philologists have it, but they won't trade. The horse traders want fifty rubles cash."

"Isn't that high?"

"It's a seller's market." The longshoreman took out a pack of Pribois, lit a cigarette, and slapped his enormous hand on the frail shoulder of the four-eyed intellectual sitting next to him. "This genius, for example, has invented a new form of serving readers. Do you like mysteries?"

"I do," Anton decided to reply.

"Oh, I don't envy you."

"Why?"

"Because there are millions like you and only one Simenon, and he writes in French. Do you read French?"

"No."

"Oh!" The longshoreman slapped the intellectual's back again. "This genius can help you out. He's translated all of Simenon's detective stories into Russian and typed them up."

"Not all of them; only some of those that haven't been published here," the intellectual countered shyly.

"And how much is one?" Anton asked.

"I'm not selling them . . ."

"He rents them. You give him a twenty-five-ruble deposit and you can read for a week. When you return it, five rubles are kept for amortization of the product and you get the rest back. Genius, right?" the longshoreman asked, puffing on his cigarette.

The intellectual readily opened his canvas bag.

"Unfortunately, all the Simenon is out right now. Would you be interested in anything from journalism? I also have Françoise

Sagan's *Lost Profile,* Trifonov's *House on the Embankment,* Russian mysteries . . ."

"Same deposit?"

"Cheaper. Just ten rubles, and three for reading."

Birukov looked through the heavy, well-bound volume. It was
a collection of mysteries published at various times in Soviet
magazines. Judging by the worn pages, the anthology had passed
through dozens of readers' hands and who knew how many more
would use it.

"Do you translate Simenon yourself?" Birukov asked as he
returned the volume.

"Yes."

"Do you know French well?"

"Perfectly. I was an interpreter for Intourist."

The longshoreman said, "He was fired for drinking."

The intellectual, blushing, wanted to respond but a bearded
man practically tripped as he walked past the bench. He stared
hypnotized at the two-volume Shukshin that lay next to the
longshoreman, and he said in a trembling voice, "Are you s-s-
selling it?"

"No, I'm not s-s-selling it," the longshoreman teased.

The bearded man recoiled as if struck. Stammering excitedly,
he started telling him that he was writing a dissertation on Shukshin, that he desperately needed the two-volume collection,
which he'd been looking for for almost two months now, and
that he was prepared to pay any amount for it on the spot.

"Will you give fifty?" the longshoreman demanded.

"R-rubles?" the bearded man said in astonishment, pulling his
wallet out of his pocket.

"Why, do you have dollars?" The longshoreman laughed and
put his broad palm over the books. "I'm not selling. I'm a bibliophile, not a horse trader."

The bearded man practically forced the money on the docker.
The longshoreman's eyes flashed angrily but suddenly softened
and, like a military commander showing the way to his men, he

extended his arm in the direction of the hairy fellows with cowboy belts who had spread out their wares on the next bench.

"Buy Pikulya's *Word and Deed* from those horse traders, and you'll get the Shukshin for a trade."

The bearded man returned with the speed of a boomerang, and Anton saw for the first time the joy of a real bibliophile who had found the edition of his dreams. A satisfied spark also glowed in the longshoreman's eyes. He patted the violet cover of the book he received in trade and looked at Birukov.

"It's a trifle, but it pleases me. My daughter is a historian, and you can't think of a better present for her birthday." Getting up from the bench, he winked at the huffy intellectual. "Make money, inventor of new forms of reader service, while the publishers catch flies! Maybe you'll build yourself a palace, like Simenon."

The longshoreman seemed to know not only the rules of the book market but its regulars. Therefore Birukov started a conversation with him about a white-haired Georgian who supposedly had promised him a new anthology of foreign mysteries. His assumption proved right. The longshoreman immediately knew whom he meant.

"You're off, pal. This isn't the season for Revaz to be here."

"What do you mean, not the season?"

"Well, in the summer Revaz works as a railroad conductor. When he finishes his travels, you'll be able to meet him. But I doubt that you'll buy a book from him here."

"His prices are too high, like those fellows?" Anton nodded in the direction of the hairy cowboys who, like long-awaited village peddlers, were surrounded on all sides by eager bibliophiles.

"Revaz is a mystery."

The longshoreman suddenly wagged his finger at an unshaven, wrinkled man with a bandaged throat who had just sold a thick volume with a new dust jacket from the Library of World Literature series for three rubles. He warned loudly, "Grisha, watch your step! If I see you do it again, I'll turn you in to the militia!"

The man scuttled into the crowd in fright.

"Oh, what a highway robber. He steals his son's books for something to drink," the longshoreman said sadly and suddenly narrowed his eyes suspiciously at Birukov. "You wouldn't be from the embezzlement and speculation squad, would you, pal?"

"Why?" Anton asked with a smile.

"Because Revaz never sells books to anyone here and never buys any. He's only interested in the speculators' prices. Like a stockholder, he just follows the market at the stock exchange."

"Why does he do that?"

"That's the mystery."

Birukov decided to show his identification. The longshoreman looked at it without special interest, moved farther away from the intellectual, who was animatedly taking deposits, and gave a sidelong glance at Makovkina, who was listening quietly.

"The wife?"

Anton nodded.

"Can I speak in front of her?"

"Fully."

"I suspect that Revaz is a CODer." The longshoreman made an intriguing pause. "Do you know what that is?"

"He sends out books COD, is that it?"

"You guessed it. You can evaluate a three-ruble book at fifteen, say? That's the prices at our market. It's a game where you can't lose and what you might call a noble speculation: you help out the buyer and you make dough."

"Where do the buyers come from?" Anton asked.

"CODers aren't afraid to spend money on letters; they know hundreds of bibliophiles in every city."

"They don't buy the books here, of course?"

"Naturally, you have to know the right places. There's no profit in buying from the horse traders."

Taking their leave of the longshoreman, Birukov and Makovkina spent half the day at the market. The people there were interesting. Experts gathered to argue about new releases; a disheveled teenager holding a crumpled ruble in his fist looked over the sci-fi books with shining eyes; a dressed-up young couple absolutely had to have the two-volume Andersen recently published by *Khudozhestvennaia literatura* and the latest edition of *Tasty and Healthful Food;* a man who looked like an actor persistently sought Vsevolod Meyerhold's correspondence; a woman, as plump as a dumpling, was prepared to buy any book on a starvation cure; a tall man who followed on her heels and looked as if he suffered from chronic ulcers was interested in *Medicinal Herbs of Siberia;* and an old man, bent with age and carrying an aluminum cane, asked almost everyone he saw for volume twelve of the magazine *Young Technologist* from last year. The market was going full force: people were trading books, people were just looking around curiously, but for the most part they were selling and buying. Revaz Davidovich never did show up.

25

After noon the sky over Novosibirsk grew dark, and by the time Birukov and Makovkina got into the bus to the cemetery, large raindrops hammered on the roof. The rain lashed the dusty sidewalks and then quickly stopped. The sun came out again. It was only in the Kuzbas region, at the very horizon, that dark storm clouds still glowered and rumbles of thunder still sighed in the distance like funereal artillery fire.

When he saw a small procession leaving at the cemetery gate, Anton thought they had missed Kholodova's funeral, but realized that for a city of one and a half million, burials were not an unusual occurrence. In the small wooden office an elderly man in a black jacket was discussing something with a grim brute of a man who was testing the edge of a trowel with a grubby finger. Little old ladies walked thoughtfully between the rows of graves.

The hearse with Kholodova's coffin drove up to the cemetery exactly at three. A truck with the headstone and fence parked next to it, and a bit farther down a bus opened its doors and the first person Anton saw coming out was balding Ovchinnikov, who was helping the musicians with their instruments. After the musicians a line of men and old women poured out of the bus for almost a full minute, and among them Anton recognized only Ksenya Makarovna and another neighbor of Demensky's with whom he had talked after Sanya's fall. Yuri Pavlovich himself, as white as a sheet, came out of the hearse. Carefully taking hold of a boy of seven or so, he set him down next to himself and then helped a weeping elderly woman get down. Fedor Fedorovich Kholodov, stooped with grief, followed the woman.

The procession moved along the cemetery to the grave. Anton and Makovkina went with everyone else.

The orchestra players broke off the melody as abruptly as they had begun. An oppressive silence followed. Standing on tiptoe, Anton saw over the heads of the old women that the coffin had been lowered into the ground. Demensky, holding the tense Seryozha, seemed to be made of stone. Tears poured down Fedor Fedorovich's pale cheeks from unblinking eyes. Ksenya Makarovna was whispering something to Sanya's mother, who had collapsed, and was holding smelling salts under her nose.

Anton stretched a little more, and amid the flowers that filled the coffin saw Sanya's face—a calm, beautiful face with a white patch of bandage that covered her wounded temple. The colorless lips were frozen in an abashed and bewildered smile.

The silent pause was dragging on, as if no one knew what to do next. Suddenly Demensky, as if recalling something very important, pushed away the child who was pressed against him and tugged at the wide gold band on his finger. It wouldn't budge. Yuri Pavlovich grimaced and pulled it off. With unseeing eyes he looked over the sad faces as if about to say something. Then he slowly sank to one knee before the coffin, lifted Kholodova's right hand, and placed the ring on her finger.

The old women stirred in front of Anton and blocked his view of Demensky. He had to find another place. While Anton moved, they shut the coffin lid. Making his way out of the crowd, Anton looked around for Makovkina. He saw her at the monument prepared for Kholodova's grave and went over to the silvery pyramid bearing an oval picture of her and a shiny copper plate. The plate was engraved with an open book and a verse on the first page.

> You won't be back,
> Won't grow gray and wise.
> But you will always be
> Young and alive in our eyes.

Birukov looked at the photo and read reproach in Sanya's eyes, staring straight into the camera.

"It's such a waste to die at her age," Makovkina said. "I feel sorry for the boy."

Anton said nothing.

The sun shone in the blue sky as if nothing were wrong. The storm's grumbling had stopped beyond the Kuzbas horizon. Grannies chatted away the time on park benches as they watched their grandchildren playing. Noisy groups of young people with guitars, transistor radios, and cassette players hurried off in all directions. Only Birukov and Makovkina walked in a depressed silence, as if they had nowhere to go and nothing to do.

Passing a phone booth, Anton called the desk sergeant and asked for the latest news. Everything was the same. Zarvantsev hadn't shown up at home yet, and Lusya Priazhkina was still swallowed up by the earth. There were no reports either from Shelkovichikha, the Stepnadze dacha, except for the fact that the thundershower that had raged all day was finally over.

Birukov was about to hang up when the sergeant said, "Golubyov wants to tell you something."

"Anton, I've been waiting for you," Slava rattled off.

"What's up?"

"You see, while looking for Priazhkina, I went to Zarvantsev's once more and found a notice in his mailbox about a twenty-ruble money order. You know those forms with the yellow diagonal stripe? What's curious about it is the notice has Zarvantsev's address but it's addressed to Revaz Davidovich Stepnadze."

"Good work, Slava," Anton said. "Here's what you have to do: first, tell all Highway Patrol cars to start looking for a Zaporozhets license number 18-18 NSS. When they find it, have them invite its owner, Albert Evgenievich Zarvantsev, to come in to CID. As for you, without wasting any time, check at the post office for how often COD payments come in the name of Stepnadze. Anything new at the Main Post Office?"

"I got receipts for the payments received by Stepnadze. The

handwriting boys are on them. They think that it wasn't Revaz Davidovich himself who got the money."

"No?"

"No."

"We'll have to look into that. Now get going; don't lose a minute. Did you have any plans?"

"I wanted to see the Yarko couple."

"You can do that later. Wait, you know what . . ." Anton thought for a second. "Try to get Taras Tarasovich and his wife to go to Stepnadze's dacha in Shelkovichikha. Have them thank Revaz Davidovich for his alleged protection for their son. Got it?"

Anton told Makovkina the gist of his conversation and offered to take her home, but she refused. Once again they walked along, grim and silent, both in their own thoughts. They walked for over an hour. In that time Makovkina spoke only once to Anton.

"Did you see how Demensky put his ring on Sanya's finger, as if she were his wife?"

"Yuri Pavlovich bought that ring for their wedding," Anton replied.

"Their wedding? I thought it was done deliberately for the funeral."

The corridors of CID were empty. The duty officer sat looking bored at his post in the lobby. Anton and Makovkina went to the desk. There was life here. The large control board's lights were flashing, telephones were ringing, patrol and detective cars were calling in on the radio—information from all parts of the city was pouring in. The information was insignificant, not at all related to the case that was uppermost in Birukov's mind.

Having listened in on about a dozen reports, Anton was about to ask Makovkina to come to the forensics lab with him, where they were working on the handwriting on the payments received by Revaz Davidovich, when the precinct inspector from Shelkovichikha called. The sergeant gave Anton the receiver. Anton listened to the hoarse voice of a no longer young man.

"There seems to have been a small brouhaha at the Stepnadze dacha," the officer said and coughed. "Revaz Davidovich had some visitors who came on the train. A thin woman and a fat man in wide trousers. Revaz Davidovich greeted them pleasantly and saw them off with curses."

"The Yarkos saw Stepnadze," Anton told Makovkina quickly, holding his palm over the phone. He went on talking to the police officer. "Where are the visitors now?"

"At the station. Waiting for the commuter train to Novosibirsk. Should I have a chat with them?"

"Don't. Let them go. And how are things in general at the Stepnadzes'?"

"The most peaceful summer residents in my district. The other houses get so noisy on the weekends that we have to intervene, but there's always peace and quiet at the Stepnadzes'. That's why I was so surprised to see Revaz Davidovich raise his voice at the company."

Anton thanked him for the information and hung up. He told the sergeant, "If there's anything new, I'll be in the lab."

The sergeant nodded. "Fine."

Dymokurov was bent over a microscope, but when he saw them out of the corner of his eye, he looked up with apparent relief and said somewhat guiltily, "That Revaz Davidovich is playing tricks. Like a circus performer."

Helping Makovkina with her chair, Anton smiled and said, "There's a joke about a circus performer, Arkady Ivanovich . . . A young man runs into a bar and says to the bartender: 'Can you pour three hundred grams of cognac into a two-hundred-gram glass?' The bartender says: 'You're nuts!' 'Can you pour a hundred and fifty each into two glasses?' 'Here you go.' The man takes an empty glass and pours the contents of the other two glasses into it—and all three hundred grams fit, there's even room left over. The bartender looks surprised. 'Are you from the circus?' 'No, you are,' the man says, wagging his finger at him. 'I'm from the embezzlement squad.' "

They all laughed. Anton picked up one of the money orders and looked closely at the even, slightly angular handwriting that gave the information from Stepnadze's passport.

"Arkady Ivanovich," he turned to Dymokurov, "this is Revaz Davidovich's handwriting, and the information is from his old passport."

Dymokurov laughed bitterly. "That's the trick, Anton Ignatievich; the handwriting is Stepnadze's but the order isn't filled out in his hand."

"And the signature?"

"Also a forgery." Dymokurov took the one order that lay apart from the others and handed it to Anton. "Here is the only five hundred rubles that Stepnadze personally picked up at the Main Post Office. Notice: the receipt is filled out with the data from Revaz Davidovich's new passport."

Makovkina, who was looking at one of the orders, asked, "Do you mean someone else was using Stepnadze's lost passport? But you have to resemble him for that."

Birukov looked at Dymokurov. "Have you examined Zarvantsev's handwriting?"

"We don't have a sample of it."

"I'll try to get you one tomorrow."

The phone rang. The forensics man answered and passed the phone to Birukov. "It's the desk, Anton Ignatievich," he said.

"Birukov?" the voice asked. "We just got a call from Zvonkova: she's been sitting in the Orbit Restaurant with Ovchinnikov for the last half hour and he's keeping two places at their table free. Zvonkova thinks he's waiting for someone."

"Where did Frosya call from?" Anton asked.

"She says she pretended to go to the ladies' room and called zero-two from the pay phone in the lobby."

"Is it a provocation?"

"Her voice was very agitated."

"I'll be there in fifteen minutes." Anton hung up and turned abruptly to Makovkina. "Natalya Mikhailovna, you'll have to play the part of my fiancée, I guess."

"To go to a restaurant?" Makovkina asked, almost in fright.

"Don't be afraid, we won't drink any vodka," Anton joked mirthlessly.

26

The second floor of the Orbit, where the main dining room was, resounded with band music while an amplified male voice affirmed optimistically:

Hope is my earthly compass,
Success the reward for daring . . .

After Makovkina had combed her hair in front of the hall mirror, Birukov took her arm and headed up the broad, old-fashioned staircase to the restaurant. It was Saturday night and the place was jammed. Without letting go of Makovkina's arm, Anton stopped in the doorway, trying to spot Ovchinnikov's tanned bald spot, when he heard a short word, like a pistol shot, coming from his right.

"Chief!"

Concentrating, Birukov squinted and found at a corner table, right at the windows, a bright pink Ovchinnikov leaning back in his chair and, seated opposite him, Frosya Zvonkova in a low-cut green dress.

Thinking that he hadn't been heard, Ovchinnikov rose to his full height and, overcoming the noise of the band, shouted, "Chief! . . . Row this way, I have an empty dock."

The people sitting around him looked over, some appalled, some amused. It was too late to think about remaining in the restaurant unnoticed. Pretending to be pleased by the unexpected meeting, Anton let Makovkina go ahead of him and started down the narrow passage along the wall toward Ovchinnikov, who was already moving back the chairs that had been pushed against the table.

"Sit down, chief," Ovchinnikov said, gesturing expansively at the free chairs. "I thought some of my soccer buddies or river pals would sail by, but this is even better—you've got a lady with you. Will you have some Extra?"

"Let me look around a bit first," Anton said with a smile as he seated Makovkina and sat down himself. "We've come in for dinner."

"Extra doesn't interfere with food consumption. We can drink to Sanya Kholodova's memory." Ovchinnikov, as if recalling something unpleasant, passed his hand over his sweating bald spot and gave Zvonkova an order.

"Get another five hundred grams."

Frosya, tense and constrained, looked at Anton worriedly and then stared at the table. "You've had enough."

"Don't be stingy, sweetie. I'll repay you when I get back to work." Ovchinnikov turned around and spoke to a passing waitress. "Galina Borisovna! Wait a second, cutie . . ."

As soon as she had taken the order, the band struck up a lively dance tune. Animated couples started for the dance floor and men made their way among the tables looking for partners. One of them, dark fuzz revealing a mustache in progress, approached Makovkina shyly. Not knowing what to do, she looked at Anton. Ovchinnikov, catching the look, started to get up in order to pick the fellow up by the scruff of the neck, like a kitten, but Anton stopped him.

"Go and dance, Natasha, until they bring the food."

Makovkina reluctantly got up. Watching her receding back with astonishment, Ovchinnikov addressed Anton.

"Your wife, chief?"

"Fiancée," Anton replied and asked, "Anatoly Nikolaevich, where's Zarvantsev?"

Ovchinnikov's eyebrows went up. "I don't know exactly. I lost track of him yesterday. We were supposed to take his Zaporozhets to the Ob Sea at six last night. I went to his house, but Alik was long gone."

"Where could he be fishing?"

"Alik's as much a fisherman as I'm a ballerina."

"Where would Zarvantsev be if he's not fishing?"

"Search me. I don't know. I went to Sanya's funeral because of him. I thought instead of sitting at home like a jerk I'll go to Yuri Demensky, give him some moral support. And Yuri looks at me like I'm a paralyzed mother-in-law. Didn't even ask me to the funeral dinner. I had to go get Frosya and talk her into coming here. I'm ashamed to admit that I'm drinking on Frosya's money. To tell the truth, I swore to myself after our last conversation: no more drinking! But today . . ." Ovchinnikov twirled an empty glass between his thick fingers. "Today when I started hammering the coffin shut at the cemetery, Sanya's little son got hysterical. He grabbed the hammer, tugging at it with all his strength, like he thought that if he got it away from me his mother would come back to life. I thought if I give up the hammer the little kid might hit me with it, if I don't it looks like I want Sanya buried fast more than the rest of them. You won't believe it but it's better to fall through the ground than to find yourself in a situation like that."

Anton took advantage of the pause to say, "Lusya Priazhkina has disappeared from Novosibirsk with Zarvantsev."

"You think Alik took her away?"

"Then where is she?"

"You can never tell what will get into Lusya's head."

"Besides you, does Zarvantsev have any friends?"

Ovchinnikov looked at the empty carafe and sighed deeply. "I wasn't going to mention this, but I have to . . . Alik became friendly with me only recently. You see, he's been trying to get a residence permit for a friend who just got out of prison—"

"Who?" Anton interrupted.

"Alik didn't tell me the guy's name, but I confess I promised to take care of it through my building management."

"What stopped you?"

Reproach crossed Ovchinnikov's face. "Chief, I have lots of
sins on my conscience, but I'm still a man. I thought I'd promise
and that's it. And if Alik treats me to Extra almost every day, it's
not like I was forcing him to do it, right?"

"Was this long ago?"

"About six weeks."

"Vasya Sipeniatin was in Novosibirsk then," Anton thought
quickly. "Demensky had bought the Crucifixion from him just
before leaving." He asked another question.

"Zarvantsev didn't ask you to do anything else?"

Ovchinnikov frowned. "I made a key for him once, but that
was a long time ago."

"What key?"

"Alik lost the key to his garage. Luckily he had a cast; otherwise he'd have had to change the lock."

"Cast?" Anton asked warily. "What cast?"

Ovchinnikov laughed. "Really, chief, you're a detective and
you don't know what a cast is? A key's impression on wax. You
can make a copy better from that than from a stencil."

"Why was Zarvantsev making impressions of his keys?"

"He said he was fooling around with wax, then tossed it in his
desk. And then it came in handy."

The "fooling around" interested Birukov mightily.

"When you made the key, did you try to open Zarvantsev's
garage with it?"

"What for? My 'firm' has no competition—Alik said the key
worked better than the factory one." Ovchinnikov thought for a
while and then, stunned by something, stared at Anton. "Chief!
Priazhkina disappeared from Novosibirsk before Alik . . . You
see, lately Lusya's been calling my apartment. The wife picks up
the phone and hears tragic sighs. No matter how much I threatened Lusya, I couldn't break her of the habit. But since that
evening when I went sniffing around Nina after the Aurora,
Lusya's calls have stopped."

"She was in the hospital from that night until yesterday."

"Too much drinking?"

"No, something else," Anton said, not wanting to reveal too much, and to stop Ovchinnikov from asking more questions, asked, "Are there any railroad workers among Zarvantsev's friends?"

"I haven't seen any. Mostly unrecognized geniuses hang around Alik: painters, actors, there's even a writer. You know, chief, let's finish this funeral conversation. You're wrong to suspect Alik and Priazhkina. It was Revaz Davidovich who messed up Sanya. I ran into Stepnadze yesterday when he was coming out of detective headquarters. I'll tell you, the old man looked like a soccer player who landed himself offside from an advantageous position through his own stupidity and who knows without the referee's whistle his goal is in vain."

The band broke off. The dancers headed back to their seats. Ovchinnikov quickly filled a glass and expansively offered it to Anton.

"Accept a penalty, chief."

"I'm on duty in an hour," Anton lied.

"Big deal. With your size a tiny shot is like a drop in a bucket."

"And the smell?"

Ovchinnikov thought for a second and stuck his hand in his pocket.

"Nutmeg. Have a bit after."

Anton laughed. "That won't help. They're very strict about this."

"Stricter than with pilots?"

"Almost."

"I don't envy you your job."

Anton and Makovkina smiled. Zvonkova seemed to give Ovchinnikov a reproachful glance and said laconically, "Chatterbox."

Leaving the restaurant, Birukov sent Makovkina home in a taxi and walked along Red Prospect, thinking. The city at night glowed with neon and the windows of high-rises blinked tiredly as they went to sleep. Reaching the first phone booth along the

way, Anton called Zarvantsev. After ten rings he hung up and
called the desk at headquarters. When the familiar voice came
on, he said, "This is Birukov. Any news?"

The sergeant hesitated for a second. "Bad news. In Shelkovichikha, not far from Stepnadze's dacha, they found Priazhkina's body."

27

Anton did not learn the results of the autopsy until the next day at the meeting in the chief's office.

A city couple out for a walk had accidentally stumbled on the dead Lusya. Priazhkina, in panties and bra, lay facedown in the water on the sloping shore of the Ina River next to the dirt road, beyond which in the deep woods rose the two-story Stepnadze dacha. Not far from the body lay the jeans with "TOLYA" on the seat, a white blouse torn on the chest, an empty Extra vodka bottle, and a can with some fish in tomato sauce still in it. The position of the corpse suggested that Lusya had wanted to bathe in the river but had fallen facedown and, deeply intoxicated, swallowed water. The autopsy confirmed this theory. However, there was another one: the drunken Priazhkina had been drowned by the simple method of keeping her head in the water. This theory was supported by two bruises on the back of the neck, which seemed to have been made by strong fingers.

After Karpenko, the medical examiner, forensics expert Dymokurov gave his report. This time his report was brief, and Arkady Ivanovich seemed embarrassed not to have more conclusive facts, after having examined the scene of the incident, that would help the detectives in the beginning stages of solving the crime.

The bloodhounds didn't find a scent to follow, and the grass matted by the thundershower did not permit Dymokurov to make any visual determinations. Within a 100-meter radius of where the body lay along the shore, there were three campfire sites with peg marks. The grass was littered with cigarette butts, newspapers, candy wrappers, cigarette packs, and matchboxes. They found six rusty cans, a toy pistol, a ballpoint pen, and even a butane lighter that had lain on the riverbank for at least a year. Basically their finds were typical of a surburban area and shed no light at all on the mysterious death of Priazhkina. All footsteps on the sandy slope were washed away by the rain. They did manage to make a plaster cast of the only footprint, left by a man's size 11 sneaker, that was under the body. However, that footprint could have been made by a total stranger.

When Dymokurov stopped talking, the division chief turned to Anton, who had been listening with concentration.

"You have questions, don't you?"

"Yes, comrade lieutenant colonel," Anton said and looked at Karpenko. "When did Priazhkina actually die?"

"Friday, around eleven P.M. One hour either way."

"Then Lusya lived only seven hours after she left the hospital . . ."

"Eight at the most," Karpenko corrected.

Anton turned to Dymokurov. "Arkady Ivanovich, was there any money among Lusya's things?"

Opening the folder, Dymokurov pointed to a crumpled and water-stained ten-ruble note. "That was in her jeans pocket."

"Why are you interested in Priazhkina's money?" the lieutenant colonel asked.

"I hadn't ruled out the possibility that Lusya bought the vodka herself and came to Shelkovichikha on the train," Anton replied. "But now I know it is impossible, because Lusya's tenner is intact. That means someone treated her to the vodka and brought her to Shelkovichikha."

"Who could have done that?"

"I think it was Zarvantsev." Anton turned to Dymokurov again. "Arkady Ivanovich, were there any signs of a parked car near the body?"

"No, but the unpaved road shows traces of car tracks. Unfortunately, the rain washed away the tread marks, but we took samples of the soil and vegetation so that we can do a spectral analysis of the tires, if necessary," he replied.

"Whom do you suspect besides Zarvantsev?" the division chief asked.

"We can't rule out Stepnadze, but according to our information, Revaz Davidovich and his wife haven't left their dacha for two days now." Anton was silent. "There is another person as yet unknown. The elevator operator in Stepnadze's building saw his wife with some thin railroad man who, disguised as Stepnadze, might have taken Priazhkina away in the Volga from the Aurora Theater. I have the feeling that Mrs. Stepnadze didn't play second fiddle in the business with the Aurora."

"What basis do you have for this feeling?"

"Nina Vladimirovna's showy alibi. While Priazhkina was riding around in the Volga, Nina was at the opera and then, risking her own reputation, she kept Ovchinnikov in her apartment until three A.M. just to have a witness to say that Revaz Davidovich was trying to get in and, consequently, that it was he who drove Priazhkina away from the movie theater."

The division chief drummed his fingers on the desk. "According to you, Priazhkina made up the story in the hospital about this conductor she knows on the Adler train?"

"It looks like it. And Lusya didn't drown, she was drowned so that she wouldn't change her story."

The chief looked away. He kept a grim silence for some time. Anton understood the silence. Premeditated murder was a heinous crime. And as a rule, it caused a lot of work and trouble.

"Do you rule out Stepnadze himself?" the chief finally asked.

"Yes, comrade lieutenant colonel," Anton replied in his former tone. "First of all, we received confirmation from Omsk that Revaz Davidovich really did visit his cousin. And second, even without such confirmation, I would still rule him out. Stepnadze is a smart and very cautious man. What someone like Sipeniatin, say, might do, Revaz Davidovich would never do."

"How about Ovchinnikov?"

"Ruled out, comrade lieutenant colonel," Anton said. "Ovchinnikov is as clear as glass to me."

"Then who is a mystery to you?"

"Two people: Stepnadze's wife and nephew. I'm convinced that they were Revaz Davidovich's accomplices in his shady deals and suddenly rebelled . . ."

"Why?"

Anton frowned. "For now I can only offer a guess. Stepnadze and his group were on the borderline of crime for a long time. They were lacking some impetus. With the appearance in Novosibirsk of Sipeniatin and Kholodova, the impetus arose, and their shady business began crumbling like a house of cards."

"So who is the 'impetus,' Kholodova or Sipeniatin?"

"One of them."

The chief drummed his fingers on the desk again. "I have the impression that Stepnadze's companions are trying to cast suspicion on him. Doesn't that seem curious to you? What are they counting on? That Stepnadze won't turn them in?"

"I think they've woven a web so complicated that they've ensnared themselves," Anton said after some thought.

Birukov left the meeting as tired as if he had taken a very important and difficult exam. He didn't attempt to guess whether the division chief had liked his answers, but in the depths of his heart he was grateful to the lieutenant colonel for the kindly and controlled tone, even though Priazhkina's death made the situation much hotter. Apparently, after many years as a detective himself, the lieutenant colonel knew very well that in times of extreme pressure nothing has as negative an effect as shouts from superiors and precautions.

Anton and Makovkina went to his office, and for a while he went through the papers on his desk distractedly, as though looking for something. The telephone rang.

Anton said grimly, "CID."

"I need Slava Golubyov," said an unfamiliar male voice.

"Who's calling?"

"Yarko from Adler."

"Hello, Taras Tarasovich," Anton said, coming alive. "Golubyov isn't in now. What should I tell him?"

Yarko started hemming and hawing. "I wanted to ask Slava to dine with us . . ."

Guessing that the work superintendent from Adler was being cautious, Anton said; "I work with Golubyov. How was your trip to Shelkovichikha with Evdokia Nilovna?"

Yarko hesitated and then sighed. "The railroad 'fixer' threw us out."

"Threw you out?"

"Yes. He greeted us pleasantly, offered us Siberian apples, but as soon as Susya put a packet of money on the table he was like a man jabbed in the rear with a needle. He started running around and shouting, threatening us with jail. Naturally we picked up our hats and beat it to the station."

"Was his wife there?"

"No. Some young thing with golden hair peeked down from the top floor once, but we didn't see his wife."

"Golden hair—that is his wife."

"She seemed awfully young for an old man," Yarko said in surprise and sighed again. "So tell Golubyov when he shows up to drop by our hotel; we'll eat here."

"I'll tell him, Taras Tarasovich." Anton hung up and looked at Makovkina. "Did you hear that?"

Makovkina inclined her head. "Even more strange . . . could we possibly be wrong about Stepnadze?"

"There's nothing strange about it. Revaz Davidovich is a smart man. You can't fool him, now that the gang's breaking up."

Right on cue, Golubyov burst excitedly into the room. With a flourish he dropped a confiscation order and a thick wad of paid CODs on Anton's desk and said in one breath, "In the last two months twenty-three money orders of twenty rubles each arrived, and each was picked up personally by Citizen Stepnadze!"

"And they all came to Zarvantsev's address?" Anton asked, examining the receipts.

"All!"

"Did Zarvantsev himself get any money orders?"

"Not one."

"How about at the Main Post Office?"

"Nothing."

The intercom interrupted their conversation. The desk sergeant reported laconically, "Zaporozhets 18-18 NSC located around Tashara!"

"Oh-ho!" Anton said, surprised. "In the opposite direction from Shelkovichikha. What is the owner of the car doing?"

"Resting in a tent. Shall we detain him?"

"Immediately. And bring him to me, and soil samples from the car to the lab."

"Right."

As he hung up, Anton's gaze met Makovkina's. "Please stay, Natalya Mikhailovna. This will be a curious conversation with a curious man." He turned to Golubyov. "And you, Slava, take a car and hurry to Shelkovichikha. Bring me Revaz Davidovich Stepnadze by evening."

28

Zarvantsev, frightened to death, made his appearance before Birukov and Makovkina. It was only after several attempts by Anton to begin the conversation that Albert Evgenievich recovered himself a tiny bit. His first intelligible sentence was, "Why have you arrested me?"

"You haven't been arrested," Anton said, trying to calm him down. "We just need to clear up a few things—"

"No, I was arrested!" Zarvantsev cried out in a ringing tenor. "My car was searched. I wasn't allowed to drive. Why?"

"To prevent an accident."

"I'm not a criminal!"

"You're very upset," Anton said patiently. "How could you drive in this condition?"

"I wasn't upset in Tashara. I'm not a criminal!" Zarvantsev cast a sidelong glance at Makovkina. "Why are you interrogating me in the presence of an outsider?"

"This is an investigator from the prosecutor's office."

Albert Evgenievich turned to Makovkina. "Comrade investigator, I am lodging an official complaint about the illegal actions of the militia. They do not have the right to suspect me of something I haven't done!"

"They don't have the right to charge you without conclusive evidence," Makovkina corrected.

Zarvantsev spun back to Anton. "Do you have conclusive evidence?"

"No," Anton said calmly.

"There, you see!"

"I do have several questions for you—"

"I won't answer them!"

"Why not?"

"Because you don't have conclusive evidence of my guilt."

"If you are guilty of something, the evidence will turn up."

"And if I'm not?"

"Then you have nothing to be afraid of. Really, why are you so wound up?"

"I'm not wound up." Zarvantsev made a visible effort to get himself under control. "I've never dealt with the militia before, that's all. I've never even been in a drunk tank, like Ovchinnikov. Understand, never! Why haven't you arrested him?"

"For what?" Anton asked quickly.

Albert Evgenievich equivocated. "Well, you know . . . Anatoly is a womanizer and . . . drinks vodka."

Birukov laughed. "That doesn't do him any credit, but that's all."

"That means you're not charging him with anything?"

"What should I charge him with?"

"Didn't Anatoly push Kholodova off the balcony?"

"No, it wasn't Anatoly."

Zarvantsev's bewilderment changed to obsequiousness. "That means my revered uncle did it! You know, Comrade Birukov, on Friday, after you left, Lusya Priazhkina called me and told me things about Revaz that horrified me, and I immediately left for Tashara."

Anton looked out of the corner of his eye at Makovkina, who was listening attentively, then asked calmly, "What horrible things did Lusya tell you?"

Looking into Anton's eyes ingratiatingly, Zarvantsev repeated Priazhkina's "confession" to the nurse's aide almost word for word and then, after some hesitation, added, "And Lusya saw Revaz Davidovich come running out of Demensky's courtyard, frightened, right after Kholodova fell. I'm telling you, Comrade Birukov, my uncle definitely tried to rape her!" He turned to Makovkina. "Forgive me, please."

Anton frowned. "This isn't the first time you've told me this theory. Why?"

Zarvantsev exploded. "Because I know my uncle's weakness for beautiful women and I want to help you."

"Priazhkina seems to have been spying on Revaz Davidovich—"

"No, she says she was on her way to Demensky's and the fall happened before her very eyes."

"What did she want at Demensky's?"

"I don't know. Apparently she used to meet Ovchinnikov there while Yuri was away."

"Did Priazhkina tell you anything else?"

"She said she was going to call Ovchinnikov and go to Shelkovichikha, to Revaz's dacha."

"Why?"

"I can't tell you that. I don't know."

"Why didn't you ask?"

Albert Evgenievich put his hand on his heart. "You see, I was frightened. I thought for conversations like this, they'll consider me an accomplice."

"Who drove Priazhkina away from the Aurora Theater in Revaz Davidovich's car?"

Zarvantsev, as if sensing a trap, grew wary, but replied without any doubt, "Revaz himself."

"Revaz Davidovich wasn't in Novosibirsk that day. He was in Omsk with his cousin."

"With Givi!" Albert Evgenievich seemed surprised. "Givi would lie if Revaz asked him to."

"The neighbors confirm it."

"Givi would pay them off to save his cousin."

"Could Nina have given the Volga to a railroad man . . ." Anton said meaningfully and dragged out the pause.

"She doesn't have any railroad men!" Zarvantsev cried out and then lowered his eyes in embarrassment. "Well, I can't speak for Nina. I do know this: that evening Nina was at the opera, where, incidentally, I spent the evening, too."

Anton asked indifferently, "Did you like the opera?"

"Not bad. They're from Moscow, after all."

"Who sang Igor?"

Zarvantsev swallowed hard. "That . . . oh, what's his name . . . You know, I'm not an opera lover, and I just don't remember the performers' names."

Birukov, taking a quick look at the silent Makovkina, calmly took out a COD money order form that Golubyov had removed from Zarvantsev's mailbox and, showing it to Zarvantsev, asked, "Can you explain the meaning of this?"

Zarvantsev took the form so gingerly it might have been hot, examined it a bit, and, returning it to Anton, grimaced. "That's my uncle trading with bibliophiles."

"Trading money?"

"No . . . He sends them books COD, they send him books the same way."

"Why do they send money orders to your address?"

Zarvantsev distractedly played with the fastener on his old leather jacket.

"Nina scolds Revaz for wasting money on trifles. So Revaz came up with this plan . . ."

"I thought you said that you and Revaz Davidovich didn't see each other much."

"The book exchange is our only link. I couldn't refuse my uncle in such a trifling matter."

Birukov took out the forms obtained at the Main Post Office and, showing them to Zarvantsev, asked, "And what is this?"

The surprise that came to Zarvantsev's face was quickly replaced with frank confusion. "I don't know, Comrade Birukov."

"In whose handwriting are the receipts?"

Albert Evgenievich, unable to believe his eyes, shuffled the forms and then, returning them to Anton, said firmly, "Revaz's."

"Who gave him such large sums?"

"You know, I don't know."

Placing a sheet of paper and a ballpoint pen before Zarvantsev, Anton said, "Write an explanatory memo about it."

Zarvantsev wiped his sweaty nose, picked up the pen uncertainly, and said in fright, "I don't know what to write!"

"I'll dictate it for you. 'To Senior Inspector of the CID Birukov. Explanation. Re the postal orders shown me that were received by Revaz Davidovich Stepnadze according to passport . . .'" Anton stopped. "Copy the passport number from the receipts. Got it? Now finish: 'I can give no explanation.' And sign it."

When Albert Evgenievich had completed his handsome signature, Birukov, looking at his old sneakers, approximately size 11, turned to Makovkina.

"The shoes have to be compared, Natalya Mikhailovna. After that, I think, we don't have to take up any more of Albert Evgenievich's time."

"You're letting me go?" Zarvantsev asked in surprise.

"Of course. But first please drop into the lab for a short time."

Makovkina filled out the form for the requisition for the lab work and, getting up from the desk, said to Zarvantsev, "Come with me."

"Where to?" he asked in fright.

"To the lab. I'll explain everything there."

"I don't know anything!"

"We don't want any knowledge from you."

"But what for? What is all this?"

"I'll explain it all to you," Makovkina repeated quietly and headed for the door.

Zarvantsev gave Anton an anxious look and followed reluctantly. As soon as the door was shut, Anton put photographs of Stepnadze and Zarvantsev on his desk and studied them intently. He was distracted from this activity only when Makovkina returned and said with condemnation, "He's an incredible coward. Aside from his looks, there's nothing masculine about him."

"His looks are interesting, right?" Anton asked.

"I wouldn't say so."

Anton showed Stepnadze's old passport to her. "Take a good look at the picture. Do you see any resemblance to Zarvantsev?"

For almost a minute Makovkina looked at the picture. "There is none."

Anton handed her the picture of Albert Evgenievich. "Compare the eyes and nose."

"A very remote resemblance," Makovkina said after another long silence. "The foreheads are completely different; Stepnadze's is broad, Zarvantsev's looks like an upside-down radish."

"What if you cover Zarvantsev's forehead with a railroad cap?"

Makovkina thought. "Then, perhaps, there would be a resemblance."

Birukov picked up the phone and asked the lab man to come in. As soon as Dymokurov entered, he asked, "Arkady Ivanovich, what do the soil samples from Zarvantsev's Zaporozhets show?"

"We're doing a spectral analysis to compare them with the soil from Shelkovichikha."

Anton handed him the photo of Albert Zarvantsev. "Very urgent request, Arkady Ivanovich. We'd like to see this citizen dressed in a railroad jacket and cap."

"We'll do it," Dymokurov said.

"And here's a sample of Zarvantsev's writing," Anton said and handed him the explanatory memo. "There's nothing there that resembles Stepnadze's handwriting, but for a handwriting analyst, this is all aces."

"Is that it, Anton Ignatievich?"

"For now."

"How's the shoe analysis?" Makovkina asked.

"Going full blast, but I can't say anything concrete yet."

Dymokurov left the office. Birukov looked at Makovkina and suddenly said, "Zarvantsev wasn't at the opera."

Makovkina replied animatedly, "I confess, I thought it was strange that Albert Evgenievich—basically an educated man, an artist—couldn't remember the name of the Moscow artist who sang the lead. And then: why does he keep trying to get his uncle charged with rape?"

Birukov thought awhile.

"That statute does not call for confiscation of the accused's property."

"You mean he's not worried about his uncle's reputation, but is worried about keeping his estate intact?" Makovkina said, quickly catching his train of thought.

"Let's not guess yet, Natalya Mikhailovna," Anton said with a sigh. "Let's hear what Vasya Sipeniatin has to say when he learns about the death of Lusya Priazhkina."

29

Sipeniatin appeared for questioning in his usual pose: hands behind his back and head down. He took a long time settling in the chair, as if intentionally postponing the start. Then he looked curiously at Makovkina, smiled at her, then glanced at the microphone and said to Anton with false heartiness, "Roll it, citizen inspector."

Anton showed him the picture of half-naked Priazhkina, lying facedown on the riverbank.

"Another corpse, Citizen Sipeniatin . . ."

"So what?" Vasya said in bewilderment. "As far as I'm concerned, they can kill half of Novosibirsk now. I'm behind bars like a trapped eagle."

Anton took out another picture, where Priazhkina was shown faceup. He asked Sipeniatin, "Recognize her?"

Sipeniatin froze. After a silence he frowned and said in feigned outrage, "What a monster is abroad in Novosibirsk! The same M.O.! Undresses broads and—"

"Who else did he undress?" Anton interrupted.

"What do you mean, who? The one whose purse was dropped off at my mother's."

"How do you know that? I didn't show you a photograph of her looking like this."

Sipeniatin was bewildered, and trying to recover from his flub, he asked quickly, "Is the sweetheart doing me in again?"

Anton put the pictures on the table.

"It's much worse, Vasily Stepanovich. It's not Zvonkova who's exposing you, but the people you're involved with."

"Vasya Sivy is never involved in group crimes," Sipeniatin said huffily. "I work one on one."

Birukov remembered the forged icon. This was the best opportunity to test Stepan Stepanovich Stukov's theory, and Anton asked, "What did you do time for last?"

"Granny's icon."

"Did you forge it yourself?"

Sipeniatin looked like he was poised for flight. "I got it that way from granny. Why?"

"You're not telling the truth, that's why." Birukov spread out about ten photographs on the desk, including pictures of people involved in the Kholodova case. "Maybe you could tell me which of these people is a master icon forger?"

"Why dig up the old stuff?" Sipeniatin grumbled. "I did my full three years for the icon."

"It's a mistake to play gentleman again when they're setting you up for the pen without a qualm."

Vasya didn't say a word, but his face revealed his inner struggle. In order to prompt his revelations, Anton had to give him some sort of conclusion, fast, even if it wasn't very significant. Anton quickly took Kholodova's purse from the safe, set it on his desk and said severely, "No, as you understand, we're not talking about three years. By the way, there was money in this purse. Where is it?"

"It was only two hundred rubles," Sipeniatin said with a smirk.

"Where did you get the three thousand?"

"A guy gave it to me."

"Who? For what?"

Apparently deciding that he had nothing to lose, Vasya sighed and pointed at Stepnadze's photograph.

"This guy. He paid me for not turning him in the last time."

"Tell me the whole story."

Sipeniatin turned to Makovkina. "Reporter?"

"Prosecution investigator," she replied dryly.

"Oh." Vasya looked disappointed. Turning back to Anton, he

explained with a laugh, "Once a pretty lady wrote about me in the newspaper. 'From the Halls of Justice,' she called the article. A pal outside sent it to me in the camp. I wanted to keep it, but some louse used it for cigarette paper—"

"Stick to the point," Anton stopped him.

"The point was like this." Sipeniatin sighed noisily. "I met this guy when my mother lived next door to Frosya Zvonkova. I sold him a couple of icons for ten each. A week later I went to the secondhand market to sell the rest. I see the guy selling my icons for a hundred each. And he sold them to some weirdos! Just as he put the money in his pocket, I come up to him. 'Hello, pops. I'm asking you to contribute fifty percent of your fee to a poor heir, otherwise the cops are waiting for you.' He handed over the hundred. I said: 'I have a better icon. Shall we sell it together?' He got antsy. 'Sell it yourself.' 'Pops, who'll pay good money to me? One look at my mug and they'll start patting their pockets to make sure I haven't lifted their wallets.' "

"So the old guy fell for it. I gave him the icon. A month later he brings it back, it's shining gold and sparkling stones. He says: 'Ask for two thousand. I'll help you.' 'How much is my share?' 'Five hundred.' We shook on it. I found a weirdo at the market. He turned the icon every which way. And he wants it and it hurts and his mama says don't do it. Then the old guy comes over all official. He checks the 'gold,' the 'stones,' tells the weirdo, 'It's worth at least three thousand, you know.' The weirdo panicked, jumped like I splashed boiling water on him, thought I'd want all three . . ." Sipeniatin laughed. "And when CID got me by the ass, I called the old guy and said two bunks are waiting for us in the camps. The guy jumped worse than the weirdo. He babbled, said, 'Take the rap. When you get back, I'll give you three thousand cash, and besides whenever you need a tenner for a drink it's yours.' I figure the old guy is an ace for me. Take care of him. If I milk him wisely, I'll live well. And I can always put him away if he finks out. That's the point, inspector."

"Who forged the icon?" Anton asked.

"I don't know," Vasya burst out.

"Why are you wasting time? There's an artist in this group . . ."

Sipeniatin was quiet, as though making up his mind whether to tell all. To hurry his thought processes, Anton said calmly, "This time you won't be able to hide your accomplice, and accessory to murder is a lot worse than icon forgery. I hope you realize that."

"I didn't meet the artist and I didn't take part in any murders," Sipeniatin said gruffly.

"And no one promised to find you a place in Novosibirsk, either?"

"What?"

The telephone rang. The usually calm Dymokurov agitatedly told Birukov that all the tests had been completed extrafast.

"Very interesting results! Everything points to Zarvantsev," the forensics expert said.

"What did the shoe comparison show?" Anton asked.

"The footprint found under Priazhkina's corpse was left by the right sneaker of Albert Evgenievich."

Birukov thought a bit and, noticing Sipeniatin's tense look, said, "Please drop by my office, Arkady Ivanovich."

Dymokurov was there in less than a minute. Noting his surprise at seeing Sipeniatin there, Birukov said calmly, "Go on, Arkady Ivanovich."

The forensics man stood next to Anton and placed one of the sheets of paper he had brought on his desk. "Here's the handwriting analysis. Instead of Revaz Davidovich, it was Zarvantsev who got the money orders." Next to the first piece of paper he put down the next. "And this is the spectral analysis. The soil taken from the Zaporozhets and the couch grass seeds found in the car's grill are identical to the soil and vegetation samples we brought from Shelkovichikha. Conclusion: Zarvantsev and his car were in the area where Priazhkina's body was found."

"How about the composite photo?"

Dymokurov put down a picture of Zarvantsev dressed in railroad uniform. "Take a look."

After a quick glance at it, Anton showed it to Makovkina. "Could be Revaz Davidovich, eh?"

"A very noticeable resemblance," Makovkina said in surprise.

Anton thanked Dymokurov, and as the lab man left, he handed the picture to Sipeniatin.

"Do you recognize the artist?"

Vasya squinted as he appraised the picture and laughed nervously. "You've got him pegged."

"Did you think we were going to play games with you?"

"I'm through playing, inspector. I don't have the trump suit." Sipeniatin tossed the picture on the desk like a losing card. "He fixed up the icon. And he murdered the nice lady who did the dive from the balcony."

"Tell it in order."

"There wasn't any order, citizen inspector. Just total disorder." Vasya frowned and grimaced. "Basically, this artist and the old guy were on my string. As soon as I got out I went to him. Hello, there, time to pay your debts. Alik was as scared as a kid. He started whining, telling me he had little work. Managed to scrape up fifty rubles and stuck me with some puny icon of the Crucifixion. I've told you who I sold the icon to and I blew the money the first night with my pals. I go back to Alik: 'Where's pops?' 'On a trip.' 'When will he be back?' 'In a week.' I had to wait, and then the militia got me by the ass. Regulation: twenty-four hours and then out of town. I went to Toguchin, got a job as a driver. The pay was good, but I wasn't used to sitting behind the wheel. I want to see my old pals. I decided to take off a week. I get to Novosibirsk, call the old guy—no answer. I go to milk Alik, the door is locked. I have a pick in my pocket. It's a snap to undo a familiar lock. I come in expecting nothing, but I sense that someone's in the room. I peek in and—Alik and Frosya's sister are making it in bed. My heart leaped—I could milk them forever with that! 'Hello, pigeons,' I say politely. 'What are you up to? Putting horns on the old man? Turning pops into a musk-ox?' Nina, naturally, split quickly, but where could Alik go? We sat down in the kitchen, finished a couple of bottles of cognac.

Alik was chewing his sleeves, whining about the old man—says he ruined his life. I could tell: he'll give me his Zaporozhets if I finish off pops . . ."

"Zarvantsev asked you to kill Stepnadze?"

"Right. 'I've lived to see it,' I thought. And right away start thinking of how to get the Zaporozhets without murder."

"What was the problem between uncle and nephew?"

"Go ask them. I didn't have time to find out—I wanted the car. So I spent the night at Alik's. In the morning we had some hair of the dog. I ask him, 'What if we manage the old guy without murder? Killing is a light punishment—one jab of a knife and it's over. Let's make the old guy's life miserable, set him up for five years in prison.' Alik shook his head. 'If they arrest Revaz, they'll confiscate his assets. Nina will be left without a cent.' I think, 'What a creep! Killing someone is nothing, but leaving a broad without baubles worries him.' Then I got an idea . . ."

Sipeniatin stroked his scabbed chin. "The last time I was in, there was a business type serving with me. A guy with brains and, I could tell, daring. He had been stealing a lot and decided to get out of it high and dry. He had a peaceful divorce with his wife, left her his property, and then got himself put away for five years for attempted rape. While he was doing his time, his former pals got double that along with confiscation of property. I told Alik about it. He thought. I ask, 'How's the old guy with women?' 'He used to be like a fly with honey. Now he's quieted down.' 'Then what's the problem! He can recall his youth! We'll find him a girlie who'll put on such a show that even the main prosecutor won't figure out what's what. I'll get pals to be witnesses who would kill their grandmothers for half a pint. Do you have a friend or should I get one?' "

"Alik liked the idea. He called the railroad barbershop and called this one over . . ." Sipeniatin pointed at Priazhkina's picture. "Her name's Lusya. She runs over, drinks cognac with us, and is ready to do anything. We agreed to pull the stunt when the old guy gets back from his trip. On the twenty-first I arrive at

Novosibirsk Central. Alik and Lusya have their eye on the old guy already, and he's chatting with a female who made my mouth water . . . I ask Alik, 'Who's she?' 'Sanya,' he says, 'is the name. She's got it in for Revaz, too. He bled her dry for five years.' 'Then what's the problem? Talk to her, let her get revenge on the old guy.' "

"Alik's eyes lit up, like a hungry wolf's. He was fired up with the business. I know the feeling. We sent Lusya back to her shave and a haircut, and we started tailing the guy and the lady. We went to the house of the guy who owes me five for the Crucifixion. It's a small world, it turns out, inspector."

Sipeniatin frowned. "Then the merry-go-round started. Pops soon left the courtyard, and Alik went up. What he and the lady discussed I don't know. I see it's getting late, have to hurry him along. I go up to the familiar door, hear a major discussion going on. I ring the bell—silence. I push the door, it's open. I come in —there's a scream. Look into the living room—the lady rushes from Alik toward the open balcony door and shouts at the top of her lungs, 'Damn you all!' I rush to help shut her mouth, and she jumps out the door! I just had time to grab her robe—it stayed in my hands. I pushed the balcony door shut with my foot, so it wouldn't be obvious from the street where the broad had fallen from. I shout at Alik, 'Why are you standing around with your mouth open? Time to split!' I stuck the robe behind the refrigerator, tripped on the briefcase that Alik drags around with him to look important. I see an open purse on the table, and in it tenruble notes and blue wool. I hated to leave it behind. I stuck the bag in Alik's briefcase and zipped off. That's how it happened, citizen inspector . . ."

"Go on," Anton said dryly.

Sipeniatin sighed and grew stubborn.

"Why go on . . . I was as scared as Alik. Who wants to serve time for murder? I explain to Alik: 'If the broad is killed, then we were born under lucky stars, because there are no witnesses. But if she makes a statement and then kicks off, we'll get a stiff sentence or maybe capital punishment.' Alik's jaw dropped. 'Call

all the hospitals,' I said. 'Find out if the broad is breathing or not.' Alik grabbed the phone and found that the ambulance took her. It turned out she wasn't killed. I thought: 'We're in it now! We have to scare the broad into keeping quiet, and scare the doctor so that he doesn't treat her too much.' The doctor was puny-looking but no coward. I decided to get out of Novosibirsk while the going was good. I went to the old guy for his debt. He counted off three thousand without a word and added a hundred for my rough time when I asked him to. The old guy has more money than chickens can peck! And the thought struck me again: 'If the old guy's money goes to Alik, it'll be all mine, without risk—mine!' I met Alik and told him, 'It's over for us. We have to get rid of the old guy whatever way we can. It would be good if his wife helped out.' Alik said, 'Nina will help, she's been wanting to get rid of the old man for a long time.' 'Well, Vasya,' I thought to myself, 'some fine company you've fallen in with! You have to be a sheep not to take advantage of these turkeys.' While Alik and I were making plans, the old guy hurried off on another trip . . ."

Birukov got tired of listening to Vasya's colorful speech.

"Why did you invite the doctor to the Aurora?" he asked.

Sipeniatin laughed bitterly.

"That was Alik who invited him. I lied to him, told him the doctor wanted a bribe. I wanted to add another thou to the old guy's money, but Alik, the cheapskate, stalled. I had to say that I would pay him out of my own money and then get it back from Alik. Naturally I didn't go to the Aurora myself; I figured the doc wouldn't show without the CID."

"Why was Ovchinnikov with Zvonkova and Priazhkina at the movie theater?"

"Frosya and the soccer player were there to confuse things, and Alik got Lusya there out of his own stupidity. You see, he wanted to check whether I met with the doc or not."

"Who drove the Volga that took Priazhkina from the Aurora?"

"Alik."

"Zarvantsev was at the opera."

"Fake. The opera was for his alibi. It was a Napoleonic plan."

"You wanted to put the blame on Revaz Davidovich?"

"Yep."

Birukov looked into Sipeniatin's eyes.

"Let's say you managed to make the facts look as if Revaz Davidovich had done it, but did you really believe that he wouldn't deny or disprove them?"

"The old guy wouldn't have been able to. I was supposed to bump him off in Omsk."

"That's it! Did you consider the possibility that he might not fly to Omsk on the basis of your telegram?"

"Alik called there and found out that the old man had arrived. But I had figured out in time that if I did in the old guy, Alik would have more on me than I did on him."

"How did you manage to register a ticket at the airport with a false passport?"

"Alik did it. When he wears a railroad uniform he looked just like the old guy."

"Where did Zarvantsev get the uniform?"

"He has a jacket and cap. And he managed to get Revaz's passport."

"How did the victim's purse get to your mother's apartment?"

"I don't know. Alik must have freaked out." Sipeniatin ground his teeth and looked at Anton openly. "When he drove off in his Zaporozhets after registering the ticket, my instincts told me that he would screw things up. He must have called Frosya disguised as me. Once I spoke to the sweetheart from Alik's apartment. He must have remembered what I call her. Alik's tops at imitating voices."

"Was Priazhkina's death planned?"

"No. Lusya was supposed to bring the old guy down under."

Anton laughed grimly. "Instead, she drowned herself."

"That's Alik's work. Lusya knew too much." Sipeniatin looked into Anton's eyes and, seeing that he wasn't believed, spoke in agitation. "Citizen inspector, there's no point in lying now. I can't get away from prison, but I'll go in just for my part, not for Alik's murder. Let him do his own time if they don't execute him. Don't think that I'm trying to get off completely. Alik and I cooked up the stew together, but let the court determine how much each of us has to eat."

"Where did you live in Novosibirsk?"

"First at Alik's. Remember the first time you were there? Alik was expecting Lusya then, that's why he opened the door to you without thinking. I was in the kitchen. When you and Alik were in the living room, I slipped out."

"Where did you live later?"

"With old pals. I'm not turning them in. None of the boys is involved in this."

Birukov was far from taking Sipeniatin's statements without a lot of salt. There was a lot that had to be checked and double-checked, but the important thing had been achieved: Vasya was telling the truth. This was apparent not only because of the facts that he gave but also by looking at him: he exuded a certain weariness, bordering on a sense of doom.

Slava Golubyov ran into the room. "Revaz Davidovich has been brought in."

"Ask him in here," Anton said and looked at Sipeniatin. "And I'm asking you not to pull any tricks."

30

This time Stepnadze wasn't wearing the full regalia of a railroad conductor but a brand new beige silk suit. Revaz Davidovich entered with such a severe and determined air that it seemed he was planning to give Birukov a lecture for disturbing him. But the sight of the glum-looking Sipeniatin made him turn back for the door with the haste of a man who had entered the ladies' room by mistake.

"Where are you going, Revaz Davidovich?" Anton said, stopping him.

Stepnadze froze instantly and turned in bewilderment. "Excuse me, dear fellow, you're busy . . ."

"We're waiting for you." Anton indicated a chair at a distance from Sipeniatin. "Sit down, please."

Recovering his composure, Stepnadze took the offered chair. Vasya Sipeniatin stared at him with the same frank curiosity that was captured in his mug shots.

"Do you know this citizen?" Birukov asked, indicating Sipeniatin.

Revaz Davidovich's gaze locked with Vasya's. For a half minute they struggled.

"Hi, pops," Vasya said.

Stepnadze turned to Birukov. "I do not know this citizen."

"What's this?" Sipeniatin said and quickly pointed to the bulging inner pocket of Revaz Davidovich's jacket. "In that pocket you have a brown wallet with ten-ruble notes. Are you going to say you don't?"

Stepnadze looked at Sipeniatin with an ironic smirk. Vasya grew nervous.

"Well, what are you staring at? Don't you understand Russian? Show your wallet with the tens in it!"

Revaz Davidovich took out a large wallet of fine-quality leather, opened it, and, rummaging in the compartments, showed Sipeniatin a one-ruble note with the same irony.

"Hid the tens?" Vasya asked quickly. "Afraid of confiscation?"

Stepnadze silently put the ruble back, shut the wallet deliberately, and, as he put it into his pocket, looked at Anton in surprise.

"I don't understand, dear fellow. What does this citizen want from me?"

"He just gave a statement that three years ago you helped him sell a forged icon for two thousand rubles," Anton said calmly.

Revaz Davidovich turned purple in outrage. "What nonsense! I've never seen this criminal before in my life!"

Sipeniatin blew up. "Watch the criminal stuff, pops! What did you give me the three thousand for last week? For my blue eyes?"

Not a muscle twitched in Revaz Davidovich's face. His outrage was passing, and he said with a smile, looking at Anton, "I didn't give this con man a penny."

"Then where did I get the three thousand?" Vasya roared.

Stepnadze turned to him very calmly. "The CID will find out whom you robbed."

"Oh, you old . . ." Vasya was stunned and roared at him, "If we end up in the same joint, you'll be licking my feet!"

Birukov called a guard. Sipeniatin, understanding without being told that his services were no longer needed, got up. Walking past Revaz Davidovich, he suggested with a malicious smirk, "Don't weave stories here—you'll get a longer sentence!"

Stepnadze stuck his right hand under his jacket, as though his heart were acting up, glanced over at the silent Makovkina, and, looking Anton right in the eyes, said excitedly, "I don't understand, dear fellow, what's been happening around me lately! I don't understand a thing!"

"Sooner or later, Revaz Davidovich, it was bound to happen," Anton said.

"I swear I didn't help sell any icons!"

"The icon is merely an overture; the opera deals with something else," Birukov said and held out a money order form. "Who sent you this money and for what?"

Stepnadze's face did not reveal the slightest hint of confusion or bewilderment. However, before replying, he examined the form, and then, when he was certain that his name was on it, replied, "This, dear fellow, was for books I sent out. I was paid for their cost."

"You need a lot of books for twenty rubles."

"I sent a lot. Besides, some of the books were bought at the market at higher prices."

"Why was the money order sent to Zarvantsev's address?"

"Alik lives in my old apartment. I'm used to that address."

Birukov thought before asking the next question.

"Zarvantsev says otherwise."

"What exactly?" Stepnadze said, leaning forward.

"That you deal in books behind your wife's back."

"Right!" Revaz Davidovich seemed happy and then lowered his eyes in embarrassment. "I was ashamed to admit it."

"Lawyers call that kind of 'embarrassment' false testimony," Anton said severely.

Stepnadze smiled guiltily. "Please forgive me, dear fellow. In the future I promise to tell the truth and only the truth as is usually demanded in a trial."

"You do all your book dealings through Zarvantsev?"

"At his address," Stepnadze corrected.

Birukov met Revaz Davidovich's anxious gaze.

"We had a warrant to check the mail in your name at the post office, and we determined that at Zarvantsev's address you get only COD money orders. In the last two months, for instance, you received twenty-three such money orders . . . Doesn't that seem a rather one-sided exchange to you?"

"I don't understand, dear fellow."

"What is there not to understand? You receive large payments, but you haven't bought a single book. Put more simply, none is sent to you."

"There was a time when they were, when I was ordering books."

"Have you kept receipts?"

Stepnadze laughed out loud. "My dear fellow, I never imagined that I would be talking to detectives about it. Book exchange is not illegal, and if you intend to charge me with speculation, then you have to be able to prove it!" Stepnadze's face went red. "I'm outraged by your fantasy!"

"You shouldn't get outraged, Revaz Davidovich," Anton replied calmly. "I'm not charging you. I'm simply trying to clear up a suspicion. As a former lawyer, surely you know that there is nothing illegal in that."

Stepnadze shrugged in confusion. "What is your suspicion based on?"

"On the facts. And it's not only your book exchange that interests us. Which of your relatives works at the Sukhumi Pedagogical Institute?"

"I don't have any relatives there."

Anton handed Stepnadze the cabled money orders from Sukhumi and Rostov. Watching Revaz Davidovich examine them grimly, he said, "The money from Sukhumi obviously comes from the woman you talked to on the beach in Adler, whose daughter you promised to get into the pedagogical institute through your relative."

Stepnadze returned the money orders from Sukhumi and Rostov very calmly, looked into Anton's eyes and sighed bitterly. "You have a wild imagination. It'll disappear as you get older."

"While I'm still young I'll try a bit more." Birukov handed Stepnadze the receipts of the money orders that Zarvantsev had gotten at the Main Post Office.

"What's this?"

Revaz Davidovich read them over and looked in amazement at the signature. Returning them, he said firmly, "I didn't receive these payments."

"Your nephew Albert Evgenievich Zarvantsev forged your signature and used your old passport to get them."

"That is impossible."

Anton showed him the conclusion of the handwriting expert. "Here, look at this."

Stepnadze took the report with a shaky hand and read it as if he couldn't believe his eyes. Rereading it several times, he returned it to Anton and said quietly, "Alik, Alik . . . What a scoundrel he is . . ."

Birukov showed him a receipt for a money order that Revaz Davidovich had cashed. "Now these five hundred rubles you received."

Revaz Davidovich shook his gray head. "I didn't get anything, my dear fellow."

"There's another handwriting analysis for this. It's hard to disagree with it," Anton said, showing him a second report.

Revaz Davidovich's face grew intense, as if he were working on a difficult mathematical problem. Having read the conclusion, he seemed to be counting up the receipts, going through them, and shrugging in confusion. Finally, returning everything to Anton, he spoke in agitation.

"I don't understand a thing! How did Alik get my old passport if I lost it a year ago? How could Alik cash the money orders using my passport if he's thirty years my junior?"

"Look at him dressed in a railroad uniform," Birukov said, showing him the composite photo.

Staring wildly at the photo, Stepnadze hissed, "What a bastard!"

"Would you like to hear what Zarvantsev had to say in his statement?"

"I would, dear fellow, very much!"

Anton pressed a button on his desk and requested a playback

of Zarvantsev's statement and then Sipeniatin's. Revaz Davidovich listened, holding his breath. It seemed that nothing else in the world held any interest for him. Sometimes he snorted, sometimes he smiled, but Anton noted that it was all fake, put on.

After Albert Evgenievich's statement came Sipeniatin's, talking about the conspiracy against Stepnadze. Revaz Davidovich, concentrating on every word, seemed to turn to stone. Now no emotion at all played on his features. Just once, when Sipeniatin mentioned that he had planned to "bump off the old guy in Omsk," did Stepnadze look at Anton and shake his head sadly.

After thanking the technicians through the microphone, Birukov turned to Stepnadze and asked, "As a former lawyer, you've probably figured out your nephew's intention?"

Revaz Davidovich put his hand under his jacket again and, grimacing, rubbed the left part of his chest—his heart must have been acting up a lot. The pause was growing oppressive, but Birukov didn't rush him. Finally Stepnadze sighed with relief and began speaking.

"I confess, dear fellow, that I've known about Alik and Nina for a long time, but I had no idea that they would go as far as murder. What base people—oh, how base!"

"We'll take care of them, but now let's clear up your case," Birukov said.

"Forgive me, dear fellow, I didn't understand . . ."

"What didn't you understand?" Anton showed him the money orders that had been left at general delivery. "As Sipeniatin says, you don't get money like that for having pretty eyes. These are bribes for helping people get into colleges. We only began investigating and have discovered all this already. And what if we dig around for a month, or two?"

Stepnadze seemed to be holding water in his mouth, and said nothing. Birukov had to go on.

"I didn't reveal what we have against you by accident. Your legal knowledge must tell you that the evidence is strong and further criminal revelations are only a question of time. The amount of the bribes will come to a high total probably, and you don't need me to tell you how high your sentence will be."

"They're not bribes. I didn't pull any strings for anyone," Stepnadze interrupted. "Crazy people sent the money. Fools, you understand; they sent it!"

"There're an awful lot of fools, it seems," Birukov said suspiciously.

"There are hundreds of them. Thousands!"

"And they all send you money?"

Revaz Davidovich hesitated no more than a few seconds. "It's impossible to get all the fools," he said, looking at Anton with mockery. "You see, I didn't do anything for them; I merely promised to."

"What did they pay you for, then?"

"For my promises." Seeing Anton's disbelieving grin, Stepnadze laughed and then spoke some more. "It's hard to believe, but to save you unnecessary work, dear fellow, I'll tell you. I don't accept bribes; I'm merely a swindler. Yes, yes! Article 147 of the Criminal Code of the R.S.F.S.R.* In trains, on beaches, in institutes and universities, I met the parents of applicants, left them my address and promised to help them—but I did nothing! I don't have influential relatives or friends, but I know the full names of the rectors of almost every institute and university, and I know many of the names of deans and chairmen of admissions committees. None of them has ever set eyes on me, and certainly none is 'my friend' . . . Out of one hundred applicants, as you know, seventy are accepted. They don't need any help, but their anxious mothers and fathers, having talked to me, feel that the acceptance didn't come without my participation and are happy to send money."

"Why did your nephew get most of the money orders?" Anton asked grimly.

Stepnadze grew flushed with rage. "Alik is a scoundrel! He stole my passport and received money intended for me. It

*Russian Soviet Federated Socialist Republic, the largest of the fifteen constituent republics of the U.S.S.R. (Trans. note.)

seemed odd to me for a long time—why had the parents wised up? And only now I see that Alik was just beating me to the post office."

"How did Zarvantsev know about the money?"

"Nina and he helped me find trusting parents. Alik got his share for that—twenty-five percent."

"Zarvantsev could have simply offered 'help' on his own."

"He doesn't have the courage to give his own name. Alik is a coward. Understand? He's a sneak. And I won't allow a nonentity like that to have use of my property! I'll leave Nina without a cent! . . . Are you going to arrest me right away?"

"In order to keep you from interfering with the investigation, I'm afraid we'll have to hold you."

"That's what I thought when the militia car came for me in Shelkovichikha." Stepnadze hurriedly pulled out his wallet, took out his passbook with a trembling hand, and gave it to Anton with determination. "Here, dear fellow, please do this according to the law. The seven thousand rubles in this account were earned honestly in the Far North. When I get out that'll be enough for me to live on to the end of my days. Everything else is subject to confiscation. The co-op apartment, the dacha, the Volga—everything! That wasn't earned through labor. Understand? Not legally!" And closing his eyes, he shook his head. "Oh, Nina-Nina-Nina-Nina! Oh, Alik-Alik! Oh, you scoundrels!"

"Revaz Davidovich," Anton said, interrupting Revaz Davidovich's emotional outburst, "I have two more questions for you."

"Go ahead, dear fellow."

"Why did Kholodova smoke so much during her conversation with you at Demensky's apartment?"

"I told you last time, she was nervous."

"Over what?"

Stepnadze grimaced. "I didn't want Kholodova to leave her job as manager of the bookstore in Cheliabinsk, and I lied to her, told her that Yuri had another woman. But please bear in mind that I didn't threaten Sanya, didn't bring up the past. We parted amicably. Sanya was planning to go to the beach." And shutting his eyes again, he shook his head. "Oh, Alik-Alik! What a scoundrel Alik is!"

"Second question." Birukov stopped in order to formulate his thoughts. "Revaz Davidovich, tell me truthfully—what made you take up a life of dishonesty?"

Stepnadze, his blank gaze fixed on the window, was silent for a long time. He worked the muscles on his high cheekbones. Finally he faced Anton and said with a feigned smile, "You see, I was accustomed to earthly goods. In the Far North I made a thousand rubles a month. When I left, my salary went down to three hundred, and when I retired, my income was even lower. I had to look for profitable sources, place a major bet, since it's a waste of time to hope for major returns on small stakes."

"Doesn't it seem to you that in betting on book speculation and fraud, you were placing a losing bet?"

Revaz Davidovich laughed bitterly. "What can you do, dear fellow . . . Jack London once said: 'Life is a game that no one wins.' "

Birukov called the guard and began filling in the warrant for holding Stepnadze. His detailed conversation with Revaz Davidovich was yet to come, and he had to prepare for it thoroughly. Calmly looking through the warrant, Revaz Davidovich signed it, bowed to Anton, and left silently with the guard. Birukov looked at Makovkina.

"That's how it turns out, Natalya Mikhailovna. Now we have to break Zarvantsev's alibi in regard to his cultural outing at the opera."

"How do you do that?"

"We'll turn to the public," Anton said, rising from his desk.

Some Novosibirsk residents probably remember how, during the intermission before the Vremya newscast one Sunday night, a quiet young man in a militia captain's uniform appeared on the screen and, pushing back an unruly lock from his brow embarrassedly, addressed the viewers without a prompter or notes.

"Dear comrades. The Ministry of Internal Affairs is urging those of you who were at the evening performance of the opera last Tuesday night and sitting near seat twenty-one in the thirtieth row to call zero-two as soon as possible."

The captain paused, repeated the request without a flub, thanked them for their attention, and disappeared from the screen.

The extraordinary appearance of a member of the militia agitated the TV audience. Suppositions and guesses abounded. Naturally none of the guessers knew that twenty minutes later the switchboard at headquarters had received sixty-four calls. Five of the callers, who gave their names and addresses, replied to the desk sergeant's question by saying that seat twenty-one in row thirty had been empty from beginning to end of the performance last Tuesday.

Albert Evgenievich Zarvantsev was arrested exactly an hour after Anton Birukov left the television studio.

31

Procedural law requires immediate interrogation of a detained suspect, and if that is impossible, then it must take place no later than twenty-four hours after detention. Birukov questioned Zarvantsev the morning of the next day, because upon his arrest Albert Evgenievich fell into a deep depression that made it pointless to try to talk to him. He had recovered by morning but fell into the opposite extreme: he became so garrulous that Anton had to be extremely patient in order to extract the essential from the verbiage.

The interrogation lasted several hours. Cowardly, weak-willed, Zarvantsev tried to mitigate his sentence by a wholehearted confession and didn't spare himself or others. At first he gave his biography at length, sparing no details, then began complaining what a bad influence his uncle, who lived beyond his means, was on him, and how finally he had seduced him with "wild earnings."

"What gave greater income—the speculation in books or the 'protection' with schools?" Birukov asked.

"The protection is a seasonal thing, but Revaz made money on books all year round," Zarvantsev replied helpfully.

"Where did Stepnadze get the books?"

"For over four years he received rare books from Kholodova. According to my calculations, Revaz made at least twenty thousand on the books Sanya sent him. But that's a drop in the bucket. My uncle knew a lot of book clerks in Adler, Rostov, Omsk, Tashkent, Alma-Ata . . . And here, in Novosibirsk, they save him a copy of every hard-to-get edition."

"Were you involved in book speculation?"

Zarvantsev lowered his eyes. "I only sold Yuri Demensky an old Bible for a hundred and fifty, which I bought from Sipeniatin for ten."

Birukov pointed to the COD money orders and receipts from general delivery. "Why didn't you get any money COD but preferred to disguise yourself as Revaz Davidovich and pick up the money orders that were sent to the Main Post Office for 'protection'? Were the amounts bigger?"

Zarvantsev shook his head. "No. The CODs came to my address and had to be picked up at a post office where they knew me personally. Besides, Revaz kept records of every book he sent out and he would have noticed if I got hold of a payment. It was easier with the protection money. Uncle had no way of knowing who would 'repay' him, and the girls working at the Main Post Office are always changing; they don't remember their clients."

"Did many of those who were promised 'protection' send money?"

"More than half. Last year, for instance, Revaz received fifty-nine payments."

"All of five hundred rubles?"

"I think there were four at a hundred and there were five or six at three hundred. The southerners, as a rule, sent five hundred."

"How much did you get instead of Revaz Davidovich?"

"I only started doing that recently."

Birukov showed him Stepnadze's old passport and driver's license. "But you've had these documents since last spring?"

Zarvantsev nodded ingratiatingly. "Yes, I took them from Revaz's dacha along with the railroad jacket. However, last year I didn't have the guts."

Birukov turned the conversation to the incident with Kholodova. Albert Evgenievich, stuttering, confirmed Sipeniatin's statement. When he was through, only a few points needed clarification.

"What was Kholodova writing in her statement to the prosecutor?" Anton asked, catching Zarvantsev's shifting eyes.

Zarvantsev, massaging his brow with long, knobby fingers, bowed his head low. "I told Kholodova that I knew about her old deal with Revaz and invited her to get her revenge on him. She grew pale, found the paper, sat down at the kitchen table, and started writing. Then she suddenly said, 'I'm writing to the prosecutor, I'll tell the whole truth about me and add what a vile thing you're proposing.' I grabbed the paper away from her. She broke the pen in half and dashed out into the living room. I went after her. Sipeniatin burst in just then . . ."

"Why did you drop off the purse at his mother's?"

"Vasya was behaving strangely at the airport. I thought he was going to turn me in to the CID. I decided to beat him to it."

"What were you removing with the turpentine from the purse?"

"Paint. There were tubes of oil paints in my briefcase. When Sipeniatin stuck the purse in there, back in Demensky's apartment, it got smeared."

Birukov laughed. "You did a professional job; you didn't leave a single fingerprint on the bag."

"I held it with a handkerchief."

"Why did you send Frosya Zvonkova over to Maria Anisimovna's?"

"Sipeniatin had told me that it's best to confuse a case as much as possible, and so I did."

"What happened to the gas in Stepnadze's Volga?"

"Nina forgot to fill up the car and in her fright said the first thing that came to mind." Zarvantsev buried his face in his hands. "The whole thing is a nightmare."

"Did you bring Priazhkina out to Shelkovichikha just to put Revaz Davidovich under suspicion?"

"Yes. After drinking a whole bottle of vodka, Lusya got hysterical, as usual. I managed to calm her down a bit and bet her a bottle of cognac that she couldn't swim across the Ina River and back. Lusya undressed, went over to the river, and fell into the water. I held her down by the neck . . . She didn't really struggle . . ."

"You made the bet hoping that she would drown on her own?"

"Yes."

"What part did Nina Stepnadze play in your affairs?"

"We love each other . . . We wanted to have a real life . . ."

Still holding his face in his hands, Zarvantsev wept. After a few more questions Anton finished the statement transcript and called the guard. Before leaving, Albert Evgenievich looked beseechingly into Anton's eyes and asked, "What will happen to me?"

"That's up to the court to decide," Anton replied.

Slava Golubyov came in soon afterward. He put more receipts of postal money orders on the desk and said in his rapid-fire speech, "I found another sixteen at the Main Post Office, and also these." Slava took three COD notices out of his pockets. "They're fresh, came in this morning."

Birukov slowly went through the stubs and smiled. "The last gasps of Stepnadze and Company."

The intercom buzzed. Golubyov quickly reached for the phone and picked it up. He said "Right!" twice, hung up, and said to Anton, "They want you—urgently—up at the general's office. With Stepnadze's money orders."

Birukov collected the receipts in a file and went out, asking Slava to wait for him. He returned in a half hour. He sat in his chair, put down the folder he had taken with him, and looked at Golubyov.

"Well? . . . Well?" Slava demanded impatiently.

"I've been ordered to turn over Revaz Davidovich's case. The Embezzlement Squad will deal with him."

"Sure, now that the case is solved!"

"There's a lot more work to be done in that case," Anton said and added, "By the way, the general called your trip to Adler 'excellent work.' "

"Auxiliary Militiaman Pashkov helped me out a lot," Golubyov said quickly and then remembered, "Oh, yes, Anton, while you were with the general, Kholodova's father called. He's very upset by his daughter's death. He said he didn't want details, just to tell him whether Sanya was guilty of anything. At my own risk, I said she wasn't."

"You said the right thing."